THE SYNDICATES BOOK VIII
DIMITRI

Copyright @ 2023 by Cala Riley
All rights reserved. No part of this publication may be reproduced, distributed, or transmitted in any form or by any means without the prior written consent of the publisher, except brief quotes used for reviews and certain other non-commercial uses, as per copyright laws. This is a work of fiction. Names, characters, businesses, places, events, and incidents are either the products of the author's imagination or used in a fictitious manner. Any resemblance to actual persons, living or dead, or actual events is purely coincidental.

Cover Design: Books and Moods
Editor: My Brother's Editor
Formatter: Dark Ink Designs

Demi Abrahamson and Jennifer Mercer for loving Dimitri enough to spend some extra time with him.

Mia,

Find a man willing to light the world on fire for you.

Love
Carla + Riley

PROLOGUE

FIFTEEN YEARS AGO

I don't understand why everyone is acting this way. Mommy would never have wanted all of these people to stand around being so serious. She liked to smile.

Nik says Mommy had to go away and that she won't be coming back. I'm not quite sure I know what he means though. Mommy would never leave me for good. She tells me all the time that if it wasn't for Nik and me, she wouldn't be as happy as she is. She wouldn't want to be unhappy. She will come back.

So instead of doing whatever these adults are doing, I'm sitting on the floor playing with my Barbie doll.

"Yes, Mr. Ken. I will marry you," I say, making the girl Barbie kiss the boy Barbie.

I think that's what they are supposed to do at least.

I've never seen my mommy kiss my father, but he has friends that come over and kiss him a lot. I'm supposed to be in bed, but when they make loud noises, I can't help but investigate. Nik says that he's supposed to be my protector and that I shouldn't seek out noises in the middle of the night.

I don't listen to him though. Mommy says that whatever boys can do, girls can do it too. Father tells me to be quiet and on my best behavior, but when he's not around, Mommy lets me do all kinds of things. She even taught me how to throw a punch. She said even though I'm young, I need to know how to defend myself.

So when Boris Makarov calls me over to the corner where he and his friends are, I don't think anything of it.

"Ivanna. Come here." His tone is demanding, like the tone my father uses.

Instead of fighting him, I walk over. My brother hates Boris. He calls him a lot of names I'm not supposed to repeat.

I'm not scared of him though. Not only can I defend myself like Mommy says, but this is my home. My brother and father are around here somewhere. This boy won't hurt me.

"Where's your brother, little Ivanna?" Boris taunts, getting some laughs from his friends.

"I'm not his keeper. Go find him yourself if you want him." I turn to walk away, but a hand pulls me back.

"With a mouth like that, it's no wonder your father hasn't sold you off yet. Tell me, does he take a belt to you when you misbehave?" Boris glares at me, his fingers digging into my skin.

"Father doesn't touch me." I hold my head up high.

He snorts. "Maybe I'll make an offer on you. Ask for early access. I'm sure by the time we marry, you will have learned your place." He looks at his friends, laughing.

"Mommy will never let that happen. She says I don't have to marry anyone I don't wanna. She said I will marry for love." I barely withhold the "unlike her" Mommy always follows that statement with.

She made me promise never to tell anyone that she doesn't love Father.

"Your 'mommy' is dead, little girl. She can't do anything to save you. Your father will marry you off. If you're lucky, it will be to a Russian."

I push him, trying to get him to release me, but his fingers only hurt me more.

"You're lying. Mommy isn't dead. She's gone for a while. She will come back." I feel my eyes start to burn.

"Who told you that lie? Your mother is dead. She's in the ground. Did you not wonder why we were at the cemetery burying a casket? How dumb are you?" he sneers.

My throat hurts now. Same with my nose. My face feels wet.

"You're a liar. Stop lying," I yell before my fist flies into his face.

The pain in my fingers hurts so bad, but I don't care. It made him let go. I take several steps back from him, seeing the anger on his face. He's going to hurt me.

I keep backing away from him quickly, scared to take my eyes off him. Then I run into something.

"What are you doing to Ivanna, Boris?"

The voice is one I recognize. It's not Nik, but the next best thing. His best friend.

Dimitri Lukin.

His hand comes down to my arm, making me wince at the bruise I know I'll have from Boris.

He glances down at me, his eyes dark and cold.

He peels the arm of my dress up so he can see the red marks from Boris's hands.

"You're going to regret touching her." Dimitri's voice is low.

I want to tell him to yell at the boys. Tell them what assholes they are.

Dimitri doesn't though. Instead, he pushes me behind him. He's only thirteen, but he's already bigger than Boris and his friends. The only person I think who could beat him up is my brother. Which makes me wonder where Nik is. He's always looking out for me.

I don't get a chance to ask Dimitri though. Instead, he jumps forward in a flash. Dimitri is on top of Boris hitting him, but I can't look away. I should run for help. Find Nik and tell him what's happened.

I stand there watching him instead. Watching Boris cry out in pain. A little part of me likes it, but I would never admit it.

Mommy says that only bad people enjoy causing harm to others.

"What the fuck is going on here?" My father's loud voice comes from behind me.

I try to curl in on myself. He only uses his mean voice when someone is in trouble.

I'm afraid that someone is Dimitri. He only beat up Boris for me.

Dimitri stops, standing over a bloody Boris. Part of me wants to smile, but I don't.

"Pakhan." Dimitri turns, bowing his head. "This boy laid hands on your daughter. I was only defending her."

Father looks down at me, making my eyes hit the floor.

"Is this true?" he asks.

I nod. "He said you were going to make me marry him and when I tried to leave, he grabbed me and hurt my arm. See?" I move the sleeve of the dress to show him.

He growls. "I would never marry you to a Makarov. Especially after he thought of damaging something that doesn't belong to him. Good job, Dimitri. Take Ivanna up to her room. I will send someone to watch over her. I think she's had enough."

Dimitri nods before gently taking my arm. It's not until we are in my room that I stop to look at him.

"Where's Nik?" I whisper.

He shakes his head. "I can't tell you that, but he asked me to watch out for you."

"It's okay. You stopped him. He is such a meanie." I look down at my hands before my eyes catch on the red in his. I gasp. "Are you hurt?"

I reach out to grab them, but he shakes his head. "They don't hurt. What about you, slugger? I saw you throw a punch."

My face hurts at how wide my mouth stretches. "Mommy taught me how. I don't think it hurt him much, but it was worth it."

He gives me a small smile. "You did good. Keep practicing. You'll get better."

I nod, then I ask him what I really want to know. "Nik said Mommy was gone, but he didn't say where. Boris said she died. Mommy is coming back, right?"

I watch him for a long time, the silence stretching. My stomach doesn't feel good. He should have said something by now.

"I'm sorry, *printsessa*. Your mom died. Nik was trying to spare you by saying she left, but I don't agree with him. You deserve to know. Your mom isn't coming back."

I stare at him until my eyes begin to water. Then what he says sinks in.

Mommy is dead. Father says when things are dead, they get buried in the ground. We buried something today.

We buried Mommy today.

My life will never be the same again.

CHAPTER ONE

Ivanna

"You look beautiful." Gregory smiles as he leans in to kiss my cheek.

I smile back. "Thank you. This place looks good."

I look up at the hole-in-the-wall bar. Gregory wanted to come pick me up from my dorm, but that would be a death sentence for the both of us.

See, I like to act like I have this nice and independent life away from the one I grew up in, but the truth is that I'm a prisoner. Even worse, it's my brother's doing.

He could have assigned any guard to me. Any of the men who work for him. Literally anyone would be better than who he chose.

Five years ago, he handed the reins of my life over to the one man who thrives on making me miserable.

Dimitri Lukin.

The bane of my existence.

So instead of letting the cute boy from class pick me up, I bribed my roommate into helping me sneak out of the dorm so I could meet him.

"Let's go inside." Gregory holds the door open, helping me inside.

The place is packed, but I don't mind. Some sports game is on the TV, making everyone cheer the closer we get to the bar.

Once there, Gregory asks for my drink order before giving it to the bartender. Several minutes later, we are settled into the corner of the bar, attempting small talk.

"What's your major?"

"What's your favorite color?"

"Favorite movie?"

Honestly, it's all so boring, but I stay and smile. I wanted this date so bad that I slipped my guard to have it. I better fucking enjoy it.

So instead of yawning like I want, I keep a smile plastered on my face, downing my drink. Gregory graciously offers to grab me a second drink.

I wait while he goes to the bar. Pulling out my phone, I smile when I see a text from Lia, my best friend. I guess she's more like a sister. I mean, she is with my brother Nikolai.

> Lia: How's the date?

I choke when I see the eggplant and water emoji as the next text. I swear I love this chick.

> Me: None of that. I know first dates are supposed to be getting to know you, but I have to admit, the man is boring.

She's typing for a few seconds before her next text comes through.

> Lia: So I guess you would be glad to know that your night is about to get a lot more exciting.

I frown.

> Me: What's that mean?

> Lia: Dimitri just left to head to your dorm. He said he had a feeling you were up to no good and wanted to lay eyes on you even though his guard swears you haven't walked out the door even once.

I snort. He's not wrong. I didn't leave via the door. The window, on the other hand....

I mean, the second story really isn't that high, is all I'm saying.

> Me: He won't find me.

> Lia: Better turn off your phone then.

I smile. Lia might be the queen to my brother's king, but she will always be my best friend, first and foremost. She has never once taken Dimitri or Nikolai's side over mine. It's what I love about her. She's loyal until the very end.

It's the same thing that drew Nik to her. She even took a bullet for him once. If I could pick any badass to be my soul mate, it would be her. Too bad she bats for the wrong team. We could have been epic.

> Me: Fair enough. I'll text you when I get home.

> Lia: You mean when he finds you.

Before I can respond, another text comes through.

> The Devil: Where the fuck are you? I swear I'm going to fucking spank your ass raw for this.

I ignore his empty threats. The man has never laid a finger on me. Even when I wanted him to.

Instead, I send him the middle finger emoji before shutting my phone off and tucking it into my pocket.

"You're way too hot to be standing here alone," a male voice says from next to me.

I turn, seeing a James Dean wannabe leaning against the wall next to me. It makes me frown because I didn't even realize he was there. I'm usually much better at situational awareness.

"I'm not alone, but thanks." I look toward the bar at Gregory. He's still waiting, but he sends a small smile my way.

"That dude? Come on, honey. You can do much better." The man leans in, making my skin crawl.

"Than you? I'm sure," I tell him, watching as Gregory abandons his place at the bar to come to my side.

"Is everything okay?" he whispers to me, looking at the man next to me.

"Peachy. This place is boring. Want to get out of here?" I ask him.

Before he can answer, the mysterious man steps in front of me. "What's the rush? The only thing boring here is your date."

For half a heartbeat, I get excited. What will Gregory do? Will he fight this man for my honor?

Gregory's face turns red. "We should go."

I deflate. Gregory is a nice guy. Too bad nice guys really do finish last. At least with me.

I think the childhood I grew up with tainted me. So while Gregory might be perfect for some, he's not for me.

"Let's," I tell him instead, slipping my arm into his.

When I go to step past douchecanoe, he doesn't move.

"Not so fast. I can show you a good time. How do you feel about alleys? There's one right out back we can get real personal with." He winks at me.

"Move," I tell him, letting go of Gregory. Gregory looks from me to the man like he doesn't know what to do.

Too soft. Gregory could never handle me, I think to myself.

"Make me." The man steps closer, his hand landing on my hip.

That's when I make my move. A well-placed knee to the balls before the heel of my hand lands on his nose, breaking it.

Only, it didn't take him down for long. Before I get three steps away with a shaking Gregory, the man grips my hair, pulling me back.

"You bitch."

Then all hell breaks loose. I'm throwing punches at the man wildly while I see other people fighting in my peripheral. I don't know where Gregory went, but I don't care at this point.

All I can do is focus on the asshat thinking he can put his hands on me.

That's when the atmosphere changed. I know the second Dimitri enters. Not only because of the way the idiot is pulled from me, but the smell of bourbon and oak that floats into my nostrils.

I've known what Dimitri has smelled like since I was six years old. Since he held me in my room as I cried over my mother's death.

Much like that day, Dimitri is defending my honor now. Only he's taking it further than I planned. I think Dimitri might actually kill this one.

"Dimitri," I yell.

He stops immediately, looking over his shoulder at me. I get a chill in my bones from the look he gives me.

Oh yeah, he was planning to kill this man for touching me. Dimitri is my bodyguard. It's his job to keep me out of harm's way, but he revels in the chaos almost as much as I do.

Some might think we are perfect for one other. We both enjoy the darker parts of life. We give as good as we get. I can't even tell you the number of times I've heard that we bicker like a married couple.

Yet, it will never happen. Dimitri made that perfectly clear years ago. So instead, he acts as my warden. The problem is, he doesn't even give me recreational time. Either it's school or home. If I leave, I can only do so with approved guests.

I'm twenty-one years old, for fuck's sake. I should be able to go have drinks with a cute boy if I want to.

"Move your ass, Ivanna, otherwise I'll keep turning your date's face into minced meat." Dimitri's dark voice causes chills to tingle down my spine.

"He's not my date. Just some asshole who thought he could lay hands on me. I had it under control." I cross my arms over my chest, tapping my foot.

The entire room is silent now. I notice that several of the Bratva men are around us, ushering patrons from the bar. I wince when I see a dazed-looking Gregory being led away, blood gushing from his nose.

Sorry, Gregory, I think to myself.

Dimitri reaches out, carefully brushing his knuckles against my cheek. "That's why you have a red mark on your cheek, right?"

I consider his words. I didn't realize it, but now that he mentioned it, my cheek does hurt.

I shrug. "It was a melee. Hard to get out unscathed. It's a little bruise."

Dimitri growls before he picks me up, tossing me over his shoulder, fireman style.

"What the fuck? Put me down." I pound on his back.

He doesn't listen to me. He never does.

So instead of wasting my energy, I let him haul me away from the bar and the prying eyes. Away from assholes who don't understand the word no. Innocent men named Gregory, who can't even handle a punch.

I let him take me away from it all and back to my prison.

Because what am I going to do? Dimitri will never let me date for real and I'll never be allowed peace.

There's no way out of this hellhole.

Ivanna Petrova will be the death of me.

I don't know when the little girl I once knew grew up to be such a wild child, but here we are.

She pounds on my back only for a moment before she gives in.

Part of me is disappointed the fight is over so soon, but the other part revels in her submission.

Not that I would ever tell her that.

Nor will I tell her that the feel of her pressed against me has me harder than a rock.

I knew something was up when she went home without a single peep to her guard. It was almost as if she was on her best behavior.

Linc fell for her shit, but I didn't. So as soon as my meeting with Nik was over, I pulled up her phone to track it.

Of course, it showed she wasn't home. Judging by the name of the bar, I'd have ventured to guess she was on a date.

I was right.

Only the fucker had his hands on her. Or so I thought. It took every last ounce of control I had to pull myself away from the man. If Ivanna hadn't called my name, I would have killed him, consequences be damned.

Instead, I'm hauling her ass to my car like the petulant child she often is.

"Do you ever get tired of pulling these stunts?" I grit out between my teeth as I lower her into the passenger seat of my car.

"Of wanting my freedom? No." She crosses her arms over her chest, making it harder to buckle the seat belt over her.

Still, I lean over and try.

It's pure agony to be this close to her and not kiss her like I want. The sweet smell of her perfume invades my senses, making me feel light-headed.

Ivanna is a temptress.

Not for the first time, I wish things could be different.

That I didn't do what I did when she was sixteen. It changed the course of our relationship, ensuring I would never get what I wanted.

Then again, she was sixteen, and I was twenty-three. To me, she was still a child. I hadn't even considered that one day I might think of her differently. Not until that fateful day she kissed me.

Oh, the things I would tell my past self if I could.

"You know, these procedures are in place to protect you. Stop being difficult."

She huffs as I shut the door. As soon as I'm in the driver's seat, she starts the argument back up.

"If that were all it was, you would let me date. I'm twenty-one years old and the only dates I've been on are ones I've snuck out for. When do I get to decide anything about my life?"

I shake my head, rubbing my face. Exhaustion hits me like a freight train.

"You chose this college," I remind her as I put the car in drive.

"Did I? Lia didn't want to be away from Nik and I didn't want to be away from her. So yes, I did, but then again, I didn't. Besides, would you have really let me move away?"

No. She doesn't need to know that though.

Truth is, Ivanna makes very good points. I should loosen the reins a bit. Let her have some more freedom to date and such. Nik has always said she could choose her own husband one day. I keep telling her that keeping her shackled to her room is a form of protection, but the truth is, it's a control thing for me. I don't want her to go out and find some asshole to marry. Even though I can't have her, I don't want anyone else to either. If I can't love her, then no one else can.

So instead, I act like the older brother she never asked for. I take her protection detail to the extreme, pushing back against Nik anytime he tries to step in on her behalf.

After all, we made an agreement five years ago.

"I need someone for my sister. Shit is getting dangerous. I don't know who I can trust." Nik rubs his hand down his face.

"What are you saying?" I tense.

I know what he wants to ask. I know I should say no. After earlier, it would be a terrible idea.

I can't though.

"Protect her. Put her needs above everyone. If it comes down to it and the bullets are flying, protect her over every single other person. Even me." He looks me dead in the eye.

"I'm your second. I can't be on babysitting duty," I remind him.

He nods. "It'll be up to you to curate a team. Only people you trust. They will protect her in your absence. I need this. I can't be the man I need to be for the Bratva and be her big brother. I need to delegate. I'm delegating it to you. The only person in this entire world who I know truly has my back."

I consider his words. I don't want to deny him, but she won't be happy about it.

"Only on two conditions," I tell him.

He nods. "What are they?"

"If I do this, it gets done my way. You won't interfere. If she comes to you begging to be reassigned, you tell her no. If she is upset with the way I do things, you tell her to take it up with me. If you want me to put her first, you need to trust that the things I do are in her best interest."

"Very well. The other thing?"

"One day she will be mine."

Nik didn't quite agree to the second one, but conceded that should she choose me, he would not stand in my way.

She will never choose me though.

"Ivanna, I'm not trying to make your life miserable. I only want to ensure your protection," I remind her. "You tend to pick pussies for men who are no good for you."

She scoffs. "I get it. You're playing the big brother role Nik couldn't because he had to become a leader. Still, I think you are being unreasonable. How am I supposed to ever find someone if you refuse to let me try? You have to see that you are overbearing."

I grit my teeth. "Would you rather be married off like cattle? The way your father would have done if he was still alive? That can be fucking arranged. Every single thing I do is for you. You think that fucker back there was a good match for you?"

I can see her shaking her head from the corner of my eye. "I told you that wasn't my date."

I scoff. "Where was your date then?"

I glance over in time to catch her wince. "He might have gotten caught in the cross fire. Last I saw, Ilya was escorting him outside with a bloody nose."

I raise my eyebrows in surprise. "That's the man you want to hitch your wagon to? A man who can't even defend you? You need someone who will burn the earth for you, Ivanna. Not some pussy too scared to throw a punch."

She's quiet a moment. "I want that. I truly do, but I can't find that if you don't let me try. Please, Dimitri. Loosen the leash and let me live."

I let out a heavy sigh as I put the car in park outside her dorm. I want to give her whatever she wants, but I can't give her this.

"Ivanna, I can't. It's a security risk—"

She cuts me off. "Bullshit. You just don't want me to be happy. You'd prefer I live a miserable, lonely life like you. Spoiler alert, Dimitri. Not everyone wants to die alone. Some of us want someone to cuddle us at night. Or to have someone to kiss and share their day with. You want to protect me, and you are. I'll give you that. I'm never in any physical danger. Too bad I'm still being hurt. By you."

She flings the door open, stepping out. I'm out the driver's door before she makes it three steps.

"Ivanna," I warn.

She tosses her hair over her shoulder, a slight sheen in her eyes.

"Don't worry, master. I'm going to my fucking room to be miserable as always."

"Ivy," I try again, using her old childhood nickname.

She shakes her head. "Don't." She sniffles. "Please, just let me go."

I watch as she turns around, walking into the building.

I wish I could.

CHAPTER
TWO

Ivanna

Tonight's the night. I'm going to finally do it.
    I wish I had a girlfriend to talk to about it. I could talk to Nik, but he'd probably kill us both.

Not that Dimitri even knows what I'm going to do.

Ever since Dimitri saved me when I was six, he has become my idol. I always followed him and Nik around when I could. Not that they let me often.

Father has them off doing errands a lot. Especially since they graduated school. I thought they would leave me and go to college, but Nik says Father won't let him go.

I think I want to go one day.

Maybe. As long as it doesn't take me away from him.

Things have changed though. Now that Father is dead, there has been a lot of tension in the house.

I'm scared Dimitri will leave.

He's no longer only my idol. He's my crush. The man I hope to marry someday.

I know our age difference will be an issue at first. I'm only sixteen and he's twenty-three. While society may look down upon it, as long as Nik agrees, we can get married. That and most marriages in families like ours have large age gaps.

So instead of chancing it, I'm planning to make my move. I'm going to finally tell Dimitri how I feel and hope he feels the same.

"Ivanna?" Dimitri's voice calls from the hall.

I jump up, looking at myself in the mirror before I run to my door. Taking a deep breath, I compose myself before opening the door.

"Dimitri, thank you for coming." I wave him into my room.

He smiles. "What do you need?"

He comes in, taking a seat on the edge of my bed. I sit down next to him, turning to face him.

My nerves are killing me. I feel like I might puke. I planned this out, but I didn't realize it would be this scary.

This will be my first kiss.

Leaning forward, I go for it, smashing my lips against his. He freezes as I pull back, my wide eyes taking him in.

"Ivanna," he says slowly, his eyes down on his hands. "Why did you do that?"

"I just love you so much and I know I'm still only sixteen, but if Nik says yes, we can be together. I know he will. He told me the other day that I get to choose. I choose you."

"You're a child. I'm a grown man. I can't be like this with you. What would people say? I'd be a pervert. I appreciate the compliment. I care about you a lot, but this can't happen."

My eyes tear up. "I love you though. Mom always said love solved all issues."

He shakes his head, standing. "Your mother was wrong. Love can't solve the fact you're too young. You're sixteen years old, Ivanna. You shouldn't even be thinking about this. You should be focused on school. I won't tell Nik, but this will never happen again. Understood?"

I sob, not looking at him. Then he takes my chin in his fingers. "Do you understand me?"

"Yes," I whisper as my heart shatters.

I SIT UP IN BED, the familiar dream making my head and heart ache. I wipe my tear-filled eyes, trying to shake off the lingering sadness.

I knew it was a long shot, but the love-obsessed teen in me wanted to believe my mom meant it when she said love would always win.

I was in love with Dimitri. I wanted him more than anything I had ever wanted. Too bad that didn't matter.

He shattered my heart.

This will never happen again.

I heard his words and took them to heart. I was ready to avoid him at all costs after that day, but the next day Nik ruined my life. He assigned Dimitri as my personal bodyguard, giving him full control of my life.

He sent me to prison without the possibility of parole.

I wish I could say things got better from there, but they didn't. That love I once held for Dimitri changed. No longer was I the silly teen that believed in fairy tales.

Instead, he made me into the woman I am today. Someone who is desperate to get a taste of freedom. Maybe not even freedom itself. I'll never truly be free with Nik running the Bratva. Freedom from him. From this aching I feel in my heart every time I have to see him. It doesn't matter how much time has passed. Every single time I'm in a room with Dimitri, all I can think about is how he broke my sixteen-year-old heart.

Last night proved that no matter what I do, he will never truly let me have what I want. He will never let me date.

He says I pick the wrong guys, but isn't that what a girl my age is supposed to do?

Go to parties. Meet random guys. Make mistakes so that one day I can be old and wise? I want memories that I can look back on fondly.

I wouldn't even care so much about it if it wasn't for the fact that it was him doing it. It hurts even more to know that my warden is the same man I once dreamed of spending my life with. Now he refuses to let me marry anyone else.

He doesn't have a choice though. Nik told me when I was sixteen that he would never force me to marry anyone. That I would have the choice.

I know he's been pressured in the past, but he has always stuck to his word.

Sitting up in bed, I glance out the window. It's still dark.

I pull my knees up to my chest, burying my face in my knees.

All I want in this world is to be loved. To have someone as a partner. Someone who sees me as an equal and chooses me over everything else.

Dimitri would have never been able to do that. The Bratva must always come first. Maybe his rejection was a blessing in disguise.

Still, it doesn't solve my current issue. If he never lets me date, then I will never find that. I won't find a kind of love like Nik and Lia have.

My eyes well with tears as I think about how caged I feel. The pressure of not having control over a single part of my life.

I want to scream, but I don't. Not only would my roommate Kiera not appreciate that, but the guard outside the door would come running in here with his gun out.

Instead, I let the tears fall as I think about all my options.

The only problem is that I only really have two.

I either live my life alone in this cage or I have to make a choice about who I want to marry.

DIMITRI

Walking into my childhood home, I smile. It doesn't feel like it used to. These walls used to hold so much sadness and anger, but Lia has breathed life into it.

Gone are the statues Nik kept only because Father had them there. She's replaced them with new art pieces, adding color to the entry area.

These aren't the only changes she's made. The entire house looks like she gave it a face-lift, erasing all those old memories.

Even the servants and guards seem happier.

That's Lia for you though. She's a ray of sunshine.

"Oh my goodness. What are you doing here? I expected you to be grounded." Lia comes rushing into the room, wrapping me in a hug.

I hug her back before pulling away.

"He probably would have tried, but I demanded to speak with Nik."

Her eyes turn worried. "Why? What happened? Does this have to do with last night?"

I wince when she brushes her finger over my cheek.

It's started to bruise, but it's not that bad. I've gotten worse in training with Lia.

"Yes and no. I've made a decision. One that won't go over well, but it's my choice and I need you to support me on it."

She looks wary. "You know I always have your back. Even when you make dumb decisions and get us into trouble."

I smile, wrapping my arm in hers as I drag her toward Nik's office.

"That's why you're my ride or die. If I go down, you're going down with me. Besties for life."

She rolls her eyes. "I wish we didn't have to go down so often though. If you get me into any more trouble, I won't be able to sit for a week."

I scrunch my nose up. "Ew. I told you I didn't need to know about that shit."

She laughs. "Come on. I know him and Dimitri were meeting this morning, so they both should be in there."

I groan. "I was hoping he wouldn't be here. I should have known better when he didn't come get me himself."

"Do I get a hint about what you are planning to do?"

I shake my head. "If I tell you, you might talk me out of it and I really need this, Lia. Like if something doesn't change, I honestly don't know if I can keep living my life this way. It's that dire."

She lays her head on my shoulder. "I'm sorry he's so hard on you. I try talking to him, but he doesn't listen. I honestly think he's into you."

I snort. "Yeah, right. That ship sailed when I was sixteen. He legit said he would never allow me to kiss him again. Pretty sure he's just taking my care to extremes. I only see one way out."

"Ivy," she starts, but we arrive at Nik's office.

"Trust me."

She nods as I knock on the door.

Dimitri opens it, his eyes narrowing on mine.

"You can beg as much as you want, but Nik won't take me off your care."

I shrug, pushing down my normal anger. "I'm well aware. That's not why I'm here."

"Let her in, Dimitri. Go check on the training. I'll talk to you later," Nik calls.

Dimitri gives me one more look before offering Lia a small smile, then leaving.

Lia runs into the office, kissing Nik while I stare at Dimitri heading down the hall.

Well, here goes nothing.

Stepping into the office, I close the door. I don't walk over to my brother. I don't think I can. My nerves are shot. My hands are shaking and I feel like I might vomit. Instead, I take the seat in front of his desk.

Sensing the seriousness, he pushes Lia off his lap. She heads around the desk to take her place next to me, her hand finding mine.

"If you're here to complain about him, I'll listen as always, but I won't interfere," Nik advises me.

I swallow hard, tears pricking my eyes. "I have made a decision, but before I tell you what it is, I have something to say. I need you to listen, really listen, without saying anything. Can you do that?"

He considers it a moment before he nods.

"I can."

Taking a deep breath, I look down at my hand in Lia's.

"I know you meant well when you assigned Dimitri to me. He's your best friend. Hell, he was my hero. He always looked out for me, even when you weren't there. I idolized him. Then things changed. You made him my warden, and ever since then, I've felt more in prison than I ever did when Father was here."

"Ivy," he starts.

I shake my head, my eyes snapping to his. "Listening, remember?"

When he sits forward, leaning against his desk, he finally nods.

"I'm listening."

"I can't breathe, Nik. I feel so contained. So out of control of my own life. I feel like I'm suffocating. You know that even when I'm in class, if a guy gets too close, one of the guards will bust in and take them into the hall for a talk. Do you know how alienating that is? Most people on campus don't even want to talk to me for fear of what will happen. My roommate only deals with it because she has to, but even she has made it known that she's requested a new room for next semester. The whole reason I wanted to go to college was to live a little before I settle down, instead the experience is being stolen from me. I'm not happy, Nik, and if this is the way life is going to continue, then I never will be." I pause, taking a deep breath. "So with all that being said, I've decided I want you to arrange a marriage for me. I want someone who doesn't live in this household. Someone who will assign their own guards and take my safety into their own hands. Nik, I want you to free me from my prison."

The entire room is quiet as I feel the tears flow down my face. Lia's hand squeezes mine as I stare at Nik.

He hasn't blinked. He looks like he's in shock.

"Nik, did you hear me? I want to be married to someone outside of your Bratva."

Nik shakes his head slowly. "I heard you, Ivy. I'm just not sure I believe it. I have turned down proposal after proposal for your hand so you could marry for love, but now you want me to arrange it anyway?"

"I'm sorry it's such a hassle for you, dear brother. If this is the only way I can escape this stifling life, then yes."

"What if it doesn't make it better? What if you find someone even more restrictive? Someone who would harm you when you are disobedient?" he asks.

I start shaking my head before he even finishes. "I would hope you would use your judgment and only pick someone who will treat me well. We don't have to be in love. Hell, he doesn't even have to like me. All he has to do is save me."

"Dimitri won't like this," Nik starts, but I cut him off.

"Dimitri is the reason for this. You promised me I could choose whoever I wanted. I need to know if you meant that," I demand.

"I did. I do," he answers quietly.

"Then arrange a marriage for me. Someone who you are allied with, but not someone who works for you. I can't see him every day anymore, Nik. I can't."

Lia pulls me in, hugging me as I sob.

"Are you sure?" she whispers.

"I'm sure, Lia. I'm at my breaking point. It's either this or I lose my will to live. I'll leave the choice up to you, Nik."

"I'll handle it," he clips out as he moves.

When I feel him kneel beside me, I pull away from Lia to look at him.

"I didn't know you were hurting this bad. I'll do it. Give me a couple of days to put feelers out, but I'll make sure you end up with someone who will treat you well. Just know that if they don't, I will go to war for you."

"I know," I tell him, letting him pull me into a hug.

What I don't say is the one thing I should say.

I wish you'd fight your best friend for me.

DIMITRI

SOMETHING IS WRONG.

I can feel it in my gut.

I knew the moment I saw Ivanna that she was up to something. Something that I'm not going to like. It rarely is with her.

So when I see Nik's name pop up on my screen, I know shit is about to hit the fan.

"What did she want?" I demand.

"Sometimes I think you forget I'm your boss," Nik mumbles. "Come to my office."

Leaving the men training, I head back inside. I expect to see Lia or Ivanna, but neither are in sight. I don't hear a sound in the house.

Pulling my phone out, I frown when I see Ivanna's tracker moving away from the house. I didn't give approval for her to leave yet. I wanted to drive her back myself.

Entering Nik's office, I know right away that something has happened. I've only seen him look this torn about something when it came to Lia.

"What happened?"

"Sit. I'll get us a drink."

"Nik, don't try any of that placating bullshit with me. Something happened. Tell me what? Did that fucker hurt her worse than I thought? I swear to fuck I should have just killed him. He doesn't deserve to breathe."

"Dimitri, sit the fuck down. Now."

He pulled out the Pakhan tone. I want to argue, but I don't. I obey like the soldier I'm meant to be.

He moves to the bar, pouring us each vodka over ice before coming back to me. He hands me a glass before taking his seat behind the desk.

"For someone so smart, I swear you go stupid when it comes to my sister," he curses.

"So she complained about me? I knew she would. Her date let her get into a fight. Not only that, but he wasn't even by her side. I can't help that she picks weak men, Nik."

Nik pinches the bridge of his nose. "Dimitri, you've smothered the girl. I don't think you see what you've done. I know you don't because I didn't see it. Not until she brought it to me."

My stomach drops at his words. "I haven't done anything to her, but care for her. Protect her."

"You've become the villain in her story. She's feeling isolated. So backed into a corner that she finally snapped. You broke her, D. She's done. Do you know why she came to see me?"

I swallow hard. "To ask you to reassign me as she always does."

He shakes his head slowly. "She asked me to arrange a marriage for her."

I blink slowly. I don't think I heard him right.

"She wants you to arrange her marriage?"

"Yes."

My mind is processing, but my lips move faster than I can think.

"Me. Marry her to me."

He gives me a sad smile. "I would if I could. I'd rather her be right here with us all the time. Unfortunately, she had stipulations. Well, only one, really. She wants to marry anyone not in my Bratva. She doesn't want to be around you anymore. You specifically."

The other shoe has dropped. She's not escaping Nik or her life.

She's escaping me.

The glass in my hand shatters as it hits the wall. I don't even remember throwing it, yet the evidence is there in the vodka trailing down the wall.

DIMITRI

"I won't let her marry another." My tone is deep and low. Dark even.

I mean every word.

"That's the problem. You never claimed her yourself, yet you keep her from claiming another. She point-blank left the decision up to me. You know what she said? She said either I arrange a marriage for her or she will lose her will to live. What do I do with that, D? I want my sister happy. I should have never made that deal with you. I thought I was doing what was best. Letting you protect her while giving you time to come to terms with your feelings for her. I was wrong."

I'm so angry that I feel like my body is shutting down. Instead of lashing out, I'm internalizing it. Letting it build.

I want to find her right now. Tell her that she doesn't get the option to leave me. I guess that's why Nik sent her away.

"You made the deal with me," I say, deathly calm.

"I did. I also said that she would be yours, but only if she chose you. You took too long, and she's not choosing you. I've held up my end of the deal."

I slam my fist on his desk. "Bullshit. I will kill anyone who goes near her."

His eyes flare. "Don't make me put you down, Dimitri. I give you leeway with how you speak to me, but I will not accept such blatant disrespect."

"Protect her even over yourself. You said that. Put her first. She's the only thing that matters, Nikolai. I will kill anyone who tries to take her from me."

Nik growls. "It's her choice to make. If you can't keep your head clear, then I'll send you away on assignment. You won't keep making her miserable."

"Stand in my way and find out how seriously I took the oath I gave you the day you gave her to me."

He stares at me as I stare at him. Neither one of us moves or says a word.

After several minutes, he finally speaks. "This is happening, D. I wish it were you, but it's not. If you truly care for her, you will want her to be happy. Make your peace with it so that you can at least help me make sure whatever fucker she ends up with will be so scared of me, no, of us, that he will never dare harm her."

I don't answer him. I can't.

How do I tell my best friend that as much as I want Ivanna happy, I can't stand the thought of that happiness coming from someone other than me? I can't.

Instead, I jump up, leaving his office.

The only noise in the house is the door slamming against the wall as I stalk back out to the training area.

Interrupting the current fight, I stand in the middle.

"Come on, you weak-ass bitches. Let's fucking fight."

CHAPTER THREE

Ivanna

I expected Dimitri to show up and lose his shit.
Instead, it's been the opposite. He's all but disappeared. I still have his handpicked guards watching me, but it's eerie.
They haven't been up my ass like normal.
I even convinced Oleg to take me out for breakfast before class. I mean, sometimes I can get them to do it, but only when Dimitri allows it.
He didn't even call Dimitri.
It has me worried when I should feel ecstatic. I'm getting the space I so desperately wanted.
Why does it make me feel empty? Sad even.
Abandoned.

Shaking my head of the thoughts, I focus on the current task. Lia asked me to come to the house. She said she had something exciting to show me.

I'm hoping it's a pregnancy test. I'd kill to have a niece or nephew about now. Someone to take my mind off the drama in my own life.

"Thank you, Oleg," I tell my guard as he opens my door.

He nods, staying by the car as I make my way up to the house.

I'm not even through the door when Lia comes at me.

"I have been waiting forever. Come on." She grabs my arm, leading me to the library.

It's her favorite room in the house.

Instead of the normal couch and armchairs, she has a nest of some sort on the ground with blankets and pillows. In the center of it all are a bunch of binders.

"Did you really call me over here for a study date?" I groan.

"No. Sit."

Doing as she asks, I pick up one of the binders. I start flipping, seeing pictures of men with details on them.

I stop on one in particular. He's fucking hot. He has dark hair with the perfect amount of scruff. His lips are full and look perfect for kissing. His clothing is impeccable. The only thing I can't tell from the photo is what color his eyes are. He almost looks too good to be true.

He's no Dimitri. A little voice in my head taunts me.

I scan his bio and see his name is Declan O'Brien.

"What is this?" I point to the picture.

She leans forward, smiling.

"Ooh yeah, I knew you'd like him. He's cute, right? Nik said he's Irish, but that we don't have beef with them, so you can marry him if you want."

"Marry him? Is this what I think it is?"

"A dossier of men for you to choose from? Why yes, it is, bestie."

I look back down at the man. He is attractive. I glance at his details.

"Chicago? What the fuck, Lia?"

"What? I told Nik I wanted all the eligible bachelors from the families that we get along with. He threw a fit, but as you can see, I won. If you are going to marry a virtual stranger, then I'm going to make sure we pick the best one we can."

My heart melts. She really is the best. As much as she doesn't want me doing this, which she told me over and over yesterday when we went for ice cream, but she is still supporting me. She's in the passenger seat, helping me navigate through this.

God truly blessed me when he gave me her.

"Thank you, Lia. With that being said, I'm going to veto anyone that doesn't live in the state at least. I didn't want to go away to college because I would have had to be away from you for a short while. I don't want to marry someone who will take me away from you for good. No matter how hot the Irishman is."

She sighs, taking the binder from me.

"This binder is out then." She tosses it outside our circle of blankets. "It's too bad though. Declan is second in line for the Irish leadership in Chicago."

"I don't need another Dimitri," I growl. "One is more than enough."

She laughs, shaking her head.

I pick up the second binder, frowning when the first picture is of Dimitri.

"I thought I said I didn't want anyone who works for him."

She glances at the binder, frowning. "I know. I put that together as a last resort."

My eyes prick as I look at Dimitri's details. His likes and dislikes. His best traits and what makes him worthy of being a husband. All things I know better than any piece of paper can tell me, yet what's missing is the reasons it will never work.

I run my finger over his photo one last time before closing it and setting it aside.

"Ivanna, are you sure you want to do this?" Lia asks quietly, taking in my somber mood.

Do I? No, but I won't tell her that. Why would I want to get married when I've never even had a boyfriend? But I feel as if I'm backed into a corner and there is no other way out. Dimitri won't allow me to date, so what else am I supposed to do? Be miserable and alone for the rest of my life? No, I'll take my chances.

I shrug. "I feel like I have no other choice."

"Nik said Dimitri didn't take it well." She keeps her voice down.

I glance at the door to be sure we are alone before I lean in. "What did he do?"

"Threw a glass against the wall. Then he took on every single guard that was training yesterday. He even made them come at him as pairs."

I swallow hard.

"My guard didn't call him this morning when I asked to get breakfast," I admit. "Did Nik take back over?"

She shakes her head slowly. "Nik said he told him to either get his head clear and perform his duties as assigned or to leave on assignment until you've made your choice."

My heart stops. Like literally for one second, I think I might be dead.

"He left?"

The question leaves my mouth in such a cracked tone that I can't believe it came from me.

Her eyes widen. "I... I don't know. I haven't seen him since yesterday with you."

I suck in a breath.

Fuck, this hurts. The pain in my chest is almost too much to bear.

I mean, I put this in motion. I planned to marry someone else, but I think a very small part of me hoped that Dimitri would lose it and demand I marry him.

My fingers itch to reach for his picture again. To see him one more time.

Lia moves to my side. "Ivy, what's going on in that head of yours?"

I sniffle. "I didn't think he'd leave."

"Isn't that what you want? Space from him?"

I consider her words as I try to process my own feelings.

"I don't know. Lia, I don't know what I want. I wanted to stop feeling stifled. A small part of me even believed maybe he wouldn't allow this. That he would finally admit what I've always known, that I'm his. It's a toxic way of thinking, I know, but I can't help it."

She runs her hand over my head as I lean on her shoulder.

"Tell me what happened. How did we get here?" she whispers.

I've never told her the history of us. I never wanted to talk about it.

I feel like I need to now.

"He was my protector. When I was six, he stepped into that role and became my whole life. Between him and Nik, my world revolved around them. Then I hit puberty. All of a sudden, I noticed how handsome he was. Not only that, but he treated me like a princess. Like every girl would dream of. I held this crush in my heart, though, because my father would never allow it. He told me I was going to marry a man of his choosing to help better the Bratva. So I dreamed about Dimitri, but didn't let myself hope. I didn't dare mention him to Father, or else Nik would be punished. Father would never lay a hand on me, but he knew hurting Nik would hurt more. If he didn't beat him, he'd send Nik on an errand he didn't want to do. So when he finally died, I was relieved, but I still didn't dare voice my desire. When I was sixteen, Nik finally told me I could choose who I wanted to marry. I couldn't have been happier. I asked Dimitri to meet me in my room. I knew he was older, but I wanted him to know I chose him. That I would be his. So when he came in, I kissed him."

I hear Lia suck in a breath, but keep going.

"That's when my life turned into a true hell. He told me he didn't see me in that way and that it would never happen again. Almost immediately, Nik made him my keeper. You've seen the rest since then. I guess that little girl inside still hoped for her happy ending."

"Oh, Ivy. You'll get your happy ending. I'm sure of it."

I pull back, wiping my eyes. "It's too late for that. All I can hope for is a decent life that allows me some freedoms. Some little bouts of joy between the darker days."

"I think we can aim for better than that. We have a whole binder full of men. Maybe one of them isn't the man you dreamed about growing up, but one might be able to be the one you need. If you'll allow him to be."

"I feel like my heart was broken at sixteen and I've never had the chance to put it back together."

"No worries, boo. You have me here now. I refuse to let you live a miserable life. Let's take a look at our options."

As she pulls the binder across our laps, I lean against her.

If it weren't for her, I don't know if I would survive.

Dimitri

I SHOULD HAVE A BETTER HOLD on myself, but right now, all I can think about is destruction.

I want to burn down the entire planet. Then at least I would know that no one would be touching what's mine.

Only the thought of her no longer being a bright light in the world stops me.

"Are you done wallowing?" Nik asks from the door to the gym.

I might have intimidated the rest of the guys away. I didn't do it on purpose. Yesterday I challenged them to fight me because I needed an outlet.

All of them.

After fighting so many of them, sometimes more than one at once, and still standing, they became wary of me. When they refused to fight me anymore, I found my way in here.

I haven't left since.

"I'm not wallowing," I grunt out, throwing punches at the bag.

"You look like shit. Did you even sleep last night?" he asks.

I might have dozed during one of my breaks, but otherwise I've been letting out all my anger. My muscles burn, but the thought of another man touching her renews the energy I've depleted.

"What do you want, Nik?"

"I want to know what you're going to do about this."

Turning to him, I throw up my hands. "What do you want me to do? You said you're marrying her off. It sounded like I didn't get much of a fucking choice in that decision. You said I make her miserable. So yeah, I'm here. Processing that shit."

"Why did you never claim her?" he asks point-blank.

"She was sixteen, Nik."

"That's when you decided you wanted her, yes. I still have questions about that, by the way."

Sighing, I move to the bench, picking up my water and downing it. After several moments of silence, I speak.

"She kissed me. At first, I was appalled. She was sixteen years old. I told her it couldn't happen and left, but the more I thought about it, the more I realized that she was there. She was at the point where she was going to be dating and kissing and everything. At the time, I put the claim on you because I didn't want any other fucker hurting her. I was looking out for her in the only way I knew how. I thought I was being brotherly, but then she went off to college and I watched her become a woman. I don't know when, but I stopped seeing her as a girl. Instead, I saw the woman I wanted to spend the rest of my life with. Even when she makes me want to strangle her to death more often than not. She wouldn't have me now though. I know that. I waited too long and burned those bridges. She hates me."

"Haven't you ever heard that there's a thin line between love and hate?" Nik asks.

"You've seen her with me. Do you really think she even likes me most of the time?"

"I think that the opposite of love is indifference. My sister is hurting so bad over this shit with you that she's willing to marry anyone outside of this family to get away from you. If she hated you, she wouldn't be running. Ivy would fight you and she'd win. I've watched you two fight over the years. As much as I hate to admit it, I see the chemistry between you two. I've noticed every time you give in and give her what she wants without letting her see it. The same way I see her concede the fight to you when she knows you're right. It's a minefield between you two, but the question is, are you willing to cross it?"

"I'd cross the pits of hell for her."

"You and I know that. You proved it when she was taken, but she doesn't. Prove it to her. She and Lia are looking through dossiers. I've asked them to come up with some men she would like to be formally introduced to. I want you there. I want you to see what she's doing and then do everything in your power to change her mind. I'm not marrying her off to another family. She belongs here. With us. Make it happen."

"If they touch her..." I trail off.

"You need to keep your anger in check. Lighten up on her. Let her have a little more freedom. Show her that you heard her and are trying to do as she asked. Maybe that will slow this train down until you can climb on."

"I might have already told her lead guard to use his best judgment and not call me for every little thing. Only the important ones."

It killed me to do it, but when Nik told me how much pain Ivanna was in, I couldn't help it. I had to give her something, anything.

I mean, this morning I still tracked her on her phone to the diner and all the way here. I know she's in the house somewhere. It's why I'm still down here. Trying my best to give her the space she so desperately wants. At least as much as I can.

"That's surprising. I didn't think you'd give in so soon," Nik admits.

"Me either, but I don't want her to get hurt. I'd do anything to take any pain away from her. I can't stand the thought of her out there without me to protect her if need be. I've felt this overwhelming need to protect her ever since I saw her punch that dickwad Boris when she was six years old. That's never going to change."

"She's not a little girl anymore, D. She's an adult who wants an opportunity to live life. I'm going to try to stall this marriage thing as long as I can, but while I do, you need to fix this."

I nod at him. "Are you telling me that as Pakhan?"

He growls. "I'm telling you that as your best friend and her brother. I can't imagine anyone I would trust more with her. I don't want her out of this house, D. Fix it. Quickly."

With that, he leaves the room, leaving me with my thoughts.

If there is even a small chance I can repair what's broken, I'll do it.

At the end of the day, she's the only thing in my life that matters.

CHAPTER
FOUR

Ivanna

I feel like we have been looking at pictures for hours. The first flip through, she had me take out any who were hard no's from the first impression. That meant all the men my father's age and any of the men who were younger than me. I didn't want to be a babysitter. I need a man who is experienced enough with life to be confident, but not cocky. I also need him to not be geriatric.

Still, looking through them all has left me feeling depressed.

My fingers itch to pick up that other binder. The one I know I shouldn't.

I must stare at it too long though because, after our third flip through, she picks it up.

"Are you sure you don't want to consider someone in-house? I can't say I'm not being selfish here. I don't want you away from us. It's bad enough that you decided to live on campus. Now you're basically moving out for good."

I sigh. "I would love to pick someone from that binder, but it wouldn't be fair to them. I would never truly be able to be with them because he would always be around. I would never get the chance to truly move past this feeling I feel for him."

Lia flips through the binder until she lands on Maxim's photo.

"What about Maxim? We both know he's awesome. He wouldn't expect anything from you. He would protect you and care for you. He's perfect for this. I really think you could learn to love him one day too."

I scrunch my nose. "Maxim is the best. Really, but I don't see him that way. Besides, doesn't he deserve to find love too?"

Lia snorts. "Oh, I'm sure Maxim finds a lot of love. Fine, not Maxim. What about..."

"No," I stop her, my hand on the page. "There is only one man between those pages I'd consider."

She frowns. "Then pick him. Demand him. Nik will make it happen."

I shake my head. "I can't. The Bratva is his whole life. I know he would accept if Nik ordered it, but that's not what I want. I don't want him to be forced to be with me. That would only make things a million times worse. Knowing I took his choice away. I would never be able to believe that anything he feels for me is real. I know you're trying to do what's best for me, but trust me when I say the ship with Dimitri has sailed. It's so far gone you can't even see it anymore."

She bites her lip for a moment before nodding. Putting down the binder, she picks up the approved binder.

"Okay, then last flip through for tonight. We have ten men left after taking out all the ones who didn't meet your specifications."

I chuckle. "You mean yours? All I said was I didn't want a grandpa or a baby. You are the one who kept going through and making choices."

She laughs. "Fine. Yes, my specifications. I need to make sure my girl is taken care of. Now let's start with bachelor number one. Yuri Golubev. He's twenty-five. He lives in Santa Rosita, California, where he's a brigadier under his uncle. He's not in line to inherit the Pakhan title, but he is still high enough up to hold influence. He's known to be ruthless on the streets, but Nik's note says that he has been instrumental in helping stop the meat markets in their city. That's promising."

She turns the binder so I can look at the picture. He's handsome. He has blond hair slicked back on his head. He also has a short beard that looks more like scruff, but it's kind of sexy. I can tell he's built from the photo provided. His broad shoulders fill out his T-shirt as if he's trying to bust out. I don't miss the tattoo on the side of his neck showing his position. His brown eyes are brighter, shining.

Still as attractive as he is, I can't help but compare him to Dimitri. Whereas Yuri is tough looking almost like a street gangster, Dimitri is more subtle. He is broad and built as well, but he dresses to look less so. He prefers to let others underestimate him. Then there are his features. Dimitri's dark hair is cut closer to his head, leaving only a little to play with, but boy, have I imagined pulling it. Then there's his facial hair. It's almost as if he shaves every morning, yet somehow he always has this five o'clock shadow. It's dark and sexy, making me want to feel the scratch of it against my face. Even better, between my thighs. The most striking part of Dimitri though is his eyes. They are dark brown, almost black. When he looks at you, it's almost as if he's staring directly into your soul. It's the reason I try not to maintain eye contact with him. I feel like he's burning me from the inside out.

Clearing my throat, I force a smile. "He's cute."

"Right? I'll star him. Next we have Boris Makarov. He's..."

"No." My eyes glance at the picture.

How did I not notice him before? I wasn't looking at names, I guess. He doesn't really look like the asshole from my childhood. He's grown up. I'd even say he was attractive if I didn't know what a douche he was.

"Oh. Um. Okay." She goes to flip the page, but I stop her.

"He doesn't look the same. Boris and Nik don't get along. When we were younger, Boris was always jealous of Nik. He would pick on me to get to him. I can't tell you how many times Dimitri beat him up. It would piss them both off if we chose him."

She looks over at me. "It would piss Dimitri off?"

I shrug. "He never liked the way Boris spoke to me. I haven't seen him since my father died. Nik cut off all contact with his family. He looks different. His hair used to be longer and he never could grow facial hair."

She smiles. "Dimitri would be pissed, Ivy."

"Okay? Are we trying to piss him off? I mean, he isn't even here, Lia."

She grabs my arm. "I'm going to ask you one question. I want you to answer honestly without weighing the options, okay?"

I nod slowly.

"If you could have anyone in any of these binders, or hell, in the entire world, who would it be?"

I suck in a breath. I know why she's asking. Still, am I ready to admit it?

"Dimitri," I breathe out quietly.

"That's what I thought. Hear me out on this. What if we choose a couple of men you're actually interested in so we are giving this a fair shot, but also pick one or two we know he won't approve of? Like, let's say Boris here."

"You want to see if it will make him jealous?" I shake my head. "I don't think it's jealousy. I think he's just overprotective and can't stand the douche."

"Maybe, but don't you want to know once and for all? Don't you want to put it all on the line one last time before you hitch yourself to someone else's wagon?"

I sigh. "I don't want to get my hopes up."

"So don't. Just throw Boris into the mix, and hell, he might surprise you."

Rolling my eyes, I concede, "Fine."

DIMITRI

We finish up looking through the rest of the men. After looking at so many pictures and debating the merits of each man, I feel like my eyes could bleed, but we got it narrowed down. All in total, with Boris, I chose four possibilities. None of them live here, but they are all under three hours away. All of them are Russian. I had never really thought about it until we started going through the binders, but I really do want someone who shares my culture and customs.

"See you tomorrow," I call over my shoulder as she walks toward Nik's office.

"Later!"

I head down the stairs to find my guard, ready for the day to end. My mind drifts back to Dimitri. Did he really leave?

I'm surprised when I run into a broad chest. Looking up, his dark eyes captivate mine, holding me hostage.

"Where are you going, *printsessa*?"

"Oh." I'm so surprised and relieved to see Dimitri that I'm not even angry at his tone. "You're here? I thought you left."

He tilts his head, studying me. "I would never leave you unprotected. Why would you think that?"

"Well, this morning, then Lia..." I shake my head. "Never mind, it doesn't matter. I'm going to find Oleg to drive me home."

He grunts, his hands still on my arms from where he stopped me when I ran into him.

"I'll take you. Oleg is training."

"Oh. Okay."

I let him lead me out the door, unsure how to feel about this. He's not getting angry with me. He's calm and collected. It's almost as if he's given up caring. I hate it. I want him to yell. To manhandle me and make me listen to him. I didn't realize it until this moment, but I live for his demands.

I never truly understood the saying you don't know what you have until it's gone. Now that Dimitri isn't being an overbearing prick, I kind of miss his sternness. My equilibrium is off. So off that I don't say a word as he loads me into his car before taking off toward campus.

Do I really mean so little to him that he can give up his control so quickly? I bet he's happy to pass on the responsibility to someone else. He can finally be rid of his burden.

I'm so lost in my head that when his hand touches my knee, I jump.

He holds up his hands. "Sorry. We are here. I'll walk you up. Vlad will be here in thirty minutes to watch over you. Can I trust you to behave?"

"You're leaving me alone?"

He nods slowly. "For thirty minutes."

"Why?" I blurt out.

He looks confused. "Isn't this what you've been wanting? More freedom? Isn't that what this whole marriage thing is about? I'm trying to compromise with you, Ivanna."

I swallow hard. "This marriage thing is more than needing you to loosen the reins. I'm tired of feeling alone all the time. The only time I truly feel like I'm not is when I'm with Lia or Nik. I can't be with them all the time. I want to find a partner. Someone who is going to treat me as an equal. This may have started as a way to liberate myself from your stifling control, but now that I've had time to think about it, it's what I need. You said it yourself, I pick losers. Men who won't be able to protect me. So I'm enlisting help. Nik won't let me marry anyone not worthy."

As I speak, Dimitri's eyes grow darker. I'm waiting for it. The explosion. It doesn't come though. Instead, he nods before getting out of the car. He doesn't speak another word until he's escorted me to my dorm room.

"Thirty minutes. I'm trusting you, Ivanna."

I nod, knowing I won't leave. I have nowhere to go. I craved this freedom so much, but now that it's here. I don't want it.

I want him.

Shaking off my thoughts, I lock myself in my room. For once, I'm glad my roommate is gone. I let the tears fall as I curl up on my bed.

My life has never been easy.

I just wish for one second it was.

Dimitri

She doesn't leave her dorm.

I know because even though I told her that she would be alone, I'm still watching. I'm always watching her. She's become my obsession.

She wants an equal. The problem is we will never be equal. She will always be way better than me. Still, she will be mine. I can't let her go. Nik and his men will have to put me down first.

So instead of focusing on that, I work on keeping myself under control. I wanted to lose it when she told me about what she wanted. How this has evolved from escaping me to actually wanting to marry someone else.

I refuse to allow it though.

While sitting in the car, I plot.

How will I win her over and prove to her that I'm the man for her? That answer comes fast enough. I'll shower her with all of her favorite things. I'll take her on dates to places she's mentioned in passing. She wants a wedding? I'll meet her at the altar. Children? The thought of having a mini Ivanna that has my blood running through her veins makes the hair on my arms stand up in equal parts anticipation and dread.

I'll woo her like she's never been wooed, no matter how much it kills me.

The bigger question is though, how do I make her believe I'm serious? How do I convince her to take a chance on me?

For five years, I've been an asshole to her. I've built walls clearly separating us from each other and tearing down any shred of hope for a future between us that she had.

I honestly don't know if redemption is possible for me at this point. Just the thought of her truly walking away makes my heart stop beating.

Knock it off, Dimitri, you'll get her.

My phone rings, pulling me out of my head.

"Ya?"

"I've set up her first date." Nik jumps right to the point.

I clench my jaw so tight I swear I hear a tooth crack.

"Who?" I grind out through clenched teeth.

Nik pauses. "I wish you were here so I could see your face when I tell you."

"Stop teasing me, Nikolai. Now tell me."

"Boris."

Boris. Boris. Do I know a Boris? My mind filters through a Rolodex of names until it finally clicks.

"No," I say, shaking my head. "Absolutely not. She would never."

"That's what I thought too," Nik mumbles. "I thought it was a mistake, so I asked Lia. She confirmed that Ivy wants to go out with Boris Makarov."

"Why? I don't understand."

"Your guess is as good as mine, but I've made the call and the date is set."

"Call and cancel. Tell them it was a mistake," I demand.

"I can't do that, D. You and I both know that. I'm just giving you a heads-up so you have some time to process this before it happens."

I stare at her dorm building. All I want to do is get out of the car and storm up to her door. Grab her and turn her over my knee and paddle her ass red until she agrees to stop this nonsense.

"D, you there?"

DIMITRI

"Do you know where he plans on taking her?"

"I don't have the details yet, but when I do, you'll be the first to know."

"He won't get a chance to be alone with her."

"I would hope not. I'll know more tomorrow and send you the information. That way, you can talk to your team and make a plan."

"Fine."

I hang up without waiting for him to respond. Dropping my phone in the cupholder I take a deep breath.

I try counting to ten, but my anger gets the best of me.

"Fuck!" I roar as I slam my palm on the steering wheel.

Boris Makarov has had a death wish for years. When we were younger, he treated Ivy like she was beneath him when really it was him beneath her.

"I'll play your games, *printsessa*. Just know if he touches you, we'll be leaving wearing his blood."

AFTER I LEFT Ivanna's earlier, I drove around for a while, trying to calm down. I knew that if I went into the training room again, he would have my ass.

"For fuck's sake, D, next time, take your anger somewhere else. The guys are still trying to recover."

Eventually, I found myself pulling into my driveway. Shutting off the car, I stare out at the house. I recently added a fresh coat of paint to the siding and shutters. As far as I'm concerned, it's ugly as fuck, but I know when the day comes and Ivy sees it, she will love it.

Getting out of the car, I look around the street. The rest of the houses are older but well-kept. I can hear children playing down the street and it brings a smile to my face.

Maybe someday I will come home to Ivy sitting on the porch with a child playing in the yard.

Shaking my head, I let myself into the house and head into the kitchen. With the news Nik dropped earlier, I know I need to be alone. After tossing my keys onto the island, I open the freezer and grab a bottle of vodka. Next, I get a glass from the cabinet and pour myself a drink.

As the silence surrounds me, I take a sip. Compared to Nik's, my place is silent, still. No one is walking around to make sure the place is secure, no radios going off with people checking in, nothing. It's such a sharp contrast to Nik's I almost don't know what to think of it. While I love the quietness and being alone with my thoughts, it's almost stifling.

I've only stayed here a few times, even though I've had the house for years. Recently I started coming by and fixing it up. Nothing too major, but making it livable. Refreshing the paint to neutral colors.

Leaning against the counter, I look around the kitchen. It's nice but doesn't get used like it should. I still need to buy some barstools for the island and fully stock the cupboards.

What would Ivy think of this place?

I smile at the thought. Not for the first time, I think about her making herself at home here. She would fill the walls with photos and art. Knowing her, she would replace my couch with one that she approved of and add throw blankets along the back in case she got cold.

She would make this house a home and I would let her.

Pushing off the counter, I walk into the downstairs bathroom. Bending down, I open the can of paint and get to work. Earlier in the week, I prepped the walls with primer. Before, the owners had it painted a hideous fluorescent orange. As I paint the walls, my anger dissipates.

I can't blame Ivy for doing what she thinks is best, even though she's wrong. For now, though, I'll bide my time and wait her out. Soon enough, she will see the error of her ways.

Once I'm done painting and have everything cleaned up, my body is aching and ready for sleep. I walk throughout the house and think about her here in my space. Her laughter would echo down the hall as I chased her into my bedroom. As I walk into my room, I stop and eye my bed. I can't help but smile as I think about her jumping into the middle of my bed and spreading her arms and legs wide, taking up the entire thing.

Shaking my head, I head into the bathroom and turn on the shower. As it heats, I take off my clothes. After tossing my clothes into the hamper, I look around. While the layout of the bathroom is fine, it needs updating. Do I get one sink or two? What about storage? Ivy's bathroom counter looks as if a bomb hit it with how many products it has on it.

"Enough, Dimitri. You have to win her over first before you can think about all that shit," I scold myself as I get into the shower.

I shower quickly and dry off. Walking into my bedroom naked, I fall face-first onto my bed and drift off to sleep, dreaming of the future.

CHAPTER
FIVE

Ivanna

Nik wasn't happy about me choosing Boris, but he allowed it. I don't know what conversation he had with Lia, but she convinced him.

That's why I'm dressed in a little black dress, ready to go to the ballet.

Why is it that all Russian men like ballet? I find it quite boring. I mean, sure, the dancers are amazing, but it's not my thing.

Still, Boris chose it, so I must go.

"You'll have four guards. Only one will be in the box with you though. You will allow them to have eyes on you at all times. They will allow minimum physical contact. You go to the ballet and then straight back home. Do you understand?"

Nik has been going over all the rules for the night for the past ten minutes. I want to be mad at him, but I know he doesn't want me to go at all. Boris has always been a problem for him. Only his family name has kept him alive.

"I understand. Thank you for letting me do this."

Nik pulls me into a hug. "You look beautiful, Ivy. I want you to be happy. No offense, but I hope Boris is not the one, but if he is, I will give him a fair shot to show me he's changed."

"Try not to worry about me. I promise I can handle this," I tell him.

He squeezes me once more before letting me go.

"I know you can. I've watched you fight before. If he tries anything, stab him in the nuts."

I snort. "You think I can get to him before my guard can?"

Nik looks over my shoulder. I glance to see who he is looking at.

My breath catches.

Dimitri is standing behind me, wearing a suit and tie. He looks like he's part of the secret service with his earpiece in his ear. Hell, my knees go weak at the sight of him.

Dimitri's jaw clenches and his hands flex as he looks me up and down.

Is he checking me out?

"I think your guard will have his hand cut off before you pull your knife out of your thigh holster," Nik whispers into my ear before straightening back up.

"Dimitri, take good care of my sister."

Dimitri nods. "Always. Are you ready?"

"Yeah. I mean, yes." I try to clear my throat.

His lips twitch as if he wants to smile, but he doesn't. Instead, he moves to my side, tucking my hand into the crook of his arm as he leads me out the door. I see my team already in the cars.

"Oleg will be driving us. Ilya and Stepan will be in the car behind us." He helps me into the car before moving around to get in the other side. "When we get there, they will survey the area before coming to get us. Boris has you in a private box. I'll be inside the box with you at

DIMITRI

all times. If you ever at any point feel uncomfortable, all you have to do is look at me and widen your eyes. I will come for you immediately. Understood?"

"I'm surprised you're allowing this," I admit softly as I get into the car.

He grits his teeth. "I didn't want to, but it wasn't my choice. Let's not get into that now. We will be there in fifteen minutes. I need to check in with the men I have on-site to make sure it's safe."

"I thought Nik said I would only have four guards?" I ask.

"You do. These men are making sure Boris isn't trying anything. I refuse to walk into this blind."

Reaching out, I touch his hand, making his gaze snap to it.

"Thank you for taking such care with my security. It's going to be fine."

He looks frozen. Almost as if he didn't know what to do or say. I'm sure it's odd for him. We usually fight.

This decision I made has put us in a weird limbo where neither one of us really knows how to act toward the other.

"Of course it will. I won't let anything happen to you." His eyes meet mine, flashing with heat.

The sudden flash of emotion shocks me enough to pull my hand back.

He doesn't comment on it. Instead, he focuses on his phone, typing away.

I look out the window and stare at the city lights and passing cars. My stomach is fluttering with both excitement and unease. Ever since I put this all into motion, I've been thinking about this moment. I've never been on a real date before, and somehow, the person who will get that first from me is the man who used to bully me as a child.

He could end up with some more firsts from you, I remind myself.

"Are you ready?" Dimitri asks as we pull into the ballet.

"As ready as I'll ever be." I smile weakly.

Dimitri grunts as he gets out of the car. He holds his hand out and I slip mine into his, letting him help me get out.

"Thank you." I drop his hand and smooth down my dress.

Dimitri holds his arm out for me and I hold on as we head toward the building. Stepping inside, I take a look at the beautiful room. The chandeliers are large and sparkling and the room is grand. Almost immediately, I spot Boris and head his way.

"Ivanna, you look gorgeous." Boris steps forward to greet me.

Dimitri's arm tightens as if he doesn't want to let me go, but after a moment, he lets me slip my hand from his arm.

"Thank you. You look quite dashing as well," I tell him, stepping forward to allow him to take my hand.

I hear a slight growl behind me when Boris brings my hand to his lips. He brushes them carefully before putting my hand on his arm.

"Shall we?"

"Yes, please."

I allow him to lead me toward the private box he's rented out. He places his hand on the small of my back as he lets me step inside first. He goes to shut the door behind him, but Dimitri is there.

"We don't need you in here. It's just us two. I can keep her safe," Boris tells Dimitri.

Dimitri ignores him, pushing his way inside. He looks around before posting against the wall where he will be able to see us the entire show. I meet his eyes. He looks angry, but he doesn't say a word.

Boris scoffs but makes his way toward me. "I thought we would have a more intimate setting to get to know one another."

I force a smile. "My safety is of the utmost importance to my brother. You understand."

He has been polite so far, but I see that glimmer of the man he once was in his eyes. He hates that my brother is superior to him. His family runs their own Bratva operation, but it's not as big or successful as ours.

"Of course. The Bratva princess. I have to admit I was surprised when my father told me that Nikolai was looking for possible grooms for you. He always rejected any requests for alliances. I've even offered myself once or twice."

"It's my choice. I'm almost done with my schooling. I know a job is out of the question for me, so I want to find my partner. Someone I can help lead with."

Boris's chest puffs out at my words. Almost as if he thinks I am talking about him. I guess I can see why he would make that assumption. I did invite him on this date.

"Did you choose me?" he whispers.

I reluctantly nod. "I did."

"Good. I'd be a good match for you. We can get married as soon as you want to. How many children do you have in mind? We will need heirs. Preferably two, one in case anything happens to the other one, but I'm open to more."

My mind whirls at his insinuation. That would mean I would need to have sex with him and while he is objectively attractive, I still remember the snot-nosed kid who hit me when I was a girl.

As much as I hate to admit it, every time I've thought about kids, I've always pictured Dimitri as their father.

I shake my head, clearing my thoughts. "Of course. I haven't chosen a husband yet though, Boris. This is a date, not a proposal."

His eyes flash with anger. His hand on mine, which I didn't even realize was there, tightens. I grimace but try to keep it from my face. I know Dimitri is watching our every move.

"Boris, I would like my hand back," I say softly.

He releases me immediately, glancing over at Dimitri with a flash of fear. It makes me want to snort. I don't know how many times Dimitri has taught him lessons over the years, but I know Boris has never gotten the upper hand. Not one single time.

"The ballet is about to start. We should be quiet," he whispers.

I nod, giving my attention to the stage. Once the lights lower, I feel Boris resting his arm over my shoulders. It makes me uncomfortable, but I don't dare tell Dimitri. I need to stick this out.

I feel his eyes on me throughout the show. At least, I imagine they are on me. I want them on me. I want him to give me all of his attention.

I'm so focused on what I want Dimitri to be doing behind me that when Boris leans over to me during the show, I freeze.

"You keep rubbing your thighs together. Are you feeling frisky? If you can slip your guard, I can take care of that itch for you."

I move my head away from him, giving him a slight smile. "I'm cold."

I say it loud enough that Dimitri hears so that Boris knows I'm not playing those games with him.

He grunts, moving back to his seat, but not before shooting a glance over his shoulder. He got the message.

A moment later, there's movement behind me. Suddenly he's there at my side, kneeling with his coat in hand.

He lays it over my lap, tucking it on either side of my legs.

"Thank you," I whisper, looking into his eyes.

He nods once, moving back to his place by the wall.

My heart is pounding in my chest.

What am I doing? Why am I here with this jackass who wouldn't even offer his jacket when a woman says she's cold? This is a mistake.

My chest feels like it's constricting. I don't know how I make it through the rest of the show. I guess because all I can focus on is my breathing. When the lights finally come on, I clap as if I watched the show, but I couldn't tell you a single part. Standing, I fold Dimitri's jacket over my arm.

"It was a pleasure, Boris," I tell him with a bit of annoyance in my tone.

"You will choose me, Ivanna. I will see you soon."

He kisses my hand once more before leaning in to kiss me. I turn at the last second, letting his lips find my cheek.

I'm suddenly pulled back as Dimitri steps in front of me.

"You should leave now, Boris." Dimitri spits his name as if it's trash.

"You should mind your business, Dimitri. Are you upset that your little doll wants someone else?"

I frown at his words.

His little doll?

"Say another word and I'll end this here and now," Dimitri's hand reaches to his hip, where his gun is in full view.

Boris lets out a nervous laugh before speaking. "My father would go to war with Nikolai. I'll leave though. We all know who she wanted to be here with tonight."

I want to say that he's wrong. The only person I want to be with is Dimitri, but I hold my tongue. Admitting that would do nothing for me except expose me as the foolish girl I am.

Boris calls one last goodbye to me before leaving.

Dimitri turns, taking his jacket before draping it over my shoulders and buttoning it in the middle. Then all of a sudden, we are moving.

"Dimitri, your weapons are in view," I whisper.

"I don't fucking care," he grunts out.

I don't say another word. All I can focus on is the fact that he has his fingers threaded between mine. He's holding my hand.

My hand.

It's like my mind can only focus on the tingling sensation from his skin on mine.

It's not until we are tucked in the SUV that I find my voice.

"What was that back there?" I whisper.

"Not now, Ivanna," he growls, typing on his phone furiously.

"You can't just dismiss me like that." I raise my voice.

He looks up from his phone with a deadly calm look. It makes me swallow hard.

"Ivanna, I'm barely restraining the need to go find Boris and slice off every piece of his body that touched you. So when I say not now, I mean not fucking now."

I want to argue, but I see the danger behind his eyes. He means his words. He's fighting some darkness right now. Something he's never once let me see before.

It's like the man in front of me is still the same one I've always known, but suddenly there's another layer to him. I thought I knew everything about Dimitri, but this one glimpse shows me I've only ever scratched the surface. The sudden need to dig further below overwhelms me. I fight it though.

Folding my arms over my chest, I don't miss the way his eyes dip to my breasts. It heats me up, but I push that down.

"Fine." I turn, facing the window, unable to allow him the last word.

I wish I knew why I was this way. Why only he works me up the way he does. Any of the other guards and I would have obeyed immediately, knowing they were doing their job, but with Dimitri, I can't seem to give him the same treatment. It's like I need to fight against him to get a reaction. I crave that attention. Even if it's negative.

When we finally pull up to the house, I don't wait for him to open my door. I jump out, running up to the door, but he catches me quickly. He turns me, pressing my back against the door as he cages me in.

I hear the other men disperse, leaving us alone.

"Why are you running, Ivanna?" His tone is low.

"I'm not running. You don't want to talk, so I'm going to bed," I huff.

I try to duck under his arm, but his hand comes up, collaring my throat as he pins me to the door. I gasp at the sudden aggression.

"I said I didn't want to talk in the car with other ears present. Now we are going to talk whether you like it or not. What was that about tonight, Ivanna? He was all over you."

"Can't a man find me desirable? Why is that so hard to believe? Why are you so against a man wanting me?"

He growls, moving his body closer as his hand tightens slightly on my throat. Not enough to cut off my air, but enough to remind me it's there. It equally pisses me off and turns me on.

"Get your hands off me, Dimitri. If you don't, I will tell Nik and he will kill you for laying a hand on me."

Dimitri laughs, but it doesn't sound right. He sounds angry. Almost as if he's barely in control of himself.

For the very first time in my life, I feel a prick of fear in his presence.

"Ivanna, you can tell your brother whatever the fuck you want. If he wants to try and kill me, let him. Why did you let Boris touch you?"

"It's a date. What do you think people do on dates? They talk and touch, and hell, most of the time, it ends in sex. Obviously, you ruined that for me."

His hand pulses on my throat, making my heart tick up a notch.

"Is dick all you wanted? Is that what you were trying to get?"

He's so close now. Closer than he's ever been to me. It's both infuriating and exhilarating.

"If you wanted dick, all you had to do was ask," he whispers.

He presses his body against mine, his erection obvious through his slacks. He runs his nose along the side of my face, inhaling my scent. When he grinds into me, I let out a small squeak.

"I have all the dick you need, *printsessa*."

He pulls the top of my dress off my right shoulder and drops a kiss there.

"Dimitri, we need to stop. We can't do this. Not here." I try to push against him, but he's a brick wall.

He continues to kiss my shoulder.

"Dimitri," I hiss.

He pulls back finally, looking me in the eye. He's fighting himself. I don't know what he's thinking, but it looks like he is on the cusp of losing it.

He takes a couple of deep breaths, still holding me against the door, his body against mine. I feel his dick twitch as he calms himself. When he finally gets himself under control, he removes his hand from my throat. For a brief moment, I miss the warmth of it.

He doesn't step back though. Instead, he grinds against me one last time.

"If you want dick, you find me. Mine is the only dick you'll ever get."

I go to argue with him, but his lips suddenly land on mine, taking the words from my mouth. It's a quick kiss. So brief that I almost think I imagined it.

"End of discussion. Get your ass to bed." He opens the door, smacking my ass hard before pushing me inside.

When the door closes behind me, him on the other side, I stand there motionless.

What the fuck just happened?

Dimitri

I SHOULDN'T HAVE TOUCHED her. I really shouldn't have, but I couldn't help it.

My self-control is something I pride myself on, yet for some reason, I feel this uncontrollable need to take her. Mark her as mine.

Maybe it's because she's changed the status quo. She's no longer content living under my rule. Instead, she's rebelling the only way she knows I cannot stop.

Nik honors his promises, especially to his family. I knew this one, in particular, would come back to bite me in my ass. I only hope I'll have more time before I have to make my move.

There's no denying how her eyes flared when I pinned her to the door. Or how she arched into my touch and her breathing picked up when my hand wrapped around her neck. The gasp she let out when I slammed my mouth onto hers and took what was mine.

The game has started. She took the first step. I've countered it.

Now I have to wait to see what she will do next.

So instead of taking her like I want, I'm going to do the opposite. I'm going to give her a taste of the freedom she craves so bad.

Dialing her main guard's number, I wait for him to answer.

"Sir," he answers.

"Oleg, I want you to allow her some more freedom. See what she does. Make sure she's never in any danger, but allow her to experience the college campus a bit more."

"Of course," he agrees immediately.

"Keep me updated. Let me know if anything happens. I want a report at the end of each day of what she does."

"Yes, sir."

I hang up the phone, not needing to relay any other information. He's probably in his quarters. When we are on Nik's property, there's no need for him to keep constant guard. There are plenty of others around to do that.

Yet I can't stop watching for her.

So after I'm sure she's crawled into her bed, I make my way up to her room. I peek inside the door, smiling at her lying in the room she grew up in. She looks so peaceful sleeping. I don't miss the fact that she has my suit jacket wrapped around her even as she sleeps. She needs me as much as I need her.

I've spent far too many nights watching over her this way without her even knowing.

Closing her door quietly, I move down the hall to the door next to hers. It's a small room with only a single bed. It was meant for the nanny when Ivanna and Nik were kids, but it's been mine ever since she was dismissed. I've spent every night so close to the girl that has become my obsession, yet I've never felt so far away.

Stripping down, I make my way to my bed situated against the wall. The same wall that her bed is against on the other side. I like feeling close to her. Knowing I will hear her if she screams out. The only thing better would be being in there with her.

Settling on my bed naked, I lean my head against the wall, imagining I can hear her breathing.

Closing my eyes, I conjure up the memory of a couple hours ago. The way her heart beat erratically made her pulse jump under my hand. Behind the slight panic in her eyes, there was heat. She is such a wild and free spirit, but she craves the domination I can bring her. She would flourish under it in the right situation.

That's what I've been doing wrong all these years. I've been trying to dominate all areas of her life, but she doesn't want that.

No, she wants to make her own choices in everyday life but submit in the bedroom. I can feel it in my bones.

She reacted so beautifully too. Even when she tried to fight back, I could feel her body giving in to me. Her legs trembled as I pressed against her.

God, the way she smelled. I've always loved her scent. She smells like strawberries and cream. Sweet and juicy.

As I remember the way her skin felt under my touch, my hand reaches down to grip my dick. I haven't gone soft since pressing her against that door. Hell, even before then.

I start to squeeze as I remember my lips on her skin. The way she filled out that tight black dress. How her breath caught when I grabbed her. The feel of her pulse fluttering under my hand as I ran my nose along her skin.

Fuck, she's intoxicating.

And she thought she could let another man touch her? She's sorely mistaken. She's mine.

I let fantasy take over reality. The way it would have gone if she had already known she was mine. The punishments I would have forced upon her.

I can see her now. Her nipples pebbled as I ripped that dress off her body. I'd never let her wear it again after wearing it for another man.

Then I would sink my teeth into the meaty skin of her neck, only biting hard enough to leave a mark. The world would know she was taken.

Then I would've pushed her to her knees, telling her to be a good girl for me.

My hand strokes my dick as I think about how she would look

down on her knees, her blonde hair falling around her shoulders. Her pretty tits moving with each ragged breath she drags into her body.

I wouldn't let her just sit there though. No, I would pull her hair back into my hand, wrapping it around my fist so I could angle her head the way I want.

Then I would grip her chin, forcing her mouth open.

Only then would I let her get a taste of me.

She would anticipate it. Beg for it with her eyes. I'd only give her the tip though.

I would wait until she's practically crying from the need she feels inside.

Sliding my dick inside her mouth, I would use her hair to dictate her pace. It would be a fast one too. I would fuck her face so hard that she'd gag. Her face would turn that pretty red as she desperately clawed at my legs, needing air. I wouldn't give it to her right away. I'd wait until the tears poured down her face, her throat swallowing on me again and again.

Then I would allow her a breath or two before I would repeat the process. The entire time she would rub her thighs together, trying to relieve the pressure.

My hand on my dick mimics the pace I would set, causing my spine to tingle.

I come hard, moaning her name as my fantasy finally finishes, with me pulling out of her mouth to cover her in my cum.

I'd rub it into her skin so that she would have to carry it with her for the rest of the day. No one would be able to get close to her without smelling me on her. It'd be the ultimate branding.

Opening my eyes, I listen for noise on the other side of the wall, but I hear nothing.

Looking down, I see the mess I've made. The cum wasted on my own skin and bedding instead of painting the object of my desire.

Not much longer, I promise myself.

I'm going to take her sooner rather than later.

CHAPTER SIX

Ivanna

"Are you going to tell me what happened last night?" Lia asks me over breakfast.

It's just us today. Dimitri and Nik had some meeting to attend with the other Bratva men. The only one left in the house is Oleg.

I glance over at him.

"Oleg, do you think maybe I could get a small piece of privacy?" I ask, knowing the answer.

It's always no. He's supposed to keep an eye on me at all times. I'm surprised he doesn't stand inside my room every night.

I suppose even Dimitri knows that's too much.

So as I wait for him to remind me of security procedures and his duty, I take a sip of my orange juice.

"Of course, Ivanna. I will be right in the kitchen. Please call if you need anything."

I choke on the orange juice, spitting it onto the table. Oleg looks concerned, as does Lia.

"Wait, you're doing it?"

Oleg nods slowly. "Your security has been reevaluated. We are going to tone it down a bit."

"Wait, do you still answer to Dimitri?"

"Of course. Is there anything else?"

I shake my head slowly, watching him leave.

Lia leans over, grabbing my arm. "How did you manage that?"

"I don't know. It makes no sense. I figured, after last night, he would be more controlling, not less. I have no idea what the hell is going on." I rest my head in my hands, looking at the table.

Lia rubs my back. "What happened?"

"Well, I had my date with Boris. Dimitri was surprisingly chill about the whole thing. Boris was a fuckboy, as I thought. You know he actually had the nerve to tell me that I looked like I needed some relief and asked me to lose Dimitri so he could provide it?"

"No way. Did Dimitri kill him on sight? Is that why you're acting so weird?"

I shake my head. "I don't think Dimitri heard him. After he said it, I told him I was cold, very loudly. Fucker just went back to watching the ballet. Dimitri gave me his jacket instead. The rest of the ballet was boring. Then when I went to leave, Boris tried to kiss me. Dimitri got all defensive. They shared some words. Something about me being Dimitri's little doll. Then Dimitri swept me out of there and refused to speak with me all the way home. I figured that would be it, but it wasn't. When we got home, before he'd even let me in the house, he pinned me against the door." I watch as her eyes widen and her mouth drops open in disbelief. "I'm telling you, Lia, he was different. It wasn't the Dimitri I'd always known. He's always calm, cool, and collected, but last night I felt like one small push and he would have lost all control."

"Oh god, that sounds so hot. I wonder if I can get Nik to pin me to a door," she adds wistfully.

"Seriously? That's my brother."

She shrugs. "I love him. What can I say?"

I snort. "Anyway, that's not even the craziest part. So he has me pinned to the door, right? Then he presses his entire body against me. His *rigid* body. I mean, I could feel every single inch and there were a lot of inches there."

Lia gasps, her hand flying to her mouth. "No way."

"Yes way. He was saying something about his dick and me, but I honestly couldn't even focus on it because all I could think was, 'This is it. Dimitri is making his move. Finally.' Only he didn't. Not really. He kissed my shoulder a few times, but then I said his name and he stopped. He kissed me. Once. Quickly. Then slapped my ass and sent me to bed. I was shocked."

"He kissed you? Holy fucking shit. He so wants you. I always knew it. Since the first time I saw you two together." Lia leans on the table, resting her chin on her hands.

I shake my head. "I'm so confused. I'm not sure I trust it. Why now? What changed for him to be like this with me?"

"You went on a date with another man, and he touched you. Men get all possessive like that. It's hot."

I roll my eyes. "Hot for you, maybe. Okay, maybe a little bit for me too, but is he possessive of me because he wants me, or is this some sick game? Is he only coming after me now because I said I wanted someone else? I don't want him to want me this way. I feel like maybe it's too late for us. How can I ever trust that this is real? I mean, he hasn't ever given any indication that he wanted me before this, yet now he's acting like a jealous boyfriend. And what about this lax security now? What is that supposed to mean? I feel like he's being Jekyll and Hyde right now and I don't like it."

"So ask him point-blank. Cut out this communication barrier you have."

I bite my lip. "I don't know if I want the answer though. My heart will shatter if I find out he is only doing this so I don't leave the family. It would ruin me."

"Babe, I'm going to be really honest with you here. That man has wanted you for a long time. Since I've moved in, at the very least. He constantly watches you and I don't think it has anything to do with your brother. I think you need to cut the bullshit and confront him."

"I'll think about it. I'm still not sure he's what I want anymore," I admit quietly.

"What do you mean?"

I let out a sigh. "Let's say he does want me for real and I choose him. He can never truly put me first. The Bratva will always come before me. I can't even be mad at him for it. It would be the same with any man in the outfit, which is why I tried dating normies. The problem is that they were too boring. I want a man to love me fiercely. To be obsessed with me and make me his entire world. I want each and every single breath he takes to belong to me. He will be mine and I will be his. I don't think I will ever find that though, because the men outside of the outfit just don't have that vibe to them. The ones inside the outfit have the vibe but can't promise me that devotion. It's a catch twenty-two. I will never win."

She gives me a sad look. "Don't give up hope. You'll find that. I promise. I can feel it deep inside me. Hold out hope."

I lean into her as she hugs me. "Thanks, Lia. As long as I have you, I know everything else will be okay."

"Same. The day I met you was the best day of my life."

"Not when you found my brother?" I snort.

She shakes her head. "Nope. It's when I found you. Our bond saved me. Without it, I wouldn't even be here."

My eyes start to tear up, so I divert my attention as usual.

"Well, don't tell Nik. He might actually kill me if he knew you loved me more."

She laughs. "Not more. Just different."

And just like that, we are back to normal. Talking about school and our daily lives.

Still, that longing inside refuses to go away.

Dimitri

I'm itching to see Ivanna, but Nik called a meeting this morning. I consider blowing it off, but I don't.

So instead of enjoying breakfast with Ivanna, gauging her mood today, I'm stuck in this conference room with three other men.

"What have we got?" Nik asks.

"A new girl has gone missing," Maxim says.

"How is this different than the others?" I question.

He frowns. "She's not low income or desperate. Ever since I put the word out that anyone approached by someone suspicious or being offered any incentive to leave with them should report it to me, things have been quiet. The money I'm offering for information seems to be helping too. This new girl is a college student."

The hair on the back of my neck stands to attention. "Which college?"

I ask, but I know the answer.

"Western U."

"Fuck," I whisper as I look to Nik.

He looks calm, but I can see the worry beneath his exterior. When Ivanna and Lia got kidnapped years ago, it about killed both of us.

"What do we know about her?" Nik asks.

"She was reported missing by her mother after she hadn't heard from her for three days. The cops are doing a search, but my contact sent it to me as soon as it hit his desk. I looked into it a bit. It's as if the girl vanished into thin air. She had gone to her academic club that evening and then poof."

Alexei speaks up. "He sent the information to me to prepare for this meeting. I looked into it too. The cameras outside of the building weren't working for a few days prior. Could have been a coincidence or a setup, but either way, the cameras didn't catch her leaving."

"We need to speak to the others in this club with her. See what they know," I say.

Nik nods his agreement. "You should do that. You're on campus the most. With Ivanna, you have a reason to be there. Try and keep it on the down-low though."

"I'll head over there after Ivanna is done with breakfast. I'll take a few guys with me and have them spread out. Talk to her roommate and see if she has any friends. Any chance she could have just run off with a boyfriend or something?" I direct the question at Alexei.

He shakes his head. "The boyfriend is accounted for and has a solid alibi. I have him on cameras and everything."

"Doesn't mean he's not involved though," Maxim interjects.

"Do your research and find out what's going on. It could be an everyday crime. It's not like every missing person is connected to this human trafficking ring, but I'd rather be safe than sorry. Report back when you hear something," Nik commands.

We all agree.

Nik and I stay seated until everyone clears the room.

The door clicks shut. "I don't like this."

"Neither do I. It's too close to home."

"And unfortunately, we can't tell them they can't go to school anymore."

Nik shakes his head. "Lia would kill me. She would tear my ass up and down on how that would be a waste of money leaving midsemester."

"She's not wrong, but it's not like the money matters at this point."

"You and I get that, but she doesn't," he says as he stands. "Go find Ivanna and head over to campus. Let me know when you find something."

"Will do."

IVANNA WAS QUIETER than normal when I took her back to her dorm. She didn't argue with me once, which is concerning. The woman is full of fire. I wanted to ask her about last night, but I could tell she was deep in her thoughts.

So I let her stay there.

When I dropped Ivanna off at her room, her roommate wasn't around. I was hoping to talk to her and see if she knew the missing girl since Ivanna and Lia had already confirmed they did not.

After leaving Oleg to look after Ivanna, I wandered around campus. Sticking to the shadows, I watched and listened.

I saw a woman selling her ADHD medication. Another taking money to write papers for others. A girl complained about her sorority sisters and how she didn't understand how one girl was accepted because of her size.

One guy was bragging to his buddies about how he banged a "hottie" last night to the point it was obvious it never happened. I found the potheads who like to sing off-key while high. Then there was a guy who had his teacher's skirt pulled up around her waist as he went down on her and she moaned his name.

Through all the bullshit, I never hear a word involving what I'm looking for. It's almost as if the students don't know that one of their classmates is missing.

Using the information from Alexei, I head over to the dorm the missing girl shares with another girl. No one answers when I knock. The girls I run into as I leave don't know much either. Seems word about this girl's disappearance hasn't been released yet, which is odd on its own. You would think campus police would be shouting it all over the campus. Or even the actual police. Shouldn't they be looking for the girl by putting her picture on every news outlet? Yet, nothing has been heard.

It doesn't sit right with me.

I let myself into the campus police station and look around. The place is quiet as I make my way into the back office. Stopping at the door, I test the knob and find it locked. I pull out the lock picks I keep in my pocket and the door pops open in under a minute.

"They need better locks," I mumble under my breath as I slip inside.

I keep the lights off even though people can't see into the room and move toward the desk. I pull out my cell phone and use the flashlight and check the papers on the desk. There are a couple reports of fights, parties, and the usual, but not a single report about someone missing.

Frowning, I sit down at the captain's desk and wake up his computer.

"Fuck," I mutter as the password-protected screen pops up. "This is why I leave this shit to Alexei."

Looking around, I notice the man has a lot of pictures of his dog, with the name Sparky on a frame. Quickly I type it in and am immediately granted access.

"Too fucking easy."

I go through the man's email. Nothing suspicious stands out. Switching screens, I start going through campus records. Before I can dig too deep, I hear the sound of footsteps coming down the hall.

Closing out of everything, I shut off the screen. Standing, I head toward the door and lean against the wall. Once the footsteps pass, I wait a minute and slip out of the hall and right out of the building.

Pulling out my phone, I shoot Alexei a text.

Me: I went into the police captain's office. There wasn't a report on the girl.

Alexei: Campus might not have one where it was reported to the city. I'll get back to you.

Backing out of the text thread, I open one with Oleg.

Me: Update?

Oleg: She's eating lunch in the cafeteria.

Slipping my phone back into my pocket, I head off campus.

There's not much else I can do here today. I head back to the compound to check on the training. I have enough pent-up frustration from last night to go several rounds with the guys.

CHAPTER SEVEN

Ivanna

This new freedom feels weird. I thought I would thrive not being watched twenty-four hours a day, but it makes me feel uneasy. That abandonment feeling only grows with the more space I've gained. I feel like I've been warm under a weighted blanket, but then all of a sudden, it's being ripped from me.

That safety net that I complained was suffocating me had become a comfort. I relied on it.

I can't even complain about it being gone because I did this to myself. This is what I wanted.

So as I sit in the cafeteria for lunch for the first time ever, I'm not sure this is where I want to be. I almost miss having Oleg with me. He usually drives me somewhere for lunch and we eat in the car.

Today I decide I want to test out my freedom. I about fall over when he says I can eat in here.

It's not as if I'm truly alone. Oleg is here somewhere. He said that he would make rounds and for me to text him when I'm ready to move.

I have no idea what to do with myself now. It's not like I have friends.

I'm sitting at a table alone while other groups are at their tables talking about their lives with one another.

If anything, this makes me feel even lonelier.

I'm so stuck in my thoughts that I don't notice her right away.

"Ivanna? Is that you?"

I startle, looking up at Kiera.

"You scared me," I tell her, catching my breath.

She laughs as she sits across from me with her own lunch.

"Sorry. I noticed you sitting here alone and thought I would join you. Where are your guard dogs?" She looks around.

I snort. "I've gained some freedom. This is where it brought me."

"The school cafeteria? You need to get out more if this is the first place you think of when you get a little freedom."

"God. You're so right about that. I doubt a party will be approved though. Even with this new freedom."

She thinks on my words a moment. "What about a club? Like an academic club, not a nightclub."

I think about it for a moment. "Actually, I could probably get that approved. What kind of club?"

She smiles. "I just joined last week, so I don't know too much, but it's like-minded individuals meeting up twice a week to discuss a variety of subjects. For some of the time, we work on schoolwork and get help from one another, but the last hour we always do these round-tables where we draw cards with different situations on them and we discuss how we would handle it. I've found it to be very entertaining. That and the professor who runs it is hot as hell. Like, I wouldn't mind doing a little extra credit, if you know what I mean." She winks.

I chuckle. "Well, that does sound interesting. What would I need to do to join?"

She shrugs. "I'll ask tonight. We are meeting again and I'll get everything you need."

"Thanks. I'll be honest, I thought you hated me."

She rolls her eyes. "I hate being confined to my room. Your guards would always give me shit when I would try to come and go with you there. Especially at night. God forbid a girl has to pee, right?"

I cringe. "I'm so sorry about that. I swear I would change it if I could."

"Sounds like you already are. I'll make you a deal. If you can get them to chill on me coming and going, I'll agree to room with you next semester. I know it's your last, but it could be fun."

My smile is even brighter now. "I would love that. I wasn't going to accept a new roommate anyway."

"Good. Listen, I need to run, but I'll talk to you tonight."

"Yes, tonight. I'm looking forward to it."

As she leaves, I smile at her back. Things are really starting to look up for me.

OLEG TEXTED EARLIER SAYING that he was bringing Ivanna home to study with Lia. From the time she arrived, I've been fighting the urge to track her down just to see her. I know it's only been a few days since I've seen her up close, but I can't help it. I want to hear her voice, to verbally spar with her. I'll take anything she gives me.

An hour ago, Nik went looking for Lia to retire for the night, so I know Ivy is alone. Moving through the house, I go room by room until I find her in the theater, watching a movie. I linger in the doorway and watch her. She looks completely at ease.

"What's this?" I ask as I step into the room.

Ivy turns around so fast she almost falls off the couch.

"I should put a bell on you," she mutters under her breath as she turns back to the TV. "It's a romantic comedy."

"Couldn't find anything else?" I ask as I take a seat on the couch next to her.

Ivy looks over at me and has a little frown on her face.

"What are you doing?"

"Hanging out with you." I shrug.

"Why though?"

"Because I want to. Do you have a problem with that?"

"Nope, no problem at all."

"Good. Now what would it take to convince you to change this to something better?"

"You're interrupting my movie night, my guy. Don't make me kick you out."

I raise my hands. "Fair enough."

We fall silent as we watch the show. It's cheesy as hell, but Ivanna has a small smile on her face the entire time. Out of the corner of my eye, I watch her. Her body is turned toward me and her legs are pulled up against her chest, covered with a blanket. She rests her head on the back of the couch.

Reaching out, I grab her ankles and pull them toward me, resting them in my lap.

"Uh, what are you doing?"

She tries to pull her legs back, but I hold them in place.

"Relax."

I wait until she stops fighting me, and then I start rubbing her feet.

"A-are you giving me a foot rub?" she asks in disbelief.

"I am."

"But why?"

"Do you want me to stop?"

Ivanna scoffs. "Not on your life, buddy. Now get to rubbing."

"Whatever you want, *printsessa*."

We fall silent as the movie plays. She watches the screen while I watch her.

"You're staring," she says after a few minutes.

"I am."

Ivanna sighs dramatically as she grabs the remote, pausing the TV. "Can I help you?"

I push down on the arch of her foot, making her moan.

Fighting back a smile, I respond, "I'm good. Unless you want to talk."

"What would we talk about?"

"Anything. Everything." I shrug. "How's school?"

"School, really?"

"Do you have anything else you would rather talk about?" I challenge.

"School is school. I'm mainly taking bullshit classes right now, just waiting until graduation."

"Are you ready to be done?"

Ivanna tilts her head from side to side. "Yes and no. Yes, because I'm ready to move on. No, though, because I've been in school for so long it will be weird not having to go every day. It doesn't help that all this schooling has been pointless. I'll never be allowed to get a job. It's just kind of intimidating."

"Change can be difficult, but I think you'll be fine."

"You think so?" she asks quietly.

"I know so." I nod. "Would you want to get a job?"

"I don't know. I mean, I took business classes with tons of out-there electives, but I'm not sure what I would even do with it." She looks down and starts playing with the blanket on her lap. "It probably doesn't matter now anyway. With these dates, who knows who I'll end up marrying. They probably won't want me to work."

I barely manage not to flinch at the thought of her moving away. "That's probably wise."

"Who knows. Maybe it's a bad idea to wait so long."

"What if you got a job at one of your brother's businesses? You would help manage one of them, or hell, do just about anything at them."

"You think so?"

I nod. "It would be a good choice since you'd always be surrounded by his men, so your safety would never be in question."

She thinks about it a moment. "I guess it all depends on who I end up marrying then."

I swallow hard, needing to control the sudden burst of jealousy. I want to tell her it doesn't matter because she's marrying me. That I would allow her to work at any one of her brother's businesses because then I know she would be taken care of. It would give her the freedom she wants yet still allow me control. The perfect compromise.

She's not ready to hear that yet though. I can tell by the way she's still talking about these dates. She hasn't gotten my message.

"How's the roommate situation? Kiera, right?" I ask, changing the subject.

Ivanna rolls her eyes. "Don't pretend like you don't know her name. Kiera's good though. We obviously got off to a rough start, but it's better now. Especially where she can get up in the middle of the night to go to the bathroom without getting yelled at by one of my guards."

"I could see how that would be difficult. So you both like that we've lightened up on the security?"

Ivanna opens her mouth and closes it several times, choosing her words carefully. "Yeah, it's nice."

She's lying. It's in the way her eye moves up and to the right when she speaks. It's her tell. Not that I would ever point it out. I like knowing when she's lying.

I don't call her out on it though. If she wanted to tell me, she would.

DIMITRI

"What else is new?" I ask her.

"Kiera invited me to join a club that she's part of." She shrugs. "I'm kind of excited to go."

My body tenses at that. Knowing that another girl went missing after going to one of those school clubs makes me wary. He never did tell us the name of it.

"Yeah? What kind of club?"

"It's called the social hour. Basically, a bunch of students get together, along with a professor. You can study for a while with different students, getting help where you need it. Then once they are done, they will do, like, roundtable discussions about current topics." She shrugs. "I don't know. Kiera seems to love it and I said I would try. Hey, why did you stop rubbing?" she asks as she jabs her toes into my thigh.

"Sorry," I say gruffly. "Do you know anything about the club's members?"

"No, but don't worry. I'm sure by the time I'm through with the first meeting, you'll have a complete report on everyone."

I'll have a full detailed report before she goes into the room, along with knowing if this is the same club the missing chick attended. I won't restrict her, but I refuse to allow her to be left vulnerable.

"Just be careful. Okay?" I murmur.

She frowns. "Is everything okay?"

"It's fine." I force a smile. "Are you staying here tonight, or do I need to drive you back?"

"I was planning on staying tonight and then getting a ride with Lia in the morning. She has a class earlier than I do, so it should be okay."

"Sounds good. Now turn your movie back on. I know you want to finish before you go to sleep."

Ivy offers me a quick smile as she picks up the remote and hits play and my mind wanders. Just the thought of her walking into that club makes me sick, but I can't tell her not to go. Not until we know more. One thing is for sure though, she won't be alone.

CHAPTER
EIGHT

Ivanna

"Are you sure I don't need to bring anything?"

Kiera weaves her arm through mine. "Relax. Like I told you before, all you need is some schoolwork and yourself. The group is pretty laid back. You have nothing to worry about."

"If you say so," I say under my breath.

I don't know why I'm so nervous but I am. Outside of group projects, I've never just hung out with people who go here with me.

"Okay, how about once we're done, we head over to the cafeteria and hit up the dessert line? Get something sweet to celebrate your first club event."

"I would like that."

"Good. Now game face, Petrova. Don't let them smell your fear, or they will start circling like sharks," she says as she opens the door.

I pause. "Wait, what?"

Kiera rolls her eyes and pulls me into the room. Thankfully no one looks our way as we step inside.

"There's Josh. Come on."

Kiera all but drags me across the room.

As soon as he sees her, his eyes light up. I look back over at her and see that she's wearing a massive smile.

She really likes this guy.

At least, that's the vibe I'm getting. She has mentioned him several times since we've really started talking.

"Hey, you made it," he says to Kiera as we come to a stop next to him.

Kiera tucks a piece of hair behind her ear. "I did."

They stare at each other, completely oblivious to the rest of us.

"Are you guys going to jump each other right here in front of us or what?" another guy says, breaking the moment.

Josh clears his throat and looks at me. "You must be Kiera's roommate. I'm Josh."

"Ivanna. I've heard a lot about you."

Josh winks over at Kiera. "All good things, I hope."

"Of course." Kiera blushes.

"I'm Chris," the strange guy introduces himself. "Welcome to the social hour."

"Ivanna. Thanks for having me."

Slowly but surely, I start to relax as others trickle into the room and introduce themselves to me.

This isn't so bad.

"Welcome, everyone!" a man says as he walks into the room. "I see some new faces with us tonight, but first look around and see if you recognize any familiar faces. Work on whatever you need to finish, and then once you're all done, we will open the floor to discussion."

Everyone moves and I stay next to Kiera. Looking around the room, I don't recognize anyone.

Do I share a class with any of these people?

Have I been so far off into my own world that I've ignored those around me?

What would Nik and Dimitri say if they knew I couldn't identify anyone from any of my classes if put to the test? They raised me better than that.

"Are you okay?" Kiera asks, pulling me out of my head.

"I'm perfect."

"Then let's get started," she says as she pulls out her computer.

I pull out a book and start some reading that I need for my lit class. This week we are discussing *Murder in the Cathedral* and it's just not for me. Something about it puts me to sleep as soon as I start reading.

Time drags by as I read. Out of the corner of my eye, I see someone approaching.

The professor crouches next to my chair. "Hey, I wanted to introduce myself. I'm Professor Lamington."

I shut my book and place it in my lap. "I'm Ivanna. Nice to meet you."

"We're excited to get to know you, Ivanna."

The way he stares at me sets me on edge and not in a good way. Objectively I can see why Kiera would find him attractive but he does absolutely nothing for me.

Awkwardly I smile as he lingers next to me, unsure of what to say.

"Hey, Teach," someone hollers from across the room, breaking the tension.

"Well, duty calls." Professor Lamington stands and reaches out as if he's going to touch my shoulder. Instinctively, I lean out of his touch.

As he walks away, I can't help but shiver. I know that if any of my guards were in the room, he would have been taken down as soon as he got close.

Is that why the interaction felt so weird? I'm so used to people staying away that when they approach it feels wrong?

Next thing I know, the study period is over and everyone puts their stuff away and starts chatting.

Professor Lamington sits on his desk and calls out. "Okay, are you guys ready?"

"Yeah."

"Yes."

"You know it," everyone choruses back.

Sitting back, I listen and watch. The professor hits different topics and allows everyone to debate without getting out of hand. It's refreshing to see people express their opinions without being called names for having differing opinions.

"Honestly, I don't know how any of you could believe pineapple belongs on pizza." Some guy shakes his head.

"I don't know, Mark, maybe because it's delicious," one girl deadpans.

"It's the perfect balance between salty and sweet. It's like heaven in my mouth," another member adds.

"I'll give you something salty for your mouth." Her boyfriend leans over and nuzzles her neck as everyone protests or cheers.

"Hey now," Professor Lamington says, getting our attention. "As good of a joke as that was and I know we're all adults, but let's keep things as PG as we can. I really don't want to have to listen to the Dean go at me for allowing sexual harassment in this club and end up shutting us down."

"But where's the fun in PG?" A guy laughs.

"I agree with you, but you know how it is." The professor shakes his head. "What else do we have to discuss today? Anyone got anything?"

Everyone shakes their head and he claps. "Alright. That's it for tonight. I'll see you all next week. You know where to find me in the meantime if you need anything."

Everyone gets up and starts leaving the room.

"So, what did you think?" Kiera asks as she falls into step next to me.

"It's definitely intriguing, that's for sure."

"Will you come back with me next week?"

"For sure, and who knows, maybe I'll join in on the discussion then."

"I can't wait to see what you bring up." She laughs.

Dimitri

"A second girl has gone missing," Maxim tells us as soon as we are all settled into the room.

I grit my teeth. "From campus?"

"She was a student, but she was taken from a nightclub downtown. It's owned by a third party not involved in our world. I don't see any connections that might be related to this. From what I can tell, she went to the bar and never came home."

Alexei confirms the story, "From the cameras, she went inside and waited at the bar. She kept looking around as if she was looking for someone. She checked her phone several times, but after an hour, she headed down the hall toward the bathroom. She never came back. I didn't see her leave the club at all. I watched the footage for the entire next day too, and not a single person looked suspicious. It's as if she vanished into thin air."

"Did you check the building schematics?"

Alexei nods before I even finish asking. "I did. The place isn't that old and it's not like it has tunnels underneath. Not unless something has changed from what they turned in to the city."

Nik frowns. "This isn't good. I want a meeting with the Polish. If they are still taking girls from our territory, I want to put the fear of God into them. We have honored our end of the deal by staying out of their business. They need to honor ours."

Nik hates the deal we made with Jan, the new leader of the Polish, but it was a necessity to avoid an all-out war. The Polish get to keep their meat market in their territory, but they agree that they will not take women from our streets. It's not perfect, but it's the best we can do publicly. Secretly, we are working with several outfits to take them down. We won't rest until the human trafficking is abolished.

"I'll arrange it," I acknowledge his order.

"Good. Maxim, I want your team posted around campus. Is there any connection this girl had with the first?"

He nods. "They shared some classes and had some mutual friends. They were also all a part of the same academic club. They call it the social hour. I talked with the members discreetly after the first girl went missing, but I didn't get a chance to talk to the teacher. I didn't want to be too obvious."

I swallow hard. Alexei had already confirmed that the group Ivanna joined was the same group that the first girl had gone missing from. I wanted to pull Ivanna from it but stopped myself. Instead, I added guards onto her without her knowledge. I'm trying not to be a tyrant, but it's hard.

"Did you do background checks? Anything come up?"

Alexei answers this time. "I checked all the names that he gave me based on other members. The students are clean. Not all of them even attend the group every meeting. As for the professor running it, he was clean as well. Professor Richard Lamington. He was born in Maryland and went to university there. He graduated with his degree and taught for a while there before moving here six years ago. He's been on the staff at the college since. He teaches social behavior theory, sociology, and philosophy. Other than seeming really fucking boring, he is squeaky clean."

"That sounds suspicious. He has never been in trouble?" I ask.

He shakes his head. "Not even a speeding ticket. I thought it was odd too, but I checked everything. If it's a fake identity, it's ironclad."

"Not everyone is a criminal," Nik jokes. "Have someone follow him around a bit. See if he is really as innocent as he seems."

Maxim nods. "Got it. I may need a few extra men. I want to send some down to the club and question the employees again."

"Take whoever you need. Alexei, keep digging into these girls. It may be a coincidence that they both go to the same college and know each other, but I have a feeling there is more to this."

"Agreed," I add. "I want you to look into everyone in the group again. I'm going to pick a few guys to roam the campus posing as students. We can try and keep an eye on them the best we can and see if they are doing anything that might be attracting this attention."

"What about Ivanna?" Nik asks.

"What about her? She has a guard on her at all times," I snap back.

"I've heard you've allowed her some freedom. Do you think this is a good time for that?" Nik looks thoughtful.

"Maybe not, but if I tighten the reins again, it's going to make her feel even more isolated. Oleg said she's begun making friends with her roommate. On top of that, she's been following the rules without complaint. That's a first for her. I don't want to break this little bit of trust we have going."

"Understood. I trust your judgment. Keep me updated and keep her safe." He nods at me once before looking to the other men. "You have your tasks. Find out who the fuck thinks they can fuck with the people in my city."

They nod and stand. I stand to follow them.

"D, before you go, we need to talk," Nik calls, holding me back.

I wait until the rest of the guys leave before I take my seat once more.

"What is it?" I ask, knowing by the look on his face I'm not going to like what he has to say.

"It's Ivanna. You'll be thrilled to know she's axed Boris from her potential suitor list."

I grimace. "Not the whole list though."

He shakes his head. "She's asked for me to set up another date with one of the remaining men."

I curse under my breath. My blood starts to boil, but I need to remain in control. If I lose it, it won't make the situation better.

"Don't do it, Nik," I manage to say.

"I have to. She's my sister. I made her a promise."

My hand comes down on the table hard, making it shake. "You made me a fucking promise."

"I did, which included the caveat that she would need to choose you as well. So don't come at me like I'm the villain. You're the one who has had years to get her to want you. You squandered them."

"She was a child, Nik. I didn't even know why I wanted to claim her yet. I just knew I couldn't handle her with another man. Back then, she was still just a little girl. One I needed to protect."

"Not anymore though, right? I won't allow you to pursue her if you're not going to give her what she needs."

"You don't have a fucking say. She's mine as much as Lia is yours. That's all I'll say on the issue. Now don't arrange the fucking date."

He frowns. "I'll put it off for a couple of days, but if she doesn't ask me to stop, I will arrange the date. I told you to make her your priority. Well, she is mine too. Her happiness means more to me than whatever strain it will cause us. It's time for you to shit or get off the pot."

"Fine. I will speak with her."

"Maybe calm down first. You look like you might lose it."

Standing, I let the chair fall to the ground. "Fuck you, Nik. You may be my boss when it comes to the Bratva, but when it comes to Ivanna, you don't tell me what to do."

With that, I storm out of there.

He might have a point though. I am going to need to calm down. If I don't, she's going to get all snippy with me and while I find it arousing most of the time, my nerves can't handle it right now.

So I spend the drive to her dorm in silence. I take deep breaths until I'm almost fully under control.

By the time I arrive, I feel ready to confront her. I thought she understood that she was mine.

I guess not, though she will by the time the night is through.

CHAPTER NINE

Ivanna

To say the last three weeks have been a total one-eighty from the life I was living before would be an understatement. Dimitri has been kind to me more often than not. He's been leaving me gifts such as my favorite candies and flowers while also giving me the space I was so desperate for.

It's such a weird combination. Part of me wants to call him and ask him why he is trying now when I am ready to move on, but the other part of me doesn't want to rock the boat. It's almost too good to be true.

It would kill me if he was only doing this out of some obligation he feels. Part of me feels as if this is too good to be true. My sixteen-year-old self is still hurt that he turned me down and I'm holding it against him. Even though, looking back, I understand.

Still, I can't help but have one foot out the door. I don't want to fall for him again, only for the rug to be ripped out from under me.

I want him to love me. To be in love with me.

We've been stuck in this limbo where I'm being the good girl he always asked of me while he allows me the freedom I've been begging for.

I'm craving the fight though. The attention that he's been neglecting to give me.

So I asked Nik to arrange another date.

It was stupid, but it was also the only way to get a reaction out of Dimitri without risking this newfound freedom.

Kiera went out with Josh tonight and told me she wouldn't be home, so I knew today would be the perfect day to make the call to Nik.

Then I sat and waited.

Dimitri didn't disappoint. Within a couple of hours of talking with Nik, Dimitri is at my door, glaring at me.

"Can I help you with something?" I ask him as I lean against the doorjamb.

He pushes me back gently, closing the door behind us as he enters my space.

"I want you to stop the dates. Tell Nik you've changed your mind," Dimitri demands.

I scoff. "Why in the hell would I do that?"

"I told you. You're mine. You won't have anyone but me. Did you think I was lying?"

I wanted this. I went so far as to make it happen. So why does it feel hollow?

Then it hits me. I wanted him to react this way, but now I don't trust it. I don't trust that it is because he wants me and not that he doesn't view me as the doll Boris accused me of being to him. Some asset for him to covet and hold away from all others.

I laugh, rubbing my hand down my face. "Lying? No. Delusional?

Yes. You can't just waltz in here rubbing your dick on me as if you are marking your territory. I'm not a fucking possession. I'm a human being. You pushed yourself on me and made your demands and then what? You disappeared. Sure, I've seen you here and there, but not once have you reaffirmed that you actually want me. This is all a game to you. You saw someone else playing with your toy and now you want it back. Newsflash, D. I was never yours to begin with."

His hand shoots out, gripping my neck as he moves in closer. "You have always been mine. I'd even go as far as saying that you were meant to be mine since the moment you were born. Maybe I didn't see it back then. You were a child. Younger than me, but now I see it. I know that you are supposed to be with me. I don't understand why you won't accept it."

I snort. "Of course you don't. It's the Dimitri show. What Dimitri says goes. Who cares about anyone else, right? Who cares how you've made me feel time and time again over the years. I'm done with this, D."

"I've told you that's not true. There is only one person who is at the top of my list and it's not myself, *printsessa*. It's you. It's always been you."

"Your words don't mean anything, Dimitri. You say I'm yours. You expect me to just fall at your feet, but that's not how real life works. This isn't some romance novel. This is my fucking life. At this point, you could say the sky is blue, and I'd wonder if you're deceiving me somehow. I can't trust you."

He let out a deep sigh. "I hear you, *printsessa*. Give me a chance. My words mean nothing to you, but my actions will prove them. Let me rebuild that trust with you. Tell Nik to pause the dates for now. I beg you."

I shake my head. "You? Beg? This isn't begging. I deserve more than this, D. I deserve a true grovel with you on your hands and knees, apologizing for all the shit you've put me through. As it stands right now, I'm not even sure I like you, let alone anything more. It's not that I can't do this with you. I don't want to."

He growls, pressing in even closer until we are sharing the same breath. "One chance. One shot. That's all I need to show you that I'm being honest with you. To prove to you that I'm all you need."

Swallowing hard, I shake my head. "You don't deserve another chance. Just... don't. Stop. Let me go."

He presses a quick, hard kiss to my lips, taking my breath away. "I'll never let you go. No matter what you do or how far you run, I'll always be there. I can't imagine a life where you aren't there annoying the fuck out of me, *printsessa*. I wouldn't want to."

"Annoying you? Really? That's how you think you're going to win me back? By insulting me?"

"It's not an insult, my love. It's a truth. The fact that you can get under my skin only proves how far I've already fallen for you. If the opposite of love is indifference, then the fire we feel between us is proof that the love we share only grows."

"I don't love you," I lie through my teeth.

He gives me a sad smile. "I can love you enough for the both of us."

I feel the anger drain out of me. I'm tired of fighting him, of having the same conversations over and over.

"Don't use words you don't understand, Dimitri. You may think you love me now because of whatever sick delusion you have in your head about protecting me, but you don't love me. If you did, you wouldn't hurt me the way you do."

I push against his chest, knowing I won't move him. Not until he lets me.

He takes a breath before pressing a lingering kiss to my temple.

"You make assumptions about my feelings for you, *printsessa*. One day you'll see how wrong you truly are."

When he steps back, I don't hesitate to duck under his arm, intent on escaping to the bathroom down the hall.

"Ivanna," he calls out, making me stop at the door.

I glance back over my shoulder at him. He looks conflicted.

"What do you want, Dimitri?" I breathe out.

"I'll give you the space you desire if you call off the dates. For now, at least."

I tilt my head, confused. "What space?"

"Freedom. More of it. Isn't that what you've been asking for years for?"

"What's the catch?"

He shakes his head. "No catch."

I consider his words a moment before nodding once.

"Okay. I'll go see Nik in the morning."

"Thank you."

Stepping outside the door, I pause to look back at him. His eyes are still on me.

Why do I feel like I just made a deal with the devil?

Dimitri

I DIDN'T WANT to make the concession, but with Ivanna, that's all I could do.

She's stubborn as fuck. I know she would go out with each and every single man she picked out, and at the end, she would pick one. No matter how she felt, she would choose one for the simple fact that she felt like she was backed into a corner and had no other options.

She's a spitfire. A wildcat.

I thought proclaiming my intentions would help ease some of her uneasiness about all of this, but I was wrong. I should have known better.

I watched as her eyes frantically looked for an escape. She didn't believe any of the words coming from my mouth. When has she ever taken me at my word? Never.

She craves her freedom so much that all I can think to do is give it to her. Let her see the real world how it really is. She's been sheltered her whole life, which is partially my fault. I wanted to keep her in a bubble to ensure she would never be harmed.

I didn't care if she hated me for my actions. All that mattered was her safety.

I see now the error of my ways. I alienated her from me. She will never believe me when I tell her that she's mine.

I need to proceed with more caution. I need to let my actions speak for themselves.

Picking up the phone, I call Nik.

"Where have you been, D?"

"With your sister. She's going to come see you in the morning. She's going to stop the dates."

Nik chuckles. "Are you bleeding? What did you do to her to get her to agree to that? There's no way you got out unscathed."

I sigh. "We compromised and made a deal. It doesn't matter. Don't you dare arrange a date for her. I'd hate to start a war."

"Whatever you say. Come back to the house. I spoke with Jan. He's willing to meet after the club closes tonight. We need to debrief beforehand."

"Why so soon? I don't like this."

"We don't have a choice. So leave Oleg to watch my sister and get your ass back here."

He hangs up, making me curse.

I don't have a good feeling about this.

Going back inside, I find Oleg outside the girls' door.

"She make it back inside okay?" I ask.

I didn't like her escaping to the bathroom, but she didn't have another choice with me in her room.

He nods.

DIMITRI

"Good. I've got something to do, so keep an eye on her. You've been doing great with allowing her some freedom. I need you to loosen the reins more. Use the whole team if you have to. Instead of posting here on the floor, starting tomorrow, I want you to surround the building and stay hidden. Ask her if she wants a ride. If not, then follow at a distance. Keep her as safe as possible while also being discreet."

"Are you sure? That will make security harder." He looks wary.

"I don't like it either, but it is the deal I've made with her. It's important, so do it."

He nods. "Of course, sir."

I consider knocking on the door to tell her good night, but I don't. The urge to see her one more time is there, but I can hear her in there talking to someone. Most likely Lia is on the phone.

Instead, I look at the door one last time before leaving.

The drive to Nik's isn't long, but it feels like it. I hate leaving Ivanna alone. Even when Oleg watches her, I often spend my nights in my car, also lingering around for any trouble.

Only when duty calls do I leave her.

Like tonight.

My gut says this isn't right. Something is going to go wrong or something. I've learned over the years my gut is often right. Nik won't listen though.

He has his own gut he follows.

So I keep my own in check. When I arrive at the house, I can tell the men are on edge.

I nod at them as I head into the house, making my way to Nik's office.

"It's going to be fine, *kroshka*. I can handle myself." I hear him murmur.

"I worry about you. You better come home to me. I won't be happy if you're hurt," Lia's voice rings out.

For a moment, I let myself be envious of their relationship. Even when Nik was fighting his feelings for Lia, they were still pulled together.

I feel like Ivanna and I are being pulled apart. I always thought she would be there waiting for me. That was my mistake. I see the errors I made now.

I'll do anything to make it work with her.

Stepping inside the office, I see Lia sitting in Nik's lap. They are still talking to one another, so I clear my throat.

"Dimitri, promise me you won't let anything happen to Nik," Lia demands, her eyes fierce.

I love seeing the fire in her eyes. It reminds me of Ivanna. I remember when Lia was more cautious of us. She grew into her role as the queen of this outfit nicely. Now she doesn't put up with anyone's shit. Not even mine.

"Of course, my liege. I would never let him come into any harm. I know you'd maim me. Ivanna would likely just end my life."

Lia narrows her eyes at me. "Are you making fun of me?"

I shake my head. "I would never dare. I will guard him with my life. You have my word."

She huffs out a breath before kissing Nik. "I expect you to climb into bed when you get home."

"Yes, *kroshka*."

She stands, stopping by me at the door. She pats my chest once.

"I think I should hang out with Ivanna a bit more, don't you? I mean, Nik would never let me out of the house without guards, so she would have to deal with that, but I miss my friend."

I give her a small smile. Nik must have told her about my call, or she was sitting there when he took it.

"That would be nice. You should call her now."

She smirks back at me. "She called me the second you left. We are meeting for lunch tomorrow."

Shaking my head, I lay my hand on her shoulder. "You're a good friend."

She nods. "Don't fuck this up. I don't want her leaving us."

"I'll do my best."

She glances over at Nik. "*Ya lyublyu tebya*."

I love you.

"*Vsegda,*" he replies immediately.

Always.

I can't wait to speak those words to my girl. I need to prove it to her first.

She leaves then, leaving us to our business.

"The men are waiting downstairs."

WE PREPARED for several hours before finally leaving the compound. Jan wanted to meet at the club, but after my insistence, Nik got him to agree to meet at a neutral warehouse on the edge of each territory.

Poe isn't necessarily involved with any specific organized crime syndicate, but he is known for being deadly. Thankfully, he offered up his space with the stipulation that any bloodshed that would occur would be multiplied on both sides by him.

We arrived first and stationed some of our guys around the grounds. It was decided that I would go in with Nik to show strength. They wouldn't think he'd expose me along with him knowing I'm his successor.

What they don't know is that we have Maxim as our backup. Not only that, but Alexei has eyes all over the place with his drones.

We are as covered as we can be.

When Jan finally pulls up, I'm surprised to see his entourage so minimal. It has me alert and ready for an ambush.

"This doesn't seem right," I whisper to Nik.

He doesn't move an inch. "Steady, D."

I want to growl, but I don't. I remain stoic as the men approach us.

"Nikolai, Dimitri, what a pleasure to meet with you. Shall we go inside? It's been a long evening. I'd like to get this meeting over with," Jan says politely.

I don't miss how rigid his guards are. I don't recognize a single one of them from his predecessor. Seems he cleaned house. Well, more than we already had when we eliminated all the men who took Lia and Ivanna.

"Of course. I've had my men set up some chairs for comfort," Nik tells the man, gesturing inside.

Jan enters with ease, but his guards look skeptical. They sense the danger here.

It's odd that Jan only brought five guards. It makes me even more uncomfortable.

Jan's guards inspect the chairs laid out, choosing the one facing the door. Once he's seated, Nik takes the seat across from him while the rest of us post along the room.

"Thank you for agreeing to this meeting. You know why I called it?" Nik asks.

Jan responds, "I have no idea, but hopefully it's because you see the merit in my business."

I barely withhold the scoff that threatens to escape. There is no merit in the meat markets.

It would be one thing if these women were willingly participating, but they aren't. I don't know a single human being who would sell themselves to another. It's the reason Nik refuses to force Ivanna into an arranged marriage. It's another form of human trafficking.

Besides, even if the women agreed to be sold, the children don't have the mentality nor maturity to make that decision themselves.

No matter what the Polish think, we would never agree to their business.

Not that we can outright say that without war. So instead, we fight them in little ways. Ways that won't lead back to us.

"I will never understand your business. I asked you to meet me because of the girls that have gone missing off the college campus recently. There have been two. They have not been seen since, nor have their phones been turned on. Seems suspiciously similar to how you obtain your women." Nik doesn't outright accuse the man, but the accusation lingers in the air.

"I see. You assume it is me. Nikolai, we made an agreement. You would stop hitting my clubs in exchange for me staying out of your territory. We have revamped how we obtain our women. If I'm even a tiny bit unsure if they have come from your territory, I release them. My men have also been made aware of the situation. They know the lethal consequences of venturing into your territory, not only from you but from myself as well. I want this to be a healthy working relationship between us. Those girls who are missing have nothing to do with the Polish."

I study his body language as he speaks. Everything points to him telling the truth, but my gut is still screaming at me. There has to be more to it than this. Who else would it be?

"You understand why I'm wary, yeah?" Nik asks, "Two young, attractive women from a very populated area going missing? Seems suspect. I must ask if you will put the word out to your men about them. Any information provided would be rewarded generously as it will also build the trust between us."

Jan nods. "I will put the word out as soon as we leave here. I know it's hard to believe, but I am not my brother. I do not thrive in chaos. I'm more of a businessman. I see the bigger picture, and in ours, we work side by side, even if it is to keep the peace."

"I wouldn't say we work together, more like tolerate each other. Help me find these girls, and that tolerance will only grow," Nik informs the man.

He nods. "Is there anything else you wish to discuss? I'm still open to paying a large sum to open a trade route through your territory."

Nik's jaw clenches just barely, but I see it.

"No. I will not allow humans to be trafficked through my territory. No amount of money will ever change my mind."

Jan sighs, "Very well. May we meet again under better circumstances."

He stands, prompting Nik to stand as well. They shake hands briefly before Jan exits the building with his guards.

Our own guards follow them, leaving Nik and me alone.

"What do you think?" I whisper to Nik.

"I think that they are skirting the truth. They might not have a hand in this, but they know who does. Hopefully, the incentive to build our relationship will be enough to get them back and find out who the true culprit is."

"He might not be outright lying, but he is involved somehow," I tell Nik. "I can feel it."

Nik nods. "We can't worry about that right now. Our number one priority is to find the girls alive and make it so they do not speak of whatever happened to them. If word gets out that these women are disappearing from our territory, it will make us look weak. We need to solve this sooner rather than later."

"I'm on it."

Nik snorts, his voice hard. "You sure? Because it seems like you're on Ivanna instead."

Turning to him, I narrow my eyes. "Do you have a problem?"

"Remember who your pakhan is, D. You're toeing a line you don't want to cross over."

His tone instantly pushes me over the edge.

Stepping into his space, I stare him in the eye. "You might lead the Bratva, but I'm not just your soldier. Don't you forget that."

"You don't forget that I can make you disappear without a trace if I choose. Watch how you speak to me."

I growl. "I'm the monster you created. You gave me this freedom to do as I saw fit. You can't go back on it now. Too much time has passed."

Nik glowers at me. "Don't make me question your loyalty."

"I will always be loyal to you, but if you make me choose, my loyalty to her will always win out."

He doesn't say another word, but I can see the anger in his eyes as he stares me down. Neither one of us is willing to back down on this.

"You two going to stand there all night?" Maxim calls out from his hidey-hole in the rafters.

I clear my throat, willingly surrendering first. Nik can't look weak in front of others. I might challenge him when we are alone, but never in front of the men.

"Maxim, did you get all that on video?" I call out.

"The meeting? Yes. Afterward, no."

I nod, knowing what he's saying. Only he witnessed me challenging our boss, and he's not going to say a word.

"Good. Let's go."

CHAPTER TEN

Ivanna

My life feels like it's spiraling out of control. When I woke up last week after that night with Dimitri, my entire life changed.

Oleg was outside my door, but he didn't act right. He asked me if I wanted a ride to school or if I'd prefer to find my own way.

Wanting to test the limits, I said I would find my own ride.

Then he left.

He left me alone.

For half a second, I was excited, but then the fear crept in. I've never truly been alone.

I figured that night I would see him again, but I was wrong. I haven't seen him since.

I feel abandoned. Alone. Even my roommate Kiera has commented on how weird it feels knowing he's not standing outside the door. She had gotten used to the security of always having a guard around.

It's not like I think I'm in danger. I'm not. There's no one lurking around the corner to grab me or anything. Hell, it's not even like I'm truly alone all the time. Kiera is here with me every night, and Lia has been making more of an effort to come see me when she's at school. It's only made me realize how much I miss her. Seeing her own guards around makes me sad though. I kind of miss the cage I fought so hard against.

The worst is when I'm walking home at night after going to the social club. Even having Kiera with me doesn't make me feel safer.

It's funny, isn't it? I wanted freedom so badly that I was willing to give anything for it, but now that I have it, I'm not even sure I want it.

I never understood the saying, "Be careful what you wish for." Maybe it's because the only wishes I made that came true were always vetted by Dimitri or my brother.

Now it makes sense.

How can I reach out to Dimitri now and tell him I was wrong? That I want my guards back.

The worst part of it all is that I feel like he doesn't care anymore.

I know it's all in my head. I'm the one who practically twisted his arm until he gave this to me, but I think I equated the level of restrictions he put on me as some sick proof of his affection.

I swear a therapist would have a field day with me. My mind is a huge fucking mess. Especially when I keep dreaming about Dimitri. I hear the words he spoke in my head every single night. Some nights he's calming me. His words make me feel warmer. Better.

Other nights, it's a nightmare. I hear his voice distorted. It's as if he's mocking me. Mocking the feelings I still harbor for him, no matter how much I wish I didn't.

Those nights are especially hard.

"You didn't sleep again?" Kiera asks me, pulling me from my thoughts.

DIMITRI

I give her a small smile. "Not really."

"Why don't you just call and ask for your guard back? Wouldn't your brother send one right away?" she asks, threading her arm with mine as we walk across campus.

"He would, but I'm afraid it would only prove that I need the restrictions. I don't want to go back to living like I did before."

She frowns. "It was really that bad?"

I sigh. "I understand the reasoning behind it. They wanted me to be safe, so they had me under constant watch. Even in high school, I always had guards around me. Everyone was so afraid of my brother that they wouldn't be friends with me for fear of accidentally upsetting me, which would then upset him. Fake politeness is something I can live the rest of my life without."

"You had Lia though."

I shrug. "I did for a while. She didn't come in until senior year. She didn't care who my brother was. I could tell by the chip she had on her shoulder. I never imagined she would end up dating him. So while I had her or, I guess, have her, it's different now. I'm happy as fuck for her, but her relationship with him changed our relationship. Like I know she wouldn't say anything if I told her something in confidence, but I also understand the strain that would put on her relationship with Nik, so I don't ask her to do that. It means that I can't always tell her everything anymore."

"Is that why you haven't had her over more?" Kiera asks as she pulls me to a stop outside the building.

"Subconsciously, I think so. I didn't even realize I stopped hanging out with her as much as I did until she started forcing her way back into my life. Jesus, I'm a terrible friend."

Kiera grabs my hand, squeezing it. "No, you aren't. You've been a great friend to me. I think you've just lived a different life than the rest of us. Remember what Professor Lamington says. Your problems are not any less than someone else's because you feel like they aren't as important."

I smile at her. "You're right. First-world problems are still problems, even if they seem trivial to others. Thank you for giving me another chance."

She steps in, hugging me.

"I'm glad I decided to look past the mean guards and get to know you. You're truly one in a million."

"You two joining us today?" Professor Lamington asks as he jogs up the stairs past us.

"Of course," I call out, pulling Kiera up the stairs with me.

Walking into the room, I smile as many of them wave or say hi to me.

This is what I was missing. Normal interaction. None of these people in this room see me as Nik's sister or Dimitri's ward.

I'm just me.

"Alright, who has homework they need to work on tonight?" Professor Lamington asks.

When no one raises their hands, he smiles. "Great. Let's dive right into it then. I've ordered pizza and drinks for us as well. You've been so good that I wanted to treat you. Don't worry, Abigail, I ordered a vegan salad for you."

She smiles at him gratefully.

"So topic number one of the night is right and wrong. I'm going to read a scenario that I pulled from the headlines and I want to discuss them with the room."

He moves some papers around until he pulls one out.

"Alright. So a female in her thirties is under fire because her nineteen-year-old daughter became pregnant and wanted to move home with her mother. The female, we will call her Jane, told her daughter that while she would help in the role of a grandmother, she did not feel it would be beneficial to have the daughter move home and use her as a crutch. As a result, the daughter carried the baby to term. She gave birth by herself in a motel room. She became homeless, making her give the baby up to the state to end up in foster care. The grandmother was contacted by foster care, but she again refused to take the child in. She feels like she did her job by raising her daughter and does not want to raise another child. Is she in the wrong?"

"She should have taken her daughter in. She's her child. Just because your child turns eighteen doesn't mean you stop caring for them. I think she's a terrible human being for turning her daughter away," Jessica speaks up.

I can see her point of view, but I see the other side too.

"Playing devil's advocate here"—I raise my hand—"we would need more information in order to make a true conclusion. I think this is one of the gray areas. Do I believe parents should love their children unconditionally? Yes, but I also believe that if you coddle your child and always rescue them from their mistakes, they will never learn from them. What did the daughter do prior to becoming pregnant to make the mother feel this way? Did she make responsible decisions or always blame her mistakes on others? With that being said, maybe the mother is not in a place mentally to take care of the child now. Not every person is meant to be a parent. Would you rather her take that child in and abuse him or her? Or would you rather her admit that she's not in the right place to take care of a child and let the state find a more suitable home?"

"Very insightful. Does anyone have a rebuttal?"

Josh speaks up. "Foster care isn't a better option. Wouldn't she rather her grandchild stay in her care? I think that what she did was wrong. Her daughter asked for help, but she refused. Now her daughter's life is falling apart, and instead of helping her, she's letting her fail."

"Don't preach the foster care system to me," I start. "My sister-in-law was in foster care and was almost raped by her foster father. With that being said, not every foster parent is bad, just like not every cop is good, or every judge is fair. Life is fluid. There are no absolutes. There's no way of saying that if she had allowed her daughter to move in and have the baby, the baby would be in a better situation. Instead of rehabilitating the mother and putting her in a halfway house for single mothers, they took the child. Did you even think about that? The foster care system is flooded with children, so they do everything within their power to keep families together. So if they removed the child, it's not because she is homeless. It's because of something else. We have very little information about her case to be able to say for sure if Jane is right or wrong because there are so many factors that would go into a decision like that. Jane could have mental health issues. The daughter could have substance abuse problems, or maybe she treated the child poorly. Until we have all the facts, we can't say for sure and even then, the only person who truly knows the motivations behind the decision is Jane herself."

Professor Lamington claps his hands.

"Very well said. That leads me to the topic for this week. Judging others."

A knock on the door interrupts him. Two men come in with the pizzas and drinks. I frown at them. They look rougher than your everyday pizza boy. They have tattoos covering their body, but they don't look like normal tattoos. They remind me of the tattoos the Russian men get when they are in prison. Except, I don't recognize any of the designs.

They don't look like guys who would work at a pizza place.

Still, they are wearing a shirt that has the pizza place's name on it.

I wish Oleg were here. Or even Dimitri. They would see what I see and vet them for me. Instead, I feel helpless. What if these men were here to hurt me? Would I even be able to fend them off? My training makes me feel like I could, but there are two of them. What if there were more?

"Hey, I grabbed you some." Kiera sets a plate and cup in front of me.

I look back to the table, seeing the men have left.

"Thanks."

She nods, turning her attention back to the professor.

He continues to drone on about why we feel we can judge others based on their decisions when we haven't lived their lives. The group discusses it as a whole, but I remain quiet, nibbling my pizza as I get lost in my thoughts.

"Do you want more?" Kiera whispers, indicating my empty drink.

I shake my head.

My stomach is upset from either the grease or the constant thoughts running through my head.

By the end of the group, I realize it's more than that. I feel dizzy.

"Kiera," I murmur, leaning against her as we walk home.

"Oh god. You're burning up. Let's get you home. I'll call us a cab."

She helps me sit down on a curb as she pulls up her phone. I hear her gasp, but I can't focus. All I can do is lay my head down on the concrete.

"It's okay. I've got her."

I hear the words, but they float away as the darkness takes me.

"Are you sure she's okay?" I hear Kiera's voice.

It's the responding one that has me trying to open my eyes. "Yes, I'll care for her."

"Okay. I'll stay at a friend's. Thank you for carrying her home."

He grunts but doesn't say a word.

Then I feel the cool cloth on my head, making me wince.

"It's okay, *printsessa*. I'm here. I'll make sure you are okay."

"It hurts," I cry out as a stomach cramp hits me.

I feel like I'm dying.

"I should take you home. You'll be more comfortable in your bed."

I try to open my eyes, but the light hurts.

"No. I don't want to move."

He sighs. "Very well."

He goes to move away, but my hand seeks his.

"Stay?" I whimper.

"I wouldn't leave you for the world. Rest. I'm going to call the doctor."

That's the last thing I remember as I fall into a deep sleep.

Dimitri

"I've taken some blood to test for toxins. I'm not sure what she's under the influence of, but she's not naturally sick. There's something else at play here."

I growl, sitting back at her side as he moves away.

"Thank you for coming so quickly. I'll send payment over this evening."

He nods, exiting the room.

Without knowing the cause, he couldn't give her anything other than a fever reducer. He said to keep her cool and try to keep her from pulling out the IV he put in for fluids.

It wouldn't matter if she did. I would put it back in. I'm combat trained for medical situations.

I hate seeing her like this though. She's curled up on her side, tears in her eyes as she shivers.

I wish I could make her feel better.

My heart wanted to crawl out of my chest into hers. I would filet my skin from the bones if it meant I could take this pain from her. I can't though so all I can do is try and care for her the best I can.

Lying next to her, I pull her until her head rests on my chest. Then I brush her hair back from her face as I continue to wipe her head with the cool rag.

I don't know how long I sit like that, using the bowl of ice water to constantly keep her head cool.

When my phone rings, I grab it, quickly silencing it. Ivanna mumbles, but burrows deeper into my chest.

I answer the phone, whispering.

"Hello."

"D, where are you? I need you to come here as soon as possible. We have a development," Nik's voice comes over the line.

I look down at Ivanna. I'm not leaving her.

"I can't come. Maxim can handle it."

Nik growls. "This isn't a request."

"I'm taking care of my number one priority at the moment. So even if you tell me it's life and death, I'm not coming."

"I swear to God, some days I want to murder you. What is so wrong with my sister that you can't possibly leave her?" Nik huffs.

I feel my anger growing, but I try to keep my tone low. "She was somehow poisoned. The doctor is checking into it, but for now, I'm not leaving her side."

Nik is silent for several long moments. I wait him out.

"What happened?" he finally asks.

"No idea. She went to her little group thing and when she came out, she wasn't feeling well. I was following her today, so I swooped in and brought her back to the dorm. I wanted to bring her to your place, but she isn't well enough to travel."

"Why didn't you call me right away?" he asks.

"She's not your responsibility. I was going to call as soon as I knew more. Now, I understand we have business, but Maxim can fill in for me. I'm not available."

"You know if she dies on your watch, I'll kill you," Nik says quietly.

"You won't have to. If she dies, I won't have a reason to live."

I hang up the phone on him and look back down at the woman in question. She owns me and doesn't even realize it.

Leaning down, I press a kiss to the top of her head.

"I will protect you at all costs. I promise, *printsessa*."

The night passes slowly, but she doesn't wake up. I use a forehead thermometer to take her temperature. For hours there's no change, but then all of a sudden, it drops. I let out a relieved breath.

"You're going to be okay," I whisper.

I'm startled when she speaks.

"Dimitri, why does my head feel like this?" she croaks out.

Reaching over, I grab a glass of water before helping her sit up.

"I didn't mean to wake you," I murmur.

She greedily drinks the water before handing it back. She looks around the room, frowning at the IV in her hand.

"What happened? Last thing I remember is eating pizza at group."

I brush the hair back from her face. It's a mess from all the sweat and water, yet she still looks like the single most beautiful creature I have ever seen.

"I'm not sure yet. You weren't feeling well."

"How did you know? Where is Kiera?"

I push her gently until she's lying back down. She immediately moves closer, putting her head back on my chest. I smile a little.

"She went to stay with a friend so you could rest."

"Don't think I don't know you are avoiding my other question," she whispers.

"I don't want to make you angry and the answer will do that."

"You were following me?"

"Yes. I wanted to check in on you discreetly."

She's quiet a moment before she snuggles even closer. "Thank you for being there."

My mouth falls open in surprise. I was sure this would be a fight like everything else with Ivanna.

Not today though.

"You must be sick if you aren't arguing with me," I comment.

"I'm too weak. Try me again later."

I chuckle. "How's your stomach? I can have Oleg grab you some chicken broth."

She considers it a moment before shivering. "No. No food. Just the thought makes me want to puke."

"Alright, *printsessa*. Rest. I'll be right here."

She pulls back slightly, looking up at me.

"Promise?"

I smile down at her. "I'll always be here. Even when you don't want me, I'll be watching out for you."

Her smile is small as she closes her eyes.

She's out within minutes, but I don't forget that smile.

When she feels better, she will be back to hating me, but in this moment, she's not afraid to need me. I'll take all I can get.

I FEEL her move but keep my eyes closed. I dozed off, but I didn't sleep deeply so I knew the moment her breathing changed. She's been lying still for five minutes, I assume trying to figure out what she's going to do now that she realizes I'm in bed with her.

She slowly crawls out of bed, moving quietly around the room. I hear her curse, making my eyes pop open.

Hers are already on mine as she messes with the IV.

"I didn't mean to wake you," she whispers.

"Let me get that for you. Do you feel better?" I sit up, moving to sit on the edge of the bed.

She lets me pull her between my legs as I carefully remove the IV, pressing a tissue to the spot to stop any bleeding.

"I feel hungover, but I don't feel sick anymore."

I nod, my hand finding her forehead. I already know she doesn't have a fever. Her temperature has been normal for hours. I wanted to touch her though.

"If you start to get a temperature again, let me know."

She frowns. "I don't remember everything, but I remember you saying you followed me. Why?"

"Why was I following you? I told you last night. I wanted to check on you. I granted you your freedom and I've honored that, but that doesn't mean I won't come check on you from time to time."

Her eyes flash with hurt. "You really pulled the guys off me? I'm unprotected?"

Standing, I move until I'm in front of her. I cup her cheek, my other hand finding her lower back as I pull her into me.

"You'll never be unprotected. Do you want the truth? It might shatter this treaty we have."

She licks her lips. "Tell me."

I let out a sigh. "My guys are still on you, but they've been instructed to give you space. Instead of being in your face, they are watching from afar."

Her eyes widen. "Where were they last night then?"

I look at her, confused. "They were there. The only reason they didn't come forward was because I was there and had you before they could."

She shakes her head. "Before. Two sketchy guys delivered pizza. I remember thinking they looked off. I thought the guards would have stopped them if they had been there, but they didn't."

"They must not have thought they were a threat. What do you remember about them?"

She rests her head against my chest, leaving me to press a kiss to the top of her head.

"Dark hair, olive skin, tattoos that reminded me of the kind guys get in prison. I didn't get a good look. They didn't even come near me or look my way. My instincts just said they were dangerous. Maybe I'm broken."

"No. Don't you dare do that. You're not broken. If your instincts said to be wary, then you follow them."

"I feel like I'm going crazy, D," she whispers.

"Why?" I'm on high alert for what she might say next.

Is someone following her? Is she a target?

"My thoughts are a mess. I wanted to move on, but then you show up like some dark knight asking me to trust you and I do trust you with everything except my heart. I think I'm finally gaining something I wanted, only to find out it's not what was missing. I don't know how to sort through how I feel half the time and then you take care of me while I'm sick. The affection confuses me. We've never been like this. We fight. It's our thing. I'm not sure how to come to terms with this sweet side of you."

I grimace. "Are you saying you don't want me to be sweet to you?"

"No. I don't know. I'm saying you are confusing me."

"I don't want that, *printsessa*. All I want is you."

She leans back, looking up into my eyes. "You mean that, don't you?"

"More than anything I've ever meant in my life," I admit.

She swallows hard. "If I agree to see you. To date you for real, there will be rules. Boundaries."

My heart starts to pound in my chest. I have negotiated with some of the deadliest men in the world, yet this woman has me more scared than any of them combined.

"Lay out your terms."

"I want to keep my freedom. I like Oleg being outside while I sleep, but otherwise, I want the guards to stay in the background. I don't mind them watching, but I still want to feel like I'm not in a cage."

"Done," I whisper, my hand caressing her cheek.

She leans into it. "I want real dates. We can go out, or you can find somewhere private to take me, but I want to be wooed the way a man would a woman he likes. I know everything about you as Dimitri, my guard, but I want to know about Dimitri, the man I might fall for."

"I've always been that Dimitri, but I agree. I'll tell you anything."

"You still owe me a grovel."

I laugh but push her back before falling to my knees. Pressing my face into her stomach, I hold her to me.

"Please forgive me, *printsessa*. I've seen the error of my ways. I've treated you poorly, but I never will again. I promise."

I hear her suck a breath in. She's quiet a moment before her hands find my hair.

"I never imagined you'd get on your knees for me."

I glance up at her with a wicked smirk. "Oh, I'll get on my knees for you anytime you want, but I promise it'll be more pleasurable than an apology."

She laughs, smacking my forehead. "Get up, you fool."

I stand but pull her into my arms.

She blows air through her lips before speaking. "I have the right to add rules or change them at any time."

"We will discuss any changes and compromise. I'll give you almost anything you ask for, *printsessa*, but I won't allow you to put yourself in unsafe situations for the sake of sticking it to me."

She considers it. "Fine. Now I appreciate everything you did for me, but I need you to leave."

"Why?" I ask quickly.

A beautiful blush covers her cheeks. "I'm gross. I want a shower and then I'm going to clean my sheets. Then I want to call Kiera and tell her she can come home. I may even gossip about you a bit. You know, normal girl stuff."

I smirk. "Only under one condition."

"What?" she asks, exasperated.

"Kiss me." I move in, but she puts her hand up to block me.

"I haven't brushed my teeth and I was sick."

I pry her hand away, cupping her cheek. "I. Don't. Care."

Then I press my lips to hers. I don't try to invade her. I don't want to push my luck. I keep my lips on hers until I feel her press back. Then I pull away.

"Our first date is tomorrow night. Be ready by seven."

CHAPTER
ELEVEN

Ivanna

"You don't have to leave again," I tell Kiera.

"I know, but I kind of liked sleeping at Josh's place."

My eyes widen. "Wait. Josh? From group Josh?"

She nods with a smile. "He saw me walking to Jessica's and offered me his bed. He's been sleeping on the floor. I'm trying to change that, so, um, can you skip group tonight? I want him to think you are still sick."

I snort. "Girl, I'll skip group for the rest of time to help you get laid. What else are friends for?"

She laughs, pulling me in for a hug. "You are so right. Besides, if I leave tonight, maybe you can see if Dimitri will take you out tonight instead."

She wiggles her eyebrows, making me blush.

"I don't know. I don't want to rush anything with him. I feel like it's been so complicated that we have to take things slow, otherwise it will only get more fucked up."

She bumps my hip with hers. "Going slow is overrated. I don't understand why you are making this so complicated. It's as easy as this. Sit him down and tell him what would make you happiest if you two were together. Tell him your hard limits. Ask him the same. Then compare. If you are compatible, then make it work. If you can't agree on anything, then cut him loose. It's not worth all the wasted time by playing the games you're playing."

"I'm not trying to play a game."

She shakes her head. "You still are. You're telling him you can't trust his words, but you aren't even giving him a chance to prove them. You're dangling what he wants in front of him with the intention of pulling it back if things get too hard for you. Love is a two-way street. There's always a give-and-take. Sometimes you might need more from him than he needs from you. Other times, it might be him being more needy. Either way, in the end it will all even out. Relationships are about making it work even when life becomes complicated because, news flash, Ivanna. Life is always going to be complicated. The question you need to ask yourself is if he's worth working through the complications to find your happiness."

"Ugh, why do you have to make sense?"

She smiles. "I only want what's best for you. After you make your decision though, I think you should let that man strip you down and worship you. The way he hauled you into his arms and practically sprinted across campus with you?" She fans her face. "Girl, if you don't want him, give a girl a shot."

A flash of jealousy hits me. She sees it, smiling wider.

"There it is. I think you already know your answer. Just don't fuck on my bed, or if you do, change the sheets."

She winks at me before she heads out the door with her overnight bag.

I shake my head, settling back on my bed.

She made a good point though. I need to stop letting sixteen-year-old me make decisions for present me. If I'm going to forgive him, I need to leave it in the past. I can't keep punishing him for not wanting me then.

So instead of taking Kiera's advice, I text Oleg.

Me: Can you drive me to Nik's?

He replies back instantly.

Oleg: Of course. I'll come up and get you.

I smile when he knocks, not two minutes later.

Dimitri was telling the truth. While my protection couldn't be seen, they were never far.

"I'm ready," I tell him, grabbing my purse.

He watches as I lock my door before letting me lead him down the hall.

For the first time in days, I feel better. I feel settled.

I feel like this is how my life is supposed to be.

"Not that I am not super excited to have you stay the night, but what made you decide to?" Lia finally asks halfway through the second movie.

When I showed up several hours ago, I just asked her to do a girls' day with me, even going as far as saying I wanted us to have a sleepover. Nik was a little peeved, but he allowed it. So while he is out with Dimitri doing something to do with the business, we are sitting here watching movies and snacking.

"I was wondering how long it would take you." I shoot her a smile. "I thought I'd make it one more movie."

She rolls her eyes. "Come on. Tell me."

I suck my bottom lip into my mouth, biting it before finally blurting it out, "I think I'm going to give Dimitri a chance."

She gasps before squealing. "Yes! Oh my god! I can't believe this is actually happening. I always knew it was going to be you two. There is no way two people fight as much as you do without having real feelings."

"Whoa." I laugh. "Calm down. I'm only giving him a chance. I didn't say I was marrying the guy."

She gives me a loaded look. "You were going to marry a virtual stranger. Dimitri is the best man in all of those binders."

"Better than your Maxim?" I tease.

She's had a soft spot for Maxim ever since they became friends while he protected her.

"Of course not, but Maxim was never for you. Dimitri, though, he's strong enough to stand against you while also caring enough to let you have your way from time to time. You balance each other out."

"You really think so?" I ask.

She nods. "For sure. He's all surly while you are a spitfire. You keep him on his toes. He could never be with a meek girl, which is all he'd find."

"He better not be finding any girls." I huff.

My mind goes back to the past. When have I ever seen him with a girl? Never. I mean, he could have left to see them, but he's never had a girlfriend.

"What are you thinking about now?"

"Do you think he's been celibate? He couldn't have been, right? Who would give up sex for years because he might end up with me?"

"If you are asking if I think he's a virgin, the answer is no, but has he been saving himself for you? Maybe. I've never seen him with anyone," Lia answers honestly.

"I know he's not a virgin. I overheard him telling Nik about some girl he had bagged when he was fifteen. They were comparing stories."

Lia scrunches up her nose. "I don't want to know about Nik's past."

I laugh. "Fair enough. Still, I wonder if he's been with anyone."

"You should ask him. He'd tell you the truth. One thing about

DIMITRI

Dimitri is he is always honest, no matter how much you wish he wouldn't be."

"You're right. Sometimes it's a pain in the ass. Maybe I will on our date tomorrow."

"Wait. Date? What? Why did you keep all of this from me?" Lia looks hurt.

I reach out, grabbing her hand. "I didn't. He told me this morning he wanted to take me on a date tomorrow. It's one of the reasons I came over. I have no idea what to wear. I was hoping you'd help me pick something out?"

"Of course. Always. I am so excited. Should we go shopping? I think we should go shopping."

Shaking my head, I pull myself up. "Let's get going then."

She jumps up, smiling so wide. "I'll let Maxim know. You let Oleg know."

I pull out my phone, texting Oleg.

> Me: Lia wants to go shopping. Will you come along?

I pose it as a question so it feels like my choice, but the truth is, he'd come along anyway. He responds that he's waiting out front.

Before I can stop myself, I type out a text to Dimitri.

> Me: Lia and I are going shopping for our date tomorrow. Any input on what I should wear?

I nibble my lip as I wait for his response. He doesn't leave me waiting long.

> The Devil: Printsessa, you can wear a potato sack and look sexy.

My heart flutters at his compliment. I'm still not sure how to handle this sweet side of him.

> Me: So the shortest dress I can find. Got it.

I add a winky face to tease him.

> The Devil: Woman, you can wear whatever the fuck you want, but just know if anyone sees what's mine, I will be committing murder.

A thrill zips through my body. I shouldn't find the idea of murder so hot, but I do. I know he will follow through with it too.

> Me: Promise?

I can't help but ask.

> The Devil: That's a fucking promise.

"What has you smiling like that?" Lia asks as she comes back into the room.

I push my smile down, looking at her. "Nothing."

She chuckles. "Sure. If you're going to sext him, please teach me your ways. I can't sext to save my life, much to Nik's dismay."

"Gross. My brother. Remember?"

She sighs. "I know. It sucks having a best friend who is related to your man. There are so many things I want to share with you, but I don't want to gross you out."

"I appreciate your withholding. Maybe we can do a trial run. We can call him Peter or something."

She shakes her head. "No way. Last thing I need is someone overhearing me talking about Peter railing me and it gets back to Nik. That would be a mess."

I shudder. "Nope. It's not working anyway. I still know you're talking about my brother."

"Alas, I guess it will not work." Lia sighs.

"You know, my roommate Kiera has become a great friend. I think you should hang out with us more. Then she can listen to your sex stories and save me the trauma."

She smiles. "Invite her shopping."

"Okay. She might not come though. She's got a boy thing."

> Me: Hey. Want to go shopping with me and Lia before your group tonight?

I ask her.

> Kiera: Thanks, but I still have class. I'll text you tomorrow.

"She's got class. We can do something this weekend."

"Sounds good. You ready to go?"

"Yeah."

For the first time in a while, I'm actually excited about my life.

Dimitri

"Everything has been silent. It's eerie," Maxim tells me as we stand watching the men train.

"No one else has gone missing?" I ask.

He shakes his head. "Not that's been reported at least. I've been keeping an eye out for any women in that age group to go missing."

"The guys haven't found anything on campus?"

"Nothing. I still think it has to do with that group. Ivanna hasn't said anything about it?"

"I haven't exactly asked. We aren't in the best place right now."

"I can't believe you even let her join the group. Knowing all the girls have been members at some point makes me think it's ground zero."

"Me too. I don't think it's a coincidence that Ivanna became sick after consuming food provided by the professor either."

"Has the doc gotten back to you?"

"Not yet. I'm going to go see him after we are done here. Did Alexei find anything on the men who delivered the food?"

Maxim is pensive. "There's no record of pizza being ordered from the pizza place to the college. Everything was either delivered to other addresses or picked up directly. We looked through the addresses provided and the cameras in the shop, but no one matching their description was found. It's sketchy. They jumped through too many hoops for it to not be connected."

"The question is who was their target. From what Oleg can tell, Ivanna is the only one who got sick. So was she the intended target? She wasn't throwing up, but it did give her a fever and had her entire body locking up. If you wanted to incapacitate someone, that would be the way to do it. They wouldn't even think anything was done to them. They'd just think they had a bug."

"I don't like this. What if that's how they grabbed the other girls? I think you should stop Ivanna from going," Maxim gives his unsolicited advice.

"Or we let her go and keep a close eye on her. They don't suspect anything right now. Why else would they have let her so close? They think she's unprotected. They don't see the guards following her every move. If she Is the target, they will try again. We will be there ready for them."

Maxim frowns. "Are you going to tell her that you're using her as bait?"

"Fuck no. I enjoy my dick where it is, thank you. I will tell her what is necessary when the time comes."

"Are you sure that's a good idea? I learned from the situation with Nik and Lia that women want to feel included. They want to be equal. By doing this, you are basically saying you don't trust her."

"Trust has nothing to do with it. She is enjoying the freedom I've given her. If I tell her, she won't feel safe. She probably would stop going and I know she'd tell that roommate of hers. It's best to keep this close to the chest right now."

"Alright. You're the boss. I hope it doesn't blow up in your face."

"Me too." I check my watch. "I'm going to head over to the doctor's place. You got this?"

Maxim smirks. "Of course I do. I think I might jump in there with them."

Shaking my head, I leave him behind, walking toward the house. When I get inside, I find Lia and Ivanna in the kitchen.

Moving to Ivanna's side, I press a kiss to her temple.

"Hello, *printsessa*. I've got an errand to run. I'll be back."

She frowns. "You said you'd pick me up at seven. That's only an hour and a half away."

I nuzzle her neck, making her squirm. "I'll be here before seven. I promise."

"You better be," she mumbles. "If you're not, I'll cause you physical harm."

I snort. "Alright, my little assassin. I'll see you in a bit."

I press one more kiss, this time to her neck, before heading out. I pause on the other side of the door a moment to hear what she's going to say because Ivanna always has something to say.

"Jesus. I think I need to go find Nik after that display. That was hot," Lia starts.

Ivanna sighs. "I know. I never thought our physical chemistry was the issue. It's the communication that's the problem. We will see if he sticks to his word and makes it back in time."

"And if he doesn't?"

"It might be irrational, but I think I'll be done. I need proof that I'm a priority."

"That's not irrational. Your feelings are valid. Do you want to go pamper ourselves until it's time to get ready?"

"Yes. Grab the wine. I need some liquid courage."

I shake my head, noting that she's already drinking. I'll have to eliminate any alcohol from our evening. I don't want her drunk.

Heading out the front of the house, I pause beside Oleg.

"Keep my girl safe."

He nods, not saying another word as I move away from him.

The drive to the doctor's office is uneventful. Still, my eye keeps straying to the clock. I won't let Ivanna down. She wants to know she's a priority. She's the top priority for me.

I just need to prove it to her.

Jogging up the steps of the clinic, I make my way past the receptionist, ignoring her protests.

Pushing into Dr. Daniil's office, I move to take a seat in his chair at his desk.

Several minutes go by before he makes his way in.

"Dimitri, I was going to call you today."

I cock an eyebrow. "Were you though?"

"Of course. I got the results back. Let me find them."

He starts to shuffle papers around his desk until he holds one up for me. I snatch it, but I don't look at it right away.

"Tell me what it says, doc."

He looks nervous. "It appears to be a normal virus, but after further inspection, it's man-made. I don't know how they did it, but they managed to make a bioweapon to take out a person by giving them a common sickness. If this was used widely, it could take out a whole city. The people would likely experience similar symptoms to Ms. Petrova. Maybe worse, depending on their immune systems."

"How do you think it got into her system?"

"I didn't observe any injection marks on her during my examination. I believe it was either inhaled or ingested. It's a simple strain of bacteria that could easily be added to a drink or on food. I believe it could even be added to a lip balm or something similar that would eventually enter the system."

Standing, I move to the doctor's side. Within seconds, I have him pinned to his desk. He gasps as he tries to get out of my hold. His receptionist bursts into the room, screaming. I pull my gun, pointing it at her as I use one hand to continue to hold the doctor down by the throat.

"Out."

She is shaking, but she shuts the door.

"This is your one and only chance, doctor. You should have called the second this information was provided to you. I should never have had to come collect the information myself. If this happens again, you'll wish you had heeded my warning. Understood?"

He chokes as he tries to respond. I let up on the pressure.

"Understood. It will not happen again."

"Good. Make sure your girl knows to keep her trap shut, otherwise I'll have to take care of her too. I'm sure your wife would do the dirty work for me when she finds out you're fucking her."

His eyes widen in fear. "What? I'm not. No. It's not like that."

I snort. "Don't lie to me, old man. It's written all over her face."

Grabbing the paper, I leave the room. I wink at the receptionist as I pass her, making her squeak in terror.

Yeah. I'm the devil. Don't cross me, I think as I head back to my car. Once inside, I snap a photo of the paper, sending it to Alexei. Then I call him.

"I just sent you a photo. Look into it for me. The men Ivanna saw somehow poisoned her. Doc says it's some kind of biological weapon. The samples are at the lab if you want to run your own tests."

"Got it. I'll look into this right now and get back to you."

He hangs up the phone as I head back to the house.

I have plenty of time to get ready for this date. My first date with Ivanna. I'm determined to make it special for her.

She deserves the world.

Too bad she's stuck with me.

CHAPTER
TWELVE

Ivanna

I can't breathe.

Standing just inside the door of my room, I try and calm myself. It's only a few minutes until seven.

Part of me is excited. I've dreamed of this for so long. I've wanted Dimitri as mine ever since I knew what hormones were. So for that part of me, this is everything I've ever imagined.

The other part of me is waiting for the other shoe to drop. That's the same part that still remembers the sting of Dimitri telling me we would never be. The same one who has been trying to escape him ever since.

What if he's late? Will I really give up on him so quickly? I told Lia I would, but they were just words.

Maybe that's why I find it so hard to take Dimitri at his word. I've used words to cover how I've felt for years. They are just pretty packaging to divert attention from the thing you are really trying to hide.

If I'm able to lie so easily, who is to say he isn't?

I look myself over one last time.

I didn't do as I threatened. My dress isn't overly revealing, but it is sexy. Sexier than anything I've ever worn before.

This is the first time I've felt like I can really dress the way I want without fear of being lectured or forced to change.

So I went with a champagne-colored dress that's floor length. It wraps across my front, hugging my breasts, but then crisscrosses across my stomach, leaving it open until it hits the skirt at my hips. The sleeves are short, only enough to cover my upper arms, with the back cut out completely.

It makes me feel like a woman for maybe the first time ever.

A knock at my door startles me.

"Yes?" I call out, swallowing hard.

"He's been waiting downstairs for ten minutes. Are you going to go out with him or not?" Lia teases.

I move to the door, opening it. She helped me get ready for a little bit, but then I asked for some privacy. I needed to really get in the right mindset for this date.

"I'm ready."

She smiles at me, hooking her arm in mine.

"Your prince awaits," she jokes.

I roll my eyes. "More like the devil."

"Who wants a prince anyway? They are too good. I prefer a little darkness in my men. It means they would be willing to do anything to not only pleasure us, but keep us safe."

I snort. "Like keep us in gilded cages."

"Maybe, but is it really a cage if I choose to lock myself inside it?"

She makes a good point. She had the option to leave. Nik was ready to put her on a bus out of town. She saved his life, altering her future. It was her choice.

Could Dimitri be mine? Would I be more comfortable with the overprotectiveness of him if I chose it on my own?

"Who knows," I whisper.

She laughs, stopping just before the stairs so that we can't be seen.

"You sure you're ready? I can make him wait. The lady is allowed to be late, you know."

I shake my head. "I'm ready."

She steps back, letting me step forward. I glance down and see Dimitri with his eyes locked on the top of the stairs. As if he is waiting for me to make my way down.

As I start down the stairs, he steps forward, waiting for me at the bottom with his hand out. His eyes take me in, the hungry look I can see in them causing my body to heat.

"You look absolutely stunning, *printsessa*," he breathes out on a whisper.

The butterflies in my stomach start fluttering at his admission. He cannot keep his eyes off me as I slip my hand into his. Once on solid ground, he keeps my hand in his as he raises it above my head and circles me. I feel the faint brush of his lips on the nape of my neck before he comes back to stand in front of me. My entire insides are in chaos. My body is tingling while the heat between my legs is roaring.

I've never felt this way before in my life.

"A fucking masterpiece, Ivanna. Truly." He looks right into my eyes.

I blush, taking in his own appearance. He's dressed up a little, but not much. He's wearing a clean, black button-down with a pair of black slacks. Nothing really out of the norm for him, but still, somehow, it looks better on him today than it has in the past.

Maybe it's my mindset. This is a date, after all. Our first date. If I am going to be honest, it's my first real date. Sure, I've gone out with guys in the past, but I was always looking over my shoulder.

I think I realize now I was always waiting for Dimitri to bust in, not because he was annoying me but because I took it as a form of affection.

"We should get going before I forget that I need to be a gentleman," he murmurs, bringing my hand to his lips to kiss.

I smile. "Maybe I don't need a gentleman."

He growls, pulling me into his chest before cupping my face. His lips descend on mine, devouring me until I'm breathless.

When he finally pulls back, I can feel his heart beating rapidly beneath my hand. He seems even more affected than I am.

"I have a plan. Let's go."

He grabs my hand, pulling me behind him. I can't withhold the giggle that slides out at how fast he's moving. Almost as if it's the only way to stop himself from ravishing me.

My thought is proven when we get to the SUV. He pushes me against the back door, pressing his lips to mine as he pecks and nibbles at my lips.

"I thought we had somewhere to go," I gasp out when he moves to showing my neck kisses.

"We do. You're just so irresistible. You're right though. We should go."

He presses two more kisses to my neck before pulling back, opening the passenger door. Once I'm inside, he leans over me, buckling my belt before stealing one more kiss from my lips.

When he shuts the door, my hand finds my lips. They are tingling from all the action they are getting. I feel giddy, like a child getting ready to open presents on Christmas. I don't remember the last time I felt this light.

It scares me.

Dimitri climbs into the driver's seat. After pulling away from the house, he reaches over, threading his fingers through mine, kissing the back of my hand before settling both of our hands on my thigh.

It's all I can focus on. The sensation of his skin against mine. The weight of his hand on my thigh. The intimacy it represents.

I thought I was ready for this, but now I'm not so sure.

My heart is beating so fast I feel like I might have a heart attack.

Will I survive Dimitri?

DIMITRI

She's being quiet, but I'm letting her process her thoughts. This has to be a big change for her.

I know it is for me. I went from always trying to control her to keep her safe to now doing whatever I can to prove to her that I'm the one she wants to be with.

It's jarring to change so suddenly, but I refuse to lose her. If I did, it would probably kill me.

So I let her be with her thoughts.

I hear a slight gasp when we finally pull up to the restaurant I chose.

Really, she chose it.

"You remembered?" she whispers.

I smile at her before climbing out. I wait until I've helped her from the SUV to pull her into my arms.

"You said if you were ever to have a boyfriend, you'd want him to pull out all the stops. When I asked you what that meant, you said you expected to be lavished with affection and taken on very public dates at restaurants. You said the Starlight Delight would be your number one choice, but you'd settle for anything as long as the man was good to you," I whisper against her ear.

"I told you that when I was fifteen years old. How did you remember that?"

"I remember everything about you. You might have just been my best friend's little sister back then, but you were still important to me.

Even though my feelings for you have changed, it doesn't mean I never cared."

She sniffles before burying her head against my chest.

"I used to dream about you bringing me here. Nik offered to bring me a couple of times, but I never wanted to come with him. It's always been a romantic thing for me," she admits quietly.

"I know. It's the same reason you denied me when I offered to take you for your eighteenth birthday. You didn't see me as a romantic partner. I'm hoping you do now," I admit.

"I said no because my heart couldn't handle you bringing my dreams to life only to tell me I was like a sister to you."

Brushing the back of her head, I tuck my head down and bring my nose to her hair, inhaling the heavenly scent.

"I wasn't ready for you, Ivanna. It sounds stupid, but I needed to prepare to be what you need."

"It's in the past. If we are going to make this work, we can't keep bringing up the past. I'm still going to be the pain in the ass you hate and you're still going to be an overbearing fool, but we will compromise. Right?"

I pull back, looking into her eyes. "I never hated you. Even when you're a pain in the ass, there isn't anyone I'd rather be with."

She gives me a small smile. "I'll remember that the next time you call me a brat."

I snort. "You know what the best part of us crossing this line is?"

"What?" she asks.

I swat her ass, making her jump into me.

"I can punish you when you're misbehaving. Now let's get inside before I decide to say fuck it and take you home."

Her cheeks are flushed, but she lets me grab her hand, leading her inside.

Immediately we are ushered back to a private table, away from prying eyes. After placing our drink orders, Ivanna rests her elbows on the table and rests her chin in her palm.

"You know you could have ordered a drink, right?" she says softly.

I raise a brow and fight back a smile. "I did order a drink."

Ivanna rolls her eyes. "I meant vodka."

"I'd rather not drink on our first date."

Ivanna's eyes go soft. "That sounds so weird."

"What does?"

"Us going on a first date."

"Is it though?" I ask as I lean back in my chair, resting my hand on the table. I fight back a smile when Ivy's eyes drop down. "Personally, I think it sounds right, inevitable, really."

"Inevitable, really?" she says, eyebrows raised.

"Really. I've known for years that we would end up down this road."

"If you've known for years, then why did you wait so long?"

"I wanted to give you time." Ivanna scoffs, but I keep going. "I'm serious. I realize that seven years isn't that big of an age gap, but I still wanted you to experience everything you could before this." I wave around the room. "So I did what I could to keep you at bay."

Ivy shakes her head. "Please don't lie to me."

"I promise you I'm not."

Ivy sits back and crosses her arms over her chest as she studies me.

"I think that you're afraid."

"Of what?"

"Losing control. Losing me."

"Do I control you? Yes, but that comes from a place of concern. Sometimes I don't think you realize the delicate position you're in with who your brother is. As for losing you? That will never happen. I won't let it." I shake my head.

The waitress interrupts us and places our drinks down. After taking our orders, she walks away.

Leaning forward, I pick up my glass and hold it up to Ivy's. "Here's to the future."

"To the future." She pauses. "So what now?"

"Now we talk about whatever you want," I say as I grab her hand, holding it on the table.

"What do you usually talk about during first dates?"

"Considering this is my first, I wouldn't know." I shrug. I see Ivy's mouth open and cut her off. "The way I see it is we don't have to go through the hassle of the awkward conversation. We've known each other so long that we can already answer most of those questions."

"Like what?"

I raise my brow. "What's my favorite color?"

"Red," she says immediately.

"And yours is yellow." I smirk as her eyes slightly widen. "I know you love adding peanut M&M's to your popcorn and you hate pure silence unless it's when you're trying to go to bed at night."

"I like my room…"

"Pitch black," I finish.

Ivanna blushes and looks away. "That should creep me out, but it doesn't."

"Like I said, I know you, Ivanna Petrova."

Her eyes come back to me. "I don't know how you sleep, but I know you check on me every night before you go to bed when we're at home. I know you drink your coffee black with nothing else added, and you really don't care for anything sweet."

My heart clenches. This. This is what's been missing between us.

"Just think of what we will learn when the walls between us fall."

Her eyes go all glossy. "I can't wait for that."

Neither can I.

CHAPTER
THIRTEEN

Ivanna

"I want to show you something. Will you go with me somewhere?" Dimitri asks once we are settled back into the SUV.

"Sure," I tell him.

I'm not even nervous anymore. Dinner was amazing. Not only was the food better than I thought it would be, but I felt like Dimitri was opening up to me in a way that he's never done in the past. I've known him my whole life, but that doesn't mean I actually know him. Hearing about his thoughts and feelings about things in the past really opened my eyes to how differently we experienced life.

When we finally pull up to a small house, I look to Dimitri with confusion.

"Who lives here?"

He smiles over at me. "I do."

I shake my head. "You live at the compound. You have the room next to mine."

He dips his chin. "I do. I spend most of my time there, but only because you are there. I've always owned this house, Ivanna. I've only ever slept here a few times. Mostly since you've been at the dorms protected by my men."

"How the hell did I not know you have a whole-ass house?"

"You never asked," he admits quietly.

That's the truth. I was so blinded by my hurt that I stopped trying to get to know Dimitri. I put the brakes on the friendship we once had and turned it into something sour.

"Will you show it to me?" I ask.

He nods before getting out of the SUV. I wait for him to come around and help me out. Then he leads me up the front steps.

The house is quaint. It's not big like the compound, but that makes it feel more homey. I never did like the house I grew up in. It always felt more like a dungeon.

This house could never feel that way.

The bright-yellow paint on the outside shines from the front porch light. The shutters are a pale pink, making me smile. I wouldn't imagine him choosing pink.

It's one of my favorite colors though, especially paired with yellow.

Did he choose it because of that?

He unlocks the door with biometrics before guiding me inside.

"That's fancy," I tell him.

My dorm has a normal key lock, and the compound is never locked since someone is always there. I've never seen anything like it.

"It's fingerprint enabled. There are only two prints registered. Yours and mine."

"Mine?" I ask, completely blown away.

He really gave me access to his home before even bringing me here? What does that mean?

"Wishful thinking. I know," he jokes.

I shake my head, letting it go for now.

My heart doesn't though. It was already half in love with him. It's fallen further with each brush of his skin against mine.

"So this is the living room." He shows me around the open space. It's sparse, with only a couch and television on the wall.

"I haven't been here enough to buy much. The kitchen is through there, but I never eat here, so there's nothing in there. There's a shed out back and a garage around the side of the house. Upstairs, it has two bedrooms. The master and spare. Want to see those?"

He's teasing, but I'm not.

I'm being serious.

"Show me where you sleep." My tone is huskier than I anticipated.

I can tell the moment it registers with him too. The humor falls from his face as he reaches out to grab my hand, slowly pulling me to the stairs. It seems like it takes forever, but only a minute has likely passed when we arrive at his room.

This is the only room I've seen so far that's dark. The rest of the house is light and airy, but his room is painted a deep blue, making it feel masculine.

It smells like him too. A bourbon-and-oak smell permeates the air as if a candle has been burned. I know it's just him though.

I once tried to peek through his items at the house to find his cologne. I found it alright, but it didn't smell like him. The scent that has been haunting me since I was a teen is something natural to him.

"I like your room," I whisper, walking over to his bed to run my fingers over the comforter.

"*Printsessa*, you need to turn around and leave if you want any hope of escaping here without finding out what my cock feels like inside of you," he warns.

The desperation in his voice sends a jolt to my center, making me sway with desire.

"I'm a virgin, Dimitri. Did you know that?" I ask.

He growls, moving closer to me. "Of course I do. I made sure of it."

"I've been saving it for someone," I tease.

I bite back a smile as I watch his jaw tense and his eyes darken.

"Someone special?"

I shake my head, turning to face him fully. "I've been saving it for you."

He's on me within a heartbeat, his hands fisted in my hair. "Are you sure this is what you want? I'm not one of those soft guys you've been trying to date. If I fuck you, I will never let you go. You know that, right?"

I did know that. I know that if I let this go further, I'm basically locking the cage I've been so desperate to escape, yet in this moment, it's all I want. I'd gladly live in here as long as he's locked in here with me.

I don't answer him with words. Instead, I step back, pulling down the arms of my dress until it falls to my waist, showing him every naked inch of my torso.

"Fuck," he curses lowly.

I continue to push the fabric down, smiling when his eyes home in on my pussy.

"You weren't wearing underwear?" His voice is husky.

I tsk. "Panty lines are overrated. Personally, I prefer to go commando when I can. Does that bother you?"

He pounces on me then, his mouth finding mine as he pushes me back until the back of my knees hits the bed.

He pulls back, gently pushing me until I'm lying back on the bed.

"This is going to hurt. It's not going to be some fairy tale first time you see in those movies you love. I'm going to prepare you the best I can. Okay?"

"Okay," I murmur, suddenly feeling shy.

Dimitri drops to his knees before pressing kisses from my ankle to my thigh. Then he does the same to my other leg.

"So wet for me." His voice is low, almost as if he's speaking to himself.

I don't get a chance to answer him though. He leans in, his tongue touching my skin, making me jump.

My heart feels like it's going to beat out of my chest while I feel that familiar ache in my clit, making me want more.

I meant what I told him. I'm a virgin, but I've touched myself so many times thinking about the man between my legs.

The reminder of that only makes my body grow warmer. When his hands reach out, opening me to him, I shudder. This whole thing is so erotic that I can't help but feel oversensitive. The touch of his tongue to my clit sends another jolt to my core, my body clenching around nothing.

"Dimitri," I murmur, trying to get him to do something more than tease me.

"What do you need, *printsessa*? Tell me. Beg for it."

Part of me wants to get angry, but I can't. Not when he's on his knees for me. The least I can do is give in. Finally stop fighting this and him.

"More. I need more," I tell him.

"More what?"

"More of you. Make me feel good. Claim me. Make me yours. Please."

He chuckles. "I'll make you feel better than good."

Then he goes to work. His tongue licks every inch of my pussy before his teeth join in, nibbling while his lips suck on me. It's such a contrasting experience that I'm not sure what to focus on. Then I feel it. His finger at my entrance.

I've never dared put anything there. I read once that even a tampon might break your hymen, so I've avoided all of it because I only wanted one person to do that for me.

He presses in gently before pulling out and spreading my wetness around me. He continues to do this until I feel his finger stop inside of me. I'm not sure how much he's managed to feed in, but it doesn't hurt. It burns a little, but that feeling has already faded.

"You saved this for me? All for me?" he asks before focusing back on my center with his mouth.

I gasp at the sensation. "Yes. Only you."

He mumbles something, but I can't hear it. Instead, he moves his finger. The next press in comes with added pressure. I clamp down on it before forcing myself to relax.

He must feel my body reacting because he moves his other hand so his finger is pressing on my clit in a circular motion.

That's enough to have me forget all about his fingers inside me. Instead, all I can feel is the building pressure warning me that I'm going to come soon. I've come from my own hand, but it's never felt this intense before. I feel like my blood is boiling. I'm actually scared of what's going to happen when I reach the point.

"Let go, *printsessa*," he demands.

Then it happens.

I scream out, my body clenching uncontrollably around his fingers as I come hard. Liquid rushes out of me as my ears grow cloudy, my eyes clamping closed.

I have no idea how long I lie like that. It could be minutes or hours. All I know is my body is jelly. I wouldn't be able to move even if I wanted to.

I can hear Dimitri talking, but his words aren't registering. They are distorted by the loss of hearing.

When my ears finally clear, he's still talking.

"Such a beautiful woman. You did so well. Watching you come is the best thing I've seen in my entire life. I could eat this pussy for every meal and still never tire of it."

"Dimitri," I croak out.

He pulls his head up from between my legs where he had been resting his head.

"Yes, *printsessa*."

"I don't think I can move."

He chuckles. "You don't need to. I'll take care of you like I always do. Do you need water?"

I nod.

"I'll be right back."

DIMITRI

He stands before leaning down to press a kiss to my lips. His are still wet with my arousal, making me feel a little bit dirty, but also turning me on yet again.

How can I feel this way so soon after something so explosive?

I watch as he leaves, his clothes still fully on. For a moment, I frown. I didn't even get to see him naked.

Leaning up, I look between my legs. My cheeks turn red as mortification sets in.

There is a huge wet spot. It looks like I pissed the bed. How can he be so chill about this?

When he comes back, I haven't moved, my eyes still wide on the spot as I try and process what I'm seeing.

"What's wrong?" he asks.

I gasp. "I peed on you."

He raises a brow. "You squirted. There's a difference. It was glorious. God, I can't wait to make you squirt on my cock."

I look up at him, shocked.

"Seriously?"

"Baby, the fact that I could make you squirt means I did my fucking job. I'm going to make you do it every single time we fuck. So get used to it."

He hands me the bottle of water already opened.

I take it, sipping on it a moment.

"You still have your clothes on," I state.

He nods slowly. "I wasn't sure you'd still want more. We don't have to rush this. I'm willing to take my time with you. You're well worth it."

"I want this, Dimitri. I've never wanted anything more." I reach out, pulling him toward me.

He lets me, fitting himself between my legs.

Then I start to unbutton his shirt.

I THOUGHT I was hard from going down on Ivanna, but apparently, I was wrong. Looking down, my cock twitches at the view of her legs spread next to mine. I watch as Ivanna takes a deep breath and raises her hands and slowly starts to unbutton my shirt. My hands flex at my sides as I fight the urge to take over.

Let her have this.

Even with her leading right now, I'm still in control. I'll let her have her fun with me, but I won't take it very far. Not now. Tonight was about her, not me. Ivy swallows hard as the last button gives way.

My hand reaches out and grabs hold of hers right as she touches my belt. She looks up at me with dilated eyes.

"Why did you stop me?"

"We're not having sex tonight."

Ivanna flinches and tries to pull away, but I won't let her.

"I don't want you to think I only took you out just to have sex," I tell her bluntly.

"But what if I want to have sex?"

Hearing the word sex roll off her lips makes me groan as her eyes drop to my covered cock.

"We will, but not tonight."

"I want to touch you," she demands.

I tip my chin up and step back. "Crawl up on the bed."

I wait until she does as I say and begin to take the rest of my clothes off. Ivanna gasps as my pants hit the ground and I come into view.

I wrap my hand around my cock and pump it once, then twice, trying to calm myself down. Letting go, I get onto the bed and lie down next to her. Ivy turns onto her side and I pull her body into mine, placing her leg over my hip.

"Lift your head."

Silently, Ivy does as I ask, and I place my arm under her head. I watch as Ivy's eyes flutter shut in pleasure. I've dreamed about having her naked body pressed against mine, but this is better than I thought it would be.

Reaching out, I brush some hair out of her face. Her eyes meet mine and without looking away, I trail my hand from her cheek, along her shoulder, down her side, until I reach between us. Grabbing my cock, I move it until it's situated right where she wants it most, without penetration. I pump my hips so I rub against her folds.

"Dimitri," she whimpers.

"Is this okay?"

"Yes."

"Perfect," I say as I do it again. "Now you're in charge. You can do whatever you want, but I can't slip inside of you. Get yourself off while rubbing against my cock, touch me, kiss me. This is all on you."

"I-I've never." She shakes her head.

"I know, *printsessa*, and that's okay. This is your time to learn, explore, figure out what we both like."

Ivanna nods and, with shaky hands, reaches over and cups the back of my head, pulling my lips toward her. Taking her lead, I lean in and kiss her.

Her tongue laps against mine as she moves her hips, rubbing my cock through her drenched pussy. God, I want to be inside her so bad, but when I walked down to the kitchen to get her water, I realized I couldn't. Not tonight. She needs proof that I love her. I can't take her until I know she believes what I say.

Gripping her hips, I pull her until she's on top of me, her hips gyrating against me.

"I need more, Dimitri," she whispers, her head falling forward until it's against mine.

Reaching down between us, I find her clit, circling it as she moves against me.

Fuck, I'm going to come with the feel of her heat against me. It's almost too much.

I refuse to come before her though. So I pick up my pace, encouraging her to do the same.

Her moans become louder, her breath stuttering with pleasure. I stare up at her, loving the way her face contorts with pleasure. Then she jerks slightly, her body losing the rhythm. I don't stop thrusting my hips though. I let her ride it out as I finally let myself go, my cum landing all over my legs and her ass.

Ivanna pulls away and falls onto her back, panting.

"Holy shit," she mumbles.

I laugh as I get out of bed.

"Hey," she calls, making me look over my shoulder. I see her brows furrow. "Where are you going?"

"I'm going to go grab you a wet washcloth to clean up."

Her eyes go wide and she moves to get off the bed. "That's not necessary. I can do it myself."

"Ivanna Petrova," I warn with heat in my voice. "If you move one more inch, I'm going to paddle your ass red and won't give you any relief after."

"B-but..."

"No buts." I shake my head. "It's my job to take care of you. Let me do it."

"Okay." She nods, blushing.

Turning back around, I head into the bathroom. Quickly, I turn on the sink and let the water warm. Without waiting, I clean myself before grabbing a new washcloth and running it under the hot water. Shutting off the water, I wring it out and head back to the bedroom.

Ivanna sits on the bed with her back against the headboard and her legs together. Sitting on the edge of the bed, I tap her knee.

"Open."

Ivanna takes her sweet time before parting them for me.

"Fucking perfection," I grunt as I wipe off her swollen lips.

DIMITRI

"You're crazy," she whispers as I move to clean my cum off her ass.

"Crazy about you."

I toss the rag toward the corner of the room before crawling back into bed and pulling her into my side.

"That's gross. You just tossed a wet towel onto the floor."

"It will be fine for now. Relax." I lie on my side and pull her body into mine.

Ivanna's head and hand instantly go to my chest.

With one hand, I hold on to her leg that she has thrown over me, and with the other, I play with her long gold strands.

"Thank you," she whispers.

"For what?"

"For not pushing and letting me take my time. I really did want you inside of me, but I think you were right. Going slow is smarter."

My hand squeezes her leg. "Let me make one thing clear. I will never push you. I can't promise you that I will always let you take your time. The thought of you doing exactly as I say and taking you as hard and fast as I want makes me fucking hard."

Ivanna giggles. "I can tell."

I ignore her comment and keep going. "But my body is yours to do with as you please. Just as yours is mine. You want to try something? I'll give it a go. But just know, once you open those doors, it's open season."

"You're ridiculous," she mumbles as she smiles against my chest.

"Am I though?"

My phone rings, ruining the moment.

"Don't answer it," Ivanna pleads as she holds on to me tightly.

"It might be important."

"Please?"

"Fine," I say reluctantly. "But if they call back, I have to get it."

"They won't."

The phone falls silent and I can feel Ivy holding her breath. As soon as it starts ringing, I pull out of her hold.

"I'm sorry." I get out of bed.

"I know." The dejected look on her face almost has me ignoring my phone.

I don't though.

Picking up my pants, I pull my phone out of my pocket and see Alexei's name on the screen.

"Yeah?"

"I need you to get to Nik's."

"I'm busy."

"Too busy to come over here and see what I have on what Ivanna was poisoned with? Or by who?"

I hang my head and squeeze the bridge of my nose. "I'm on my way."

I hang up as I stand. Moving, I start to get dressed.

"Dimitri, no," Ivanna begs as she crawls across the bed toward me. "Please don't go. Not tonight."

After slipping on my pants, I turn toward her and cup her cheek. "I wish I could stay, but I can't. You know that."

It kills me as I watch the devastation cross her face. Especially after what we just shared.

"Do you want to stay here, or would you like me to take you home or to your dorm?"

"Will you come back here tonight?" she asks, not meeting my eyes.

"I want to say yes, but I can't make any promises." I shake my head.

"Then take me back to campus, please."

Ivanna gets off the bed and starts to get dressed. For a moment, I watch her and hate who I am. I wish I could stay in bed with her all night and hold her. I wish I could make her promises that I can't.

Especially not when it has to do with her.

She knows the score.

Getting my ass into gear, I finish getting dressed.

"Ready?"

"Yeah."

Reaching out, I grab her arm and turn her toward me. "I'm sorry."

"So am I."

CHAPTER
FOURTEEN

Ivanna

My phone vibrates on my desk as I work on my homework.

"Are you going to keep ignoring that?" Kiera asks.

I turn and face her. "I'm not feeling very talkative right now."

"Are you going to tell me what happened? You seemed so excited before you left to go home yesterday and then when you came back last night, you were the exact opposite."

"I'm still processing."

Kiera pauses from putting stuff into her backpack and looks at me. "Just answer one thing for me, please."

I nod.

"He didn't do anything to you that you didn't want, right?" she asks reluctantly.

My eyebrows rise. "Are you asking if Dimitri raped me?"

"You said it, not me."

I shake my head. "No, he would never." I sigh. "Honestly, the date went better than I thought it would."

"But..."

"But the reality of who we are smacked us in the face. That's all I'm saying."

Kiera frowns as she puts her bag over her shoulder. "I know I don't know what happened, but maybe don't think too hard on it."

I frown. "What do you mean?"

"Look, I've only known you since the start of the school year. I don't know as much about you as I should, but that's okay." She rushes as I open my mouth. "But what I do know is that the feelings between you two are mutual. His eyes are on you when you're not paying attention. It's hard going from friends to lovers. You would think it would be easy, but it's not." She smiles awkwardly. "Honestly, I wouldn't recommend it, but with you two? I think it would be worth it."

"What are you saying, Kiera?"

"I'm saying maybe don't be so hard on yourself or him when things don't go the way you want them to." She looks down at her watch. "I got to go. Will you be okay?"

"Yeah, I'll see you later," I say absentmindedly.

As the door closes, I stare out the window and think about everything she said.

I've known Dimitri my entire life. He's the guy who kept me at arm's length for years yet made sure nothing ever happened to me. He was there waiting in the wings. Last night was better than I thought it would be. There was nothing awkward about it. Unlike my date with Boris, I was completely at ease with Dimitri.

Then he showed me his home and everything that happened after.

I sigh. It was perfect. Not exactly what I thought was going to happen, but perfect. The way he cleaned me after. I feel my cheeks flush just thinking about it. In the end though, reality hit us in the face.

I hate soft guys. They just don't do it for me. I thought I wanted someone a little rough around the edges and who understands the Bratva life, but at the same time, I don't want my man crawling out of bed in the middle of the night to do someone else's bidding.

It made me feel cheap and not important. I want to be someone's number one priority and with Dimitri, I just don't know if that's possible. As much as I hate to admit it.

My phone vibrates again and I reluctantly pick it up and read the text.

> The Devil: Stop ignoring me or I'll bust into your room.

Quickly I unlock my screen and open the chat.

> Me: I need time.

> The Devil: Don't pull away from me now, printsessa.

I hate the lead feeling in my stomach. I want him more than anything, but at the same time, I feel like my mind is so messed up. Why can't I be rational? Why am I the way I am?

Pocketing my phone, I head to the door. Oleg isn't outside, which is a reminder of how hard Dimitri has been trying.

Still, remembering the way he left brought up that familiar abandonment feeling that I've lived with my whole life.

I send a quick text to Oleg asking him to drive me to the coffee shop.

He answers back right away, telling me he will meet me downstairs.

After a quick trip to the coffee shop, I tell him I'm going to walk in the quad on campus. He of course follows me.

I've noticed that unless I specifically ask them to get lost, they do what they feel is best. It does feel nice to know that they are making their own judgment calls instead of following Dimitri's.

Maybe that's why I feel the way I do. Years of conditioning from his need to control me.

I sigh, hating the sadness that hits me. I stop, taking a seat on a bench to wallow in my thoughts.

After taking a sip of my coffee, I tip my head back and let the sunshine hit my face.

Maybe all you need today is a little vitamin *D*.

"Ivanna, is that you?"

Turning my head, I open my eyes and see Professor Lamington standing next to me with his hands in his pockets.

"Yeah, it's me." I smile awkwardly.

Without asking, he moves and sits on the bench next to me. Right fucking next to me. Instinctively, I slide over, putting some space between us.

"Oh, sorry." He chuckles.

"It's fine," I say as I look around. I find Oleg approaching with a frown on his face, ready to remove me from the situation.

"How are you today?"

"I'm good, and you?" I ask as I slightly shake my head. Letting Oleg know I'm fine.

His scowl deepens, but he listens, standing right within range.

"Can't complain. It's a beautiful day, isn't it?"

"It is."

"Are you coming to the social hour this week? We've missed you the last couple meetings."

"I plan on it."

"Good." He smiles. "I have a few discussion points already picked out that I think you guys will enjoy."

"I look forward to it."

I don't know what else to say, so an awkward silence falls over us.

"I'm sorry, is this not okay?" he asks, pointing between us.

"It's fine. Sorry, my mind is elsewhere," I lie smoothly.

He nods knowingly. "Ah, on schoolwork, I presume."

"You would be right," I lie easily again.

"Well then, I better let you go. I just wanted to stop and say hi."

"Thanks."

"I'll see you soon," he says as he stands.

"Bye."

I watch him as he walks away and feel Oleg approach from the other direction.

"Was that Professor Lamington?"

"It was," I say as I look over at him.

Oleg has a line between his brows as he watches the other man retreat. "Be careful."

I tense. "Why? What do you know?"

"Nothing." He shakes his head. "I just don't like that group after what happened."

"It had to have been the food," I say more to myself than to him.

"Are you sure about that?" He pauses, making me question everything. "Let's head back to your room. I don't like you being out in the open for so long, sitting in one place."

I sigh as I stand. "Party pooper."

We walk side by side back to my room without speaking a word. As Oleg catalogs everyone we walk by, I enjoy my coffee without having to be aware of my surroundings.

"I'll see you later," I say as I unlock my door.

"Ivanna," Oleg says right as I step inside.

"Yeah?"

"How about you put that man out of his misery and text him back?"

I roll my eyes as I shut the door. Even when Dimitri's not around, the bastard finds a way to be at the forefront of my mind.

Dimitri

I stare at the screen of my phone, fuming. I want to strangle Ivanna for ignoring me. I know she's safe, but only because her location keeps changing and Oleg's updates. I'm mad that last night was ruined. I'm pissed that after tracking down the pizza guy, it took almost all night to break him. No matter how much we tortured him. We would have searched the place listed on his driver's license to speed things along, but Alexei found out that a single mom who has no association with him lives there now.

Finally, as the sun was coming up, he gave us his address.

"Do you think he was lying when he said no one would be here?" Maxim asks quietly as he stands at my side.

"I don't believe anything men like him say." I pause as I finish picking the lock. "With how quiet this place is though, I'd say he was telling the truth." I slip the picks back into my pocket and unholster my gun.

Reaching out, I lay my hand on the doorknob and look over at Maxim. At his nod, I open the door and we quietly enter the apartment. Maxim makes a gagging noise as the smell hits us. Looking around, I shake my head at the sight. The place is covered in empty take-out containers and alcohol bottles. We keep all the lights off as we clear it room by room. Once we know it's safe, we holster our weapons.

"This place is fucking disgusting. How can people live like this?"

"I never could," I confess.

"Where do you want to start? And do you want to turn on the lights?"

I look over at the windows and shake my head. "It's a full moon and bright as fuck in here. Use your flashlight if need be. If you stumble across any papers, take them to the bathroom and look in there. I'll take the front. You take the back."

"Sounds good." Maxim moves down the hall to get to work.

I walk over to the island and start going through the shit he has piled high. It takes everything in me not to find a trash bag and clean this bastard's apartment.

I find receipts from food places on the counter along with overdue bills. After glancing at the stack, it looks like this guy is behind on everything and about to lose this place.

The owner's going to need to hire a hazmat crew before renting it back out, I think to myself.

I continue moving through the apartment, finding a cell phone that's fully charged, which is interesting considering we found one on him.

"My, my, why do you need two phones..." I murmur to myself as I power it on.

"I found a laptop," Maxim says as he comes down the hall.

"And I found a second phone."

"Only guys up to shady shit have more than one," Maxim says, reading my mind.

My phone vibrates in my pocket and I grab it, reading the text.

Alexei: he said check the ice maker.

"You've got to be kidding me." I shake my head as I move into the kitchen.

"What's wrong?"

I don't respond as I open the freezer. Grabbing the ice tray, I take it right over to the sink and dump it.

"People really hide shit in their ice machines?"

"Apparently," I mutter as I reach toward a Ziplock bag.

"I thought that was something only done in movies." He shakes his head. "What is it?"

"It looks like a piece of paper with names and shit and a flash drive. Let's get it back to Alexei and he can tell us more."

"Sounds good."

"Hey, I have something. Nik will be here any minute," Alexei says, bringing me back to the present. "Did you get any sleep?"

"I'll sleep when I'm dead," I tell him as I rub my jaw.

Alexei hums but doesn't voice his opinion.

Again I look down at my phone that's on the table. Tapping the screen, I see that she still hasn't responded. Unlocking it, I send out a quick text.

> Me: Stop ignoring me or I'll bust into your room.

I hold my breath as I see little bubbles pop up, letting me know she's going to respond.

> Printsessa: I need time.

> Me: Don't pull away from me now, printsessa.

"Tell me what you have," Nik demands as he walks into the room.

I relax slightly as I slip my phone into my pocket. I know I have to make it up to her for leaving in the middle of the night, but at least she's responded.

"Honestly, I couldn't believe it when I saw it."

"What?" I ask, the feeling of dread hitting me all at once.

"Let me start at the beginning." Alexei shakes his head. "They've been grabbing women and men from other schools around the city. Six of them, to be exact, outside of the one we already knew about. None of them have been reported as missing or anything. Most of them are people who wouldn't be missed. It seems the college is a recent development. We were so sure it was only women being taken, but after seeing men on the list, I went back and found six other male students who had gone missing."

"Then why change it up to a college student?" Nik frowns.

"I don't know." Alexei shakes his head.

"You said the ones that they took before haven't been reported, right?" Maxim says.

"Yeah."

"What if they were testing the drug on them?" Maxim says.

Nik picks up, nodding. "That way, they wouldn't damage the

actual product. Street workers and poor kids aren't missed and are prime to use for trafficking."

"Innocence sells." I cringe as the words roll off my tongue.

"Exactly." Maxim tips his chin.

"And now that they know the drug works, they are moving full speed ahead," Alexei says, shaking his head. "I thought we did fucked-up shit, but damn."

"What else did you find?"

"I'm still searching the computer and flash drive. Right now, I'm digging deeper into both phones for anything that could have been deleted. But I do have something." Alexei looks at me hesitantly before looking over at Nik. "Do you want the good news or bad news first?"

"Bad," Nik says right as I say, "Good."

Alexei looks over at Maxim. "Tiebreaker?"

Maxim rolls his eyes as he leans back in his chair. "Fuck it, good."

"Good news. Ivanna wasn't the primary target. Bad news, her roommate Kiera was."

"Motherfucker."

"Goddammit!"

"Oh shit."

Rings out through the room.

"That means," I say through gritted teeth. "That they will try again. She sure as shit isn't safe on campus."

"I would guess that they will try and take her again," Alexei confirms. "As for their safety though, you know Ivanna is good unless she loses her security detail."

"You need to up it," Nik demands. "Add more men while you're at it."

I shake my head. "If I do that, she will hate me. She's been enjoying the little bit of freedom she's gotten lately. I can't take that from her right now unless absolutely necessary."

"I would say this is pretty fucking necessary," Nik scoffs.

I ignore him and look at Alexei. "Ivanna isn't the target that we know of, right?"

He shakes his head. "No. As far as I can tell, they didn't even realize there was a mix-up."

"If they didn't know they drugged the wrong person, then maybe they aren't the ones who grab the girls," Maxim muses.

"I'll call her myself and tell her to get her ass home. She can't stay there anymore," Nik rants.

"You will do no such thing," I say, calmer than I feel. "You left her safety in my care. It's my call, not yours."

Nik stands up so fast his chair goes flying back as he points at me. "Then I hope it's not your call that gets her taken for the second time, or worse yet, killed."

I watch as Nik stalks out of the room before slamming the door closed behind him. I hear Alexei and Maxim talking quietly between themselves, but I can't hear them over the sound of my pulse in my ears.

I hope I'm not making the wrong call. Because losing Ivanna would be the end for me.

CHAPTER FIFTEEN

Ivanna

"Are you sure you don't want me to cancel?" Lia asks for the fifth time.

"No way. You and Nik deserve a date night. If I had known, I wouldn't have come over tonight. Don't feel like you need to entertain me. I was missing home, is all."

She pulls me in for a hug. "Call me if you get lonely and I'll come back."

I snort. "Lonely in a house filled with soldiers? Unlikely. Go before Nik gets mad."

She smirks. "I like when he gets mad. Usually, he tends to spank me."

"Jesus, Lia. Go already." I fake a gag.

She laughs but takes off.

I let the smile fall from my face. I came here because Kiera was going to Josh's place for the night and I didn't want to be alone. I didn't think about the fact that Nik and Lia might have plans.

Dimitri has still been blowing up my phone, but he hasn't pushed his way in. He's given me the space I wanted.

Only that space is starting to drive me a little mad.

Making my way through the house, I find my way to the one room that hasn't been touched since I was a child.

Stepping inside, I flip on the lights.

It still looks the same as the last time she was in here.

Moving to the center of the room, I slowly sit in the middle, staring at all the paintings surrounding me.

My mother loved to paint. Father didn't approve but allowed her this hobby as long as it was out of his way. So she turned this little hole-in-the-wall room into her art studio. There are no windows. I think it was meant to be a walk-in closet, but she made it work.

My eyes burn as I allow myself to think about her. I haven't done this in years. When I was young, I didn't understand, but I do now. This was her escape from the life that she was forced into. She used to tell me to find my joy where I could. As a young child, I didn't know what she meant, but as I grew older, I realized how cold the world could truly be.

"I don't know what to do," I whisper to her ghost, hoping like hell she's still here.

A shiver hits my spine as if I can feel her with me. I know it's all in my head, but I cling to it.

The tears start to flow quietly.

"You always taught me to stick up for myself. You taught me to fight back at such a young age. Then you left me. I know it wasn't your fault, but you left. I needed you. I still do."

I suck in a breath, trying to stop the sobs from taking over.

"I took each one of your lessons to heart. You said to find a man who loves me. How am I supposed to know what love looks like? You weren't here to teach me."

Looking down at my hands, I conjure up one of the few memories that stuck in my head.

"Why does the princess need the prince to save her?" my child voice asks my mother.

She rubs her hand down my head. "She doesn't. She could save herself if she wanted, but she loves the prince, so she allows him to prove it by putting his life on the line to save hers."

"How do you know she loves the prince?"

"The narrator tells us that she does. See right here." She points to the words.

I'm still learning to read, so it takes me a second to grasp what she's pointing at.

Right there, in front of me, is exactly what she said.

"Do we have people who tell us when we love someone?"

She shakes her head. "This isn't real life, baby girl. It's a story. A fairy tale. The only person who can tell us if we are in love is ourselves."

"How do we know we are in love then?"

Leaning down, she presses a kiss to the top of my head. "Love isn't exact. There's no one formula to follow. Each person feels it differently."

I frown, not understanding all the words she's saying.

She laughs, shaking her head. "You will know you are in love when no matter how many people you meet and look at, there is only one that you think of. When your heart beats faster and you feel funny in your tummy when you think of them. You hold out for that. Don't settle for anything less."

"Will he love me too?"

She tickles me, making me laugh before pulling me into her arms. "He better love you. Ivanna, you are such a special girl. There's no way any man can resist loving you. You'll know he loves you when he makes you his number one priority over everything else in this world. You will be the center of his life as he will be the center of yours. When you find him, hold on to him and never let him go."

"Printsessa." His voice brings me back to the present.

Turning, I see Dimitri standing at the door. His eyes are hesitant.

Everything my mother told me about, I feel it with Dimitri. The only box he hasn't checked is making me the center of his world.

If this is what love feels like, I don't think I want it anymore.

"I'd rather be alone," I whisper, my throat raspy from crying.

He moves into the room, closing the door behind him as he folds his frame down onto the floor next to me. It's hard with such little space, but he does it with such grace.

Does he have to be so perfect?

"You're crying." His tone is soft as he reaches out to brush the tears from my cheek.

I shake my head, moving back. "Just thinking about my mom."

He nods solemnly. "She was an amazing woman."

Looking around the room again, I murmur, "I'm surprised this room was never cleared out."

"Your father wanted to, but Nik and I stopped him. We told him we had done it and then locked it until you were older. We wanted you to have a piece of her."

My eyes shoot to his at his admission. "Really?"

Reaching out, he clasps my hand in his. "Really. I know you might not believe this, but back then, I felt so protective of you. I told myself it was because of Nik, but the truth is, I saw this girl who needed someone to be in her corner. I decided that would be me. I meant what I said before. You were always a child to me. I never had any other thoughts about you back then, but now I do. You've grown into such a beautiful woman. Your mother would be proud of you."

I sniffle at his words. I hope he's right. I feel like all I do is make a mess of my life.

"Why are you here?" I ask, remembering that I'm avoiding him.

"To see you. I've given you space, but I can't stay away for long. I've never been able to," he admits.

"I had this idea in my head," I start. "This vision of what it would be like when we finally got together. It's all I've ever wanted. You disappointed me, Dimitri."

He winces at my words. "I'd never want to disappoint you. Tell me what I did and I'll make sure it never happens again."

I laugh humorlessly. "You shouldn't make promises you can't keep."

He cups my cheek, moving in closer. "I'll keep it. Tell me what I did."

I suck in a breath before finally laying all the cards on the table.

"I'm tired of this game we are playing. I want out. I gave something to you the other night. I let you touch me and while it felt good, you left afterward. You made me feel cheap. Used. I don't ever want to feel that way again. As much as I wanted that, I don't think you can give me what I need."

He swallows hard. "It was regarding your safety, Ivanna. I would have never left for anything else."

"You say that, but if Nik calls, you have to go. I understand that. I really do, but it's not what I want. I was a fool to think this could work."

"We can work. You come first, always *printsessa*."

"I wish I could take you at your word, but I grew up in this family, Dimitri. I know what it entails, and that's not putting your wife first."

He shakes his head. "You think running off to marry some idiot in the same line of business is going to be better? They aren't going to care for you at all."

"Oh, I know. I know that what I want is a pipe dream that will never come true. There is only one man who has ever taken my breath away. Who has made my stomach feel like a million butterflies have taken root, making it their home. I had one shot at the fairy tale love my mother told me to strive for. It's you, Dimitri, but I realized too late that if I give in to you, I'll be setting myself up for a lifetime of disappointment. I now understand why my mother always looked haunted. She'd given herself to a man who would never love her the way she deserved. At least, if I pick my prison, I'll have some control over where I end up."

Pulling me into him, Dimitri rests his forehead on mine. "Don't do this, Ivanna. Please don't."

"I want to be happy, Dimitri. I don't think you can make me happy."

The look on his face is pure devastation.

My heart breaks a little more for the man in front of me.

Dimitri

"I WANT TO BE HAPPY, Dimitri. I don't think you can make me happy."

Her words are like a kick to the nuts. I feel ill.

She doesn't think I can make her happy.

All because I made the foolish mistake of leaving her the other night. I should have told her the truth right then. Maybe even have taken her with me.

Fuck, I'd give anything to go back and make a different decision.

I'm losing her. I can see it in her eyes.

I need a Hail Mary.

So I suck up my pride and I let words flow through my lips unbidden.

"You were poisoned at that group you go to. That night, Alexei had found one of the men you saw there. I left to question him about it. I needed to know why he targeted you. I don't think you realize this innate need I have to protect you at all costs. I would literally give you my last breath as long as it meant you kept breathing. You want the heart from

DIMITRI

my chest? I'll carve it out and hand it to you on a silver platter. You think these are just words, but they aren't. I have no idea how I can prove it to you. What do I need to do for you to realize that I'm so desperately in love with you that I can't even breathe without you near me?"

Her eyes are wide at my admission. I'm sure it surprises her. She's never heard me speak in such a way, but I'm desperate. I need her to understand what she means to me.

"Why are you saying this now?"

I laugh, shaking my head. "Everything I do, I do for you, *printsessa*." I pull her hand to my lips, kissing it briefly. "I know I've fucked up along the way. I held you too tightly. I made you feel suffocated. I couldn't see the error of my ways, but I see it now. I'm going against everything inside me to give you what you've told me you need. You want space? I'll fight against every molecule in my body in order to give it to you. I went against your brother in front of Alexei and Maxim yesterday to fight for you. He wants to put you back into the cage you've only just been able to get out of. I refused him. I will do it again. I never want you to feel so trapped that you would make a decision to take yourself away from me. You're mine, Ivanna. Whether you like it or not, you've been mine for a long time. I made mistakes, but you've taught me that I can learn from them. Give me a chance, damn it. You don't get to leave me. Not like this."

Her breaths even out as she takes in everything I've divulged. I've laid it all out on the table. Our game of cat and mouse truly over.

"You fought Nik?" she whispers.

I nod. "You're in danger, Ivanna. People have been coming up missing from your campus. We have no idea who is taking them or where they are going. You're protected at all times, of course. I'd never leave you without people around who can help you if you are in need, but there is a level of worry that should be there. You need to be cognizant of your surroundings. I don't want you to hesitate to call your guards or me if you feel something is off. If you can promise you will lean on me. On my men, then I'll promise that I will never lock you inside that cage again. I will fight for you until my dying breath. Can you make that promise to me?"

She sucks her lip into her mouth. "I have a stipulation as well."

I smirk at her. "Of course you do, you little spitfire. Let me have it." I pull her into me until she's sitting in my lap.

"Hey," she protests.

"Hush. I love when you fight me but now is not the time. What is it you need, *printsessa?*"

She tucks her face into my neck. "If you decide to make changes to my safety, I want to know about them. I want to be able to voice my opinion, and I want you to actually take it into consideration. I also want the right to request you review your measures at any time, especially if I feel they are unfair."

It's strangely mature for us. Sitting here discussing things so civilly. I almost miss her claws, but having her submit is even better.

"Deal."

She presses her lips to my neck, making my dick grow harder in my pants.

"Good. I also want texts when you are going places and when you are done. I don't need to know what you are doing, but if we are going to be together, then I want that peace of mind."

My smile grows wider. "I can do that. Can I ask the same of you?"

She's silent a moment. "Yes. I mean, you have guards following me though."

"I do, but it would mean more to me if I heard from you."

"I'll text you then. Dimitri, if this is going to work, you are going to have to do better at communicating with me. No more caveman bullshit. I need honesty from you. There are things about the Bratva that you won't be able to tell me and I don't want to know those things, but if it pertains to me, I need you to tell me. I need this to be an open and honest relationship. If it becomes toxic, I will leave. You understand that, right?"

I squeeze her tighter. "I will try my best to be better at communicating with you. I know it's not a promise, but it's the best I can do right now. I know I'm going to fuck up again. I'm going to have to change for you and I'm happy to do it, but I may have moments where I'm that Dimitri you hated."

She pulls back, pressing a kiss to my lips. "I never hated you. Even when I wanted to, all I could feel for you is the love that blossomed when I was six and grew into what it is today."

I nip at her bottom lip, making her giggle. "Good. I couldn't stand the thought of your hating me."

"Then why were you such a dick?"

"I figured you hating me was better than letting anything happen to you. I really don't think you understand my need to do everything within my power to keep you safe."

"Well, how about we balance keeping me safe with keeping me happy?"

I chuckle. "Deal, *printsessa*."

CHAPTER
SIXTEEN

Ivanna

Dropping my bag onto the floor, I fall face-first onto my bed. I didn't sleep well after tossing and turning all night thinking about Dimitri. When I finally gave up on sleep this morning, I ordered the biggest coffee I could before heading off to class. The first one went by fine, but by the second, it was all I could do to keep my eyes open. The teacher happens to be so monotone that half the class nods off.

I close my eyes, just for a second.

The next thing I know, a pounding on my door startles me awake. Looking over at the clock, I see that two hours have gone by. Getting up, I stretch and feel a million times better.

"Dimitri? Is everything okay?" I ask as soon as I open the door.

He reaches out and runs his thumb from my lip to my chin. "You have a little drool right here," he says, making me wince. "I would ask you why you weren't answering your phone, but I can see now that you were sleeping."

"Yeah, I was in desperate need of a nap," I say as we walk into the apartment, the door shutting behind us.

He tilts his head to the side as he studies me. "Everything okay?"

"Uh-huh. What's up?"

"Does something have to be wrong for me to stop by?"

"No..."

"Good." Dimitri looks away and licks his lips before looking back at me. "Do you have any plans tonight?"

"I was just planning on hanging out around here. Why?"

"I want to take you somewhere."

"Do you think that's a good idea?"

Dimitri frowns. "Why wouldn't it be?"

"Because the last time we went somewhere, you ended up getting called away," I point out.

Dimitri sighs. "You know I can't help that, Ivanna."

I shrug my shoulders as I cross my arms over my chest.

"I'm sorry that hurt you. I can't promise it won't ever happen again, but I would like to think that, before that, our date went well, right?"

"Yeah."

"And you enjoyed yourself." He raises a brow.

I hum as I feel my cheeks flush. Enjoyed would be an understatement.

"So come with me again. I promise it will be worth it."

I take a deep breath as I weigh my options. I can either go with him and see what he does next, or I can sit at home alone, pining after him.

"Where do you want to take me?"

"It's a surprise." He smirks as he rubs his hands together.

"That doesn't tell me what I need to wear."

Dimitri eyes me up and down, checking me out. "You can wear that or change. We'll be outside, so maybe bring a sweater of some kind."

"Okay, when do I need to be ready?"

"Now."

I raise my eyebrows. "You want to take me on a date but not give me time to get ready? Do you even know me at all?"

"It's just going to be us. There's no need to paint your face or do your hair."

"But what if—"

"Ivanna," Dimitri cuts me off. "Will you just trust me?"

Trust him. Do I?

Yes.

My feelings? Not so much. Still, I give in.

"Okay. Give me like five minutes." I turn, running out of the room.

Leaving my bedroom door open, I head right into my closet. I slip off my favorite pair of leggings and grab a pair of panties and slip them on.

"Damn." Looking over to the side, I see Dimitri leaning against the doorframe, watching me.

I raise a brow. "Do you mind?"

"Hey, you're the one who offered a show."

Rolling my eyes, I reach forward and grab a pair of jeans that make my ass look fantastic. I bite back a chuckle when I hear Dimitri groan as I lean over, putting them on nice and slow.

If he wants a show, I'll give him one.

After buttoning the jeans, I whip off my shirt and slip off the sports bra.

"Fuck me, Ivanna. If you don't cut it out, then I'm going to take you right now, right here."

I wink over my shoulder. "I mean, there is a bed. When in Rome, right?"

"Ivanna..." he warns as he adjusts himself.

As bad as I want to test his control, I really do want to know what he has planned for us. I slip on a bra that matches the panties and a band T-shirt.

"Remember when we went?" I ask, sticking out my chest so he can see the All-American Rejects T-shirt.

"I do." He nods. "You were a pain in my ass and insisted on being in the front row in the very middle of the stage."

"You caged me in and kept everyone back."

"I did and I'd do it again."

I dip my head and hide my smile as I turn back toward my closet.

"Shoes?" I ask over my shoulder.

"Something you can slip on and off."

Nodding, I grab a pair of sandals. After putting them on, I head into the bathroom. My hair is a mess after sleeping on it, so I run a brush through it before braiding it over my shoulder. I wet down a Q-Tip and clean up my eyeliner that smeared a little bit when I slept. Stepping back from the mirror, I eye myself.

Not my best work but definitely better than I was ten minutes ago.

Walking back into my room, I find Dimitri standing next to my bed with my purse in one hand and a sweatshirt in the other.

"Thank you," I say as he hands them over.

"You're welcome. I grabbed your phone off the charger and put it in there. Need anything else?"

"Not that I know of." I shake my head.

Dimitri smiles as he grabs my hand and starts pulling me toward the door. "Then let's go."

Something about that smile does something to me. It makes me feel all light and fuzzy. He doesn't smile at me often, but when he does, I fucking love it.

"Are we going to the beach?" she asks after an hour has passed with us heading in the direction of the ocean.

"I don't know, are we?"

Ivanna reaches over and smacks my chest, making me smirk.

"Such a smart-ass," she says under her breath.

"Better than being a dumbass." I shrug.

Ivanna sits up in her seat as we pull into a driveway and park.

"Whose house is this?"

"A friend's," I say as I shut the car off. "Stay there."

I get out, round the hood and open her door.

"Thank you," she says as she places her hand in mine.

"Anytime. Got everything you need?"

"I think so."

Instead of pulling her toward the door of the house, I pull her toward the back gate.

"Seriously, Dimitri, if your idea of a date is a little B&E, we need to have a serious talk," she hisses quietly the farther we go.

"Stop worrying," I say as I pull her farther. "Now close your eyes."

She does as I ask, and I walk her through the yard. Once we get to the place I want, I stop and turn toward her.

"Open your eyes," I say quietly.

Ivanna opens her eyes and her mouth falls open.

"Dimitri..." she gasps, her hand moving to her mouth. "This is gorgeous, but I don't think we are supposed to be here. See, someone has a date set up," she says, pointing to the blanket and pillow situation happening on the beach.

"That someone is us," I tell her as I pull her forward.

Ivanna squeals and runs forward, dragging me with her. As soon as she reaches the blanket, she kicks off her sandals and sits down.

"You brought me on a date to the beach?"

"A private beach," I point out.

"I-I... how did you know?" She shakes her head in wonder.

"Believe it or not, Ivanna, when you speak, I listen," I say as I sit down next to her. "This is me proving to you again that I know you and what you want."

"How old was I when I even talked about wanting a date like this?"

"Sixteen. You told me that you wanted a date on the beach. Somewhere no one would interrupt. You wanted to watch the sunset in the arms of whoever you were with."

"So you're making it happen."

"I am, and before you ask, don't worry. We have permission to be here."

"The only thing we're missing is food."

"That will be delivered down to us whenever we're ready."

"Pizza on the beach?"

Reaching behind one of the pillows, I pull out a chilled bottle of champagne. "Do champagne and pizza really go together?"

"I mean, they could." She shrugs.

"Well, I was planning on some appetizers, some of those spicy tuna rolls you like, California rolls, and some bacon-wrapped dates, which are mainly for me. Then for dinner, we're having Thai glazed salmon served with rice pilaf. Dessert is lemon meringue pie." I pause. "Unless you prefer ordering pizza of course."

"Don't you dare?" she says with a shaky voice. "We're having some of my favorite things for dinner? Really?"

"Really."

Ivanna licks her lips as she stares at me.

"What are you thinking about, *printsessa*?"

"I need you to kiss me. Right now."

I set down the bottle of champagne and pull her close, instantly covering her lips with mine. Ivanna's hands go to my neck and she lightly pulls my hair. When I pull away, Ivanna's mouth chases mine, making me laugh.

"What's so funny?" She pretends to glare, but I can see the amusement in her eyes.

"Tell me, what would you rate this date so far?"

"Hmm..." she hums as she taps her lips. "I would say a solid eight out of ten. You haven't opened that bottle of bubbly yet, the food could be bad, and the night is young." She hesitates a moment, looking down. "You could get called away."

"What if I told you that everyone knows not to call tonight unless it's life or death?"

An emotion I can't quite name crosses over her face as her nostrils flare.

"T-that would probably make it a ten. Even if you bought horrible takeout."

Reaching to the side, I grab the two glasses and hand them to her. After she takes them, I pick up the bottle and get to work opening it. When the cork shoots out, Ivanna giggles, making my heart stutter.

If I can hear her make that sound every day, I'll die a happy man.

"What are we toasting to?" she asks after I fill the glasses.

Taking mine, I hold it out between us. "Anything you want."

"To the future," she says softly.

"To the future," I say as we click our glasses together.

Ivanna turns back toward the ocean and falls silent. The sound of the ocean roars as we enjoy each other's company. It's peaceful.

Pulling out my phone, I text the caterer before slipping it back into my pocket. A few minutes later, the sound of approaching footsteps has Ivanna looking over her shoulder.

"Good evening, Mr. Lukin, Miss Petrova," the caterer says as she sets everything down in front of us.

"Thank you so much for bringing this down here," Ivanna says.

The caterer shoots her a smile. "It's my pleasure. I hope these appetizers are to your standard. If you need anything else, just send me a message," she says to me. "Dinner will be brought down ten minutes after sunset unless asked otherwise."

"That sounds wonderful. Thank you," Ivanna says.

I tip my chin. "Thank you."

As the caterer walks away, Ivanna sets down her glass. "I don't know what I want to start with first. They all look so good."

"I'm glad you think so."

Ivanna looks over at me with a soft look on her face. "Have I told you thank you for doing this yet?"

"You don't need to thank me."

"But I do."

"You never have to thank me for taking care of you. For doing everything within my power to keep you safe yet make you happy at the same time. It's all selfish, you see. Making you happy makes me happy."

Ivanna looks away with a small smile on her face as she picks up a spicy tuna roll.

"What are you smiling about?"

"I was just thinking you've given me two killer dates so far. I can't wait to see what else you have up your sleeve." She winks.

I toss my head back and laugh. "Just wait, printsessa. You haven't seen anything yet."

CHAPTER
SEVENTEEN

Ivanna

"I'm so excited to meet Kiera," Lia says as we walk arm and arm.

"You've met her before," I say with laughter in my voice.

Lia rolls her eyes. "You know what I mean. I've never hung out with her."

"Well, now's your chance."

I open the door to the coffee shop and Lia walks in ahead of me. As we wait in line, I spot Kiera toward the back of the shop and wave.

She smiles when she sees us.

"Hi, what can I get you two today?" the barista asks as we step forward.

"Can I get a medium cinnamon dolce latte, please?" Lia asks.

"Of course." She smiles at Lia before turning to me. "And for you?"

"A large hot white chocolate mocha, please."

The barista nods. "Name?"

"You can put Lia on both."

"All right, we will call you when it's ready."

"Thank you," we say in unison.

Moving, we walk toward the back of the shop.

"Hey!" Kiera says as we approach.

"Kiera, this is Lia. Lia, this is Kiera," I say, waving between them.

Lia laughs. "It's nice to actually meet you."

"Right? It's almost as if Ivanna didn't want us to meet," Kiera teases as we sit.

"Har har." I smirk as the barista calls Lia's name. "Be right back."

"Thank you," I tell the barista as I reach for the cups.

"You're welcome." She smiles kindly.

Right as I go to grab the second, a hand comes down, startling me. "Oh, sorry."

I look up and see Professor Lamington.

"It's okay." I smile awkwardly as I take the cup.

"Great minds," he says as he grabs his to-go cup.

The name on the cup catches my attention as I hum.

"Have a great day, Ivanna."

"You too," I mumble.

Why did he grab a cup with someone else's name on it?

Not my problem, I think as I shake my head and approach the table.

"How was class?" I ask as I sit down and slide Lia her coffee.

"Thanks," she says quietly.

"It was fine." Kiera shrugs before looking at Lia. "So, tell me all the things."

"What do you want to know?" Lia asks as she brings her cup to her mouth, taking a sip.

"How did you two meet? I want to hear about all the trouble you've gotten into together. You're married to her brother, right?"

"Okay, so I met Ivy in high school..." Lia starts.

I listen to her tell our story from the beginning. The more she talks, the harder it is to keep myself from laughing out loud about how she glosses over some things, like the fact we were kidnapped or that when she and my brother met, it was because she crawled through his bedroom window where he held her at gunpoint.

Kiera leans forward, completely absorbed in everything Lia is saying. "And her and Dimitri?"

"Dimitri was, or I guess still is, her bodyguard and works for her brother. Nik and he are best friends and grew up together."

"Oh..." Kiera's eyes widen. "So it's a best friend's little sister situation."

Lia snaps her fingers and points at Kiera. "Exactly. Only they denied it until about five minutes ago."

"I love it," Kiera says wistfully as she rests her chin on her palm.

"I'm glad someone does."

"Please," Lia scoffs. "You wouldn't know what to do if he took his attention off you."

"The way he looks at you could set off a fire alarm," Kiera adds.

"Just because there's chemistry doesn't mean it's right." I shake my head, but I can't resist the smile on my lips.

Lia turns in her chair and crosses her arms, facing me. "How did the date go?"

"It was fine." I shrug. Lia raises a brow and waits, making me fidget.

"Okay, it was more than fine. I was worried about him being called away again. I wouldn't have been able to take it again. He didn't though. He told me he told everyone he was unavailable unless it was true life or death."

Understanding fills Lia's eyes. "Ivanna, you can't hold that against him."

"Why not? I want to be his priority. I'm still not sure that's even possible." I pick at my fingers, not meeting her gaze.

She understands the struggle more than anyone. She's basically married to the head of it all.

Lia closes her eyes and shakes her head. "You know that's not his fault. It's work."

"I mean, Lia's right," Kiera says. "Imagine if the roles were reversed. Would he hold it against you if you got called away because of your job? Hell, would you want to be with a man that tries to stand between you and your career? Maybe cut him some slack."

Looking down at my coffee, I think about it. I know logically they are right, but I can't help that little bit of anxiety still lingering.

"I need a napkin. I'll be right back." Lia jumps up to go grab one.

Kiera reaches out, gripping my hand. "He's a great guy. You can tell from the way he looks at you that he would move mountains for you. Don't run away because you're scared. Life will happen from time to time, but if you truly care for him, you'll stick it out and make it through it."

I nod, feeling a little better at her words. She's right, of course. We can work through this. He's making changes to accommodate me, so can't I do the same for him?

Lia comes back, napkins in hand.

Sensing the change in vibe, she smiles at Kiera. "So where are you from? You don't really strike me as a Cali native."

"Chicago, actually." Kiera smiles.

"You didn't want to stay in the Midwest?"

Kiera shivers. "God no. I hate the snow. Besides, my parents actually got relocated out here for work."

"What do they do?" Lia asks.

As they fall into an easy conversation, my mind drifts back to our previous conversation.

Is it fair of me to judge Dimitri so harshly? We really did have a great time last night.

After we finished dinner, we lay on the beach and watched the stars. It was romantic. I thought we would fool around some more, but after kissing me a few times, he took me home.

I feel like I'm the reason for that. I feel like he won't make that move again until I do.

Am I ready for that?

"Hey." Lia nudges me. "Are you with us?"

"Yeah." I shake my head. "Sorry, I was thinking about an assignment I have due tomorrow."

"Ugh," Kiera groans. "I have to go to the library later. I was an idiot when I was younger and went easy my freshman and sophomore years instead of buckling down then so I would be free now."

"Too busy partying," I tease, making us laugh.

"I can't deny I was a frequent flier at the frat houses." She winks.

"Frat houses, hmm..." Lia hums with a smile on her face. "I remember when Ivy snuck out and went to a frat party our freshman year."

I cringe just thinking about it.

"What happened?" Kiera asks, looking between us.

"Well, from what I heard," Lia says lightly. "Dimitri showed up, and they got into a fight. She tried to push him into a pool, but he grabbed her and tossed her over his shoulder and carried her out."

"Wait!" Kiera cries out. "That was you? He slapped you on the ass as he walked out and told you to be a good girl and stop wiggling."

"You were there?"

"Uh, yeah," Kiera says with wide eyes. "None of us could look away from you two. It was seriously hot."

"We're never going to live that down." I groan as I shake my head.

Lia hits her shoulder against mine. "Could be worse."

"That is true." I nod.

Kiera's phone beeps and she looks down at the screen. "Shoot, I got to go." She looks at Lia. "It was nice finally getting to hang out with you. We should do it again sometime."

"Definitely." Lia smiles.

Keira looks at me. "I'll see you at home?"

"I'll be there."

"Bye," she says before dashing out of the coffee shop.

"I like her. We can keep her. Now which man are we gonna pair her with?" Lia asks.

I shake my head. "She's in love with another, I'm afraid, but we can still keep her. She's a good friend."

Lia bumps me with her shoulder. "Good. You deserve more of those."

I smile back, happy I finally made it here.

Dimitri

NIK IS GRUMBLING as I pull up to the warehouse.

The entire drive over, he's been pestering me on why I wanted to come here, but it's really not any of his business.

Getting out of the car, I ignore his thousandth complaint about it being the middle of the day and how I usually do this shit at night.

He's not wrong, but I have plans tonight. I want to go see my girl.

"Why are we here, D?" Nik asks as we stroll around the open warehouse.

"I didn't ask you to come, so I have no idea why you are here," I retort, going back to looking at the women's section.

"You said you were going to visit Hansel. Of course I came. I want to know what you can possibly think we are missing from our armory."

"I'm not here for us, asshole."

He comes over to my side, looking down at the hairpins I've been staring at.

"Wait, are you buying that for my sister?"

"Fuck yeah, I am. She doesn't have enough switchblades and she can't always carry them. Sometimes she wears shit where she can't hide them."

"You are such a fucking goner," he says as he thumbs a blue one.

"Whatever. I'm sorry if I know what my girl likes. She's going to love it."

He pats me on the shoulder. "Oh, for sure. She's always been an odd duck. If you bought her a diamond, she'd probably tell you to shove it up your ass, but give her a weapon? Yeah, she's going to fall in love with you."

I glare at him. "She already loves me."

"Oh? She's not still questioning shit? Lia said she still wasn't sure about you."

My heart clenches at his words. "She did?"

"That was two weeks ago, but yeah. She had coffee with her and that friend of Ivanna's. Said that she liked you but was still acting like it wasn't a permanent thing."

"You're just now telling me this?" I spit at him, angry at myself more than him.

"Hey, that's your deal. Don't you always tell me to mind my business?"

He has a point. I have said those words to him more times than I can count over the years.

"Well, it is none of your business. Ivanna and I are getting along fine. We've come to an agreement of sorts. She understands she's mine and that I'm going to do everything I can to make her happy and keep her safe at the same time."

"How's that going?"

I sigh. "Not as great as I'd like. It kills me to leave her so vulnerable, but I'm managing. She seems happier. Not miserable anymore."

"She hasn't asked me to find her a husband, so that's positive." He chuckles.

I punch his arm, making him chuckle harder.

"If you ever insinuate that you will find her another man ever again, I will kill you."

He snorts, "I should be mad at you for saying that, but it's how I'd feel if anyone tried to take Lia from me. I'm glad you finally came to your senses. I was worried I'd lose my sister for a minute there."

I nod. "Speaking of, I know you want us to live at the compound, but I think Ivanna and I want to live at my place."

He freezes before looking over at me. I continue to go through the hairpin knives, finally finding one I like. It's beautiful but simple. Something easily looked over.

"Why would you want her to be out in the world like that? You don't have the protection I do."

"I have my team, and we've kept her safe in the dorms. My place will be even easier to protect. Besides, I think she likes the freedom. Not to mention, that house holds a lot of unpleasant memories for her. I want to give her a fresh start. Somewhere we can build a life without being overshadowed by shit that brings us down."

He's quiet as I make my way toward the switchblade knives. They are Ivanna's favorite. I pick up a couple to keep on hand just in case I fuck up. Some women want flowers, but my girl would melt over a knife.

"It makes sense. I'll keep her room at the compound though. She's always welcome back and you are as well. If we go into lockdown, you will stay with us."

"Of course. I would never put her safety at risk."

"So this is serious. You've talked to her about it?"

"Not necessarily. I mentioned that my home is hers. She seemed receptive. I don't want to rush things with her. She's still skittish. I get it. I've fucked up before. Made her doubt my feelings for her. I have some work ahead, but by the time she finishes her last semester, she will be ready to move in with me. If I have anything to say about it, she'll be ready to marry me too."

Nik shakes his head. "The best of luck to you. She's a spitfire, that one."

I laugh. "She's a Petrov. I'd expect nothing less."

That's the damn truth too.

DIMITRI

I knew the moment I decided she was mine that I would have a fight on my hands and I wouldn't have it any other way.

Seeing the fire in her eyes when she's angry brings out the fire inside me. To some, it may seem toxic, but to us, it's passion.

It's proof that we care so much about one another that we literally combust.

It's the tangible evidence that we wouldn't be able to live without one another, for who would challenge us the way we do one another?

No one.

That's why she's mine.

My woman.

My *printsessa*.

My forever.

CHAPTER
EIGHTEEN

Ivanna

Chilled and soaked to the bone, I walk into my bedroom and drop my things. Instantly I turn around and head into the bathroom, turning on the shower. My wet clothes plop onto the floor, making me cringe. Picking them up, I set them into the sink.

I'll deal with them later.

Moving the curtain back, I get into the shower. The hot water stings my skin, making me hiss.

Laying my head against the wall, I let the water rush over me as I replay the day. First, I woke up late because my alarm never went off, making me almost late for one of my classes. Then during the next lecture, my computer started doing the circle of death.

When I walked out of class, Oleg demanded to know what was

wrong and who hurt me. As soon as I was done unloading on him on my way to my final class, he looked like he regretted asking. During that one, I had to take notes by hand and it was a shit show. Thankfully one of the girls next to me offered to send me hers.

On the way home, it started to downpour, leading me to now. Pushing off the wall, I hurry through my shower routine and get out. After wrapping my towel around me, I head into my room to get dressed. Once in a pair of sweats and a hoodie, I walk toward my desk but stop when I see something sitting on top of it.

"What the hell," I mumble under my breath.

Stepping forward, I run my hand over the fruit logo before picking up the note.

Printsessa,
You're welcome.
Call me.
-Dimitri

My breath catches.

"How..." I shake my head. "Oleg, of course."

Bending down, I grab my phone out of my bag and then crawl onto my bed.

Me: The laptop is too much.

As I wait for his reply, I grab the computer and take it out of the box.

My phone vibrates and I pick it up once the laptop starts updating.

The Devil: It's nothing and you know it.

Me: Thank you.

The Devil: I wanted to be there, but your brother needs me. You're welcome, printsessa.

Dropping my phone, I lean back against my pillows and start thinking about how I could pay him back. For years Dimitri has been behind the scenes, making my life easier.

What can I do for him?

Suddenly an idea comes to mind and I jump out of bed. Grabbing my wallet and my phone, I leave the dorm as I call Oleg.

"Is everything okay?" he asks as soon as he picks up.

"Yeah, I have a favor though."

"What's up?"

"Can you take me to Dimitri's place?"

He agrees quickly, even stopping at the grocery store for me. It doesn't take us long to make it to his place, my biometrics opening the door as he told me it would.

I won't lie, I got a little thrill from it.

"I'll wait out here," Oleg informs me.

I nod, making my way into the house.

Heading into the kitchen, I set the bags down and get to work. Digging through his cabinets, I find a pot and pan. Setting the pan on the stove, I take the pot and fill it full of water before placing it on the burner.

"Hey Google, can you play nineties gangster rap?"

Everything falls away as I start to cook and dance around the kitchen. Before I know it, the spaghetti is done. I push it off the hot burner and let it cool. Moving around the kitchen, I start to clean up my mess.

Taking a step back, I preheat the oven and prep the bread to make garlic bread. Once the oven is hot, I put it in and set a timer. With the kitchen clean and fifteen minutes to spare, I let myself wander through Dimitri's place.

The home is clean and looks hardly lived in. Skipping his bedroom, I head right into his master bathroom. It looks the same as the last time I was here. There are a few things on the bathroom counter and a towel over the rack. The only thing in the drawers is a tube of toothpaste and an unopened pack of razor blades. Under the sink is a four-pack of toilet paper.

Heading into his bedroom, I come to a stop as I stare at his bed. I can feel myself flush as I think about what he did to me on that bed.

"You saved this for me? All for me?" he asks before focusing back on my center with his mouth.

I gasp at the sensation. "Yes. Only you."

The way he looked at me, eyes nearly black, consumed with desire.

He raises a brow. "You squirted. There's a difference. It was glorious. God, I can't wait to make you squirt on my cock."

I look up at him, shocked.

"Seriously?"

"Baby, the fact that I could make you squirt means I did my fucking job. I'm going to make you do it every single time we fuck. So get used to it."

Looking away from the bed, something on his nightstand catches my attention. Walking over, I pick up the book. My breath catches when I see the title. *And Then There Were None* by Agatha Christie. It's one of my all-time favorites. Opening it, I flip through the pages and see they are well worn with notes in the margins. My heart beats so fast that it feels like it could beat out of my chest.

He's read it, and more than once, if the creased pages are anything to go by.

Setting it down, I walk around the room, opening his drawers and looking under the bed. The room is spotless. His clothes are folded and put away. His nightstand holds a tube of ChapStick, a knife, and an extra charger. Not even a box of condoms.

"Well, that was anticlimactic," I murmur as I walk back toward the kitchen.

After pulling the garlic bread out of the oven, I set it on a hot pad. After placing a serving in a bowl, I put it in the microwave and put the rest in a Tupperware container before putting it in the fridge. Opening one of the drawers, I find a piece of paper and a pen and write a quick note. Setting it on the island, I look around the kitchen one more time.

Everything looks the way it should.

I know it's not much, but I hope my small gesture surprises him the way he did me today.

Dimitri

Stepping into the house, I come to a stop. Closing my eyes, I groan. The smell of garlic and tomato sauce fills the air.

Oleg told me she stopped by here, so instead of going to her like I normally would, I came here to investigate. I expected the walls to be painted pink or some other girly shit to attempt to annoy me.

Instead, it smells like she cooked.

Heading into the kitchen, my eyes instantly go to the dishes drying in the sink. Placing my keys on the counter, I pick up the handwritten note.

> D,
> We need to stock your kitchen.
> There's food for you in the microwave and leftovers in the fridge.
> Don't get used to me cooking for you.
> -Ivy

I chuckle as I set the paper down and shake my head. That fucking girl. As my food heats, I lean against the counter. When Oleg called earlier, I thought something was wrong. That something had happened to Ivy.

"Yeah? Is everything okay?" I ask as soon as I answer.

"Depends on who you're asking," Oleg grumbles.

"Oleg," I snap. "I'm a little busy here, so if you could get to it, that would be great. Is Ivanna okay?"

"She's in class, but she's upset."

"About what?"

"I'll save you the twenty-minute rant I got, but to sum it up, during her last class, her computer decided to take a shit and doesn't work anymore."

"And you're calling me why?"

I move to pinch the bridge of my nose but stop when I see the blood on my fingers.

"I figured you might want to surprise your girl, is all..." he trails off.

I grunt as I kick the guy who thought he could skip out on paying us our cut of protection money. "That's not a bad idea. As soon as I'm done here, I'll stop by the store and get her one."

"Make sure it's top of the line. My sister would say go big or go home."

"Yeah, yeah..." I say as the man cries out.

"Hey, do you think we could switch places? I'll do collections. You watch your girl."

"Nice try," I say as I hang up.

The microwave beeps, bringing me back into the moment. Grabbing my plate and a fork, I start to eat.

I knew when I walked into the house that she would be gone, but I can't help but wish she was still here.

If she were, I could be eating with her. We could cuddle on the couch and I'd let her watch one of those silly romance movies she adores so much. I wouldn't even make fun of them too much.

This house could be a home.

Our space.

Somewhere we build a life.

Moving to the sink, I wash my plate and put the leftover garlic bread in a Ziplock bag. I shut off the lights as I move through the house toward my bedroom. Stripping my clothes, I put them in the hamper and brush my teeth. Once ready for bed, I crawl under the covers. I itch to head over and watch her, but I don't.

Instead, I pick up my phone and call her.

I won't lie. There's a small part of me that is feeling nervous about calling her.

We have never talked on the phone much.

I want to give her this experience. I stole the dating experience from her by not allowing her to see anyone else.

I want to give her back as much of it as I can, but only if it's with me.

"Hello?" she answers groggily.

"I'm sorry, *printsessa*. I didn't mean to wake you," I tell her, keeping my tone low.

I know how she is when she just wakes up. Any little noise is like grating on her skin.

"No, I'm glad you called. Where are you?"

"Home. Oleg said you had been by, so I wanted to see what you did. Thank you for dinner. It was delicious."

"Mmm. Good. You are always doing things for me, I wanted to do something for you."

My heart warms at her words. "You existing does everything I need, Ivanna."

"Stop being sweet. It weirds me out."

I chuckle, making her laugh too.

"Do you want me to let you go back to sleep?" I keep my voice soft.

"No. Talk to me. I miss you."

"I miss you too. Are we keeping Kiera up?"

"She's with Josh. I think it's love. She spends more time there than here anymore."

I smirk. "Good. What are you wearing?"

She laughs. "Really? Is that what we are doing?"

"One of the things you were always upset with me for was taking away experiences for you. Tell me, *printsessa,* have you ever wanted to have phone sex with your boyfriend?"

I hear her quick intake of breath. "Is that what you are? My boyfriend?"

"I'm your forever, baby, but yes, for now, I'm your boyfriend. That is until I can make you my wife."

"D, you can't say things like that. It makes me feel funny."

"Funny how?" I ask.

"It makes me think I can actually be happy."

"We are happy, Ivanna. We will fight and shit will get tough, but we will always be happy. I promise."

I hear her sigh before she speaks. "I'm wearing your T-shirt. One I stole from your dresser and sprayed your cologne on. Nothing else."

My dick is harder than a fucking flagpole at her admission. My woman is lying in bed in my clothing.

Fuck, I wish I was there.

"I need a photo. Not of your naked body. Anyone could hack that. Send me a picture of you in my shirt."

"Okay."

I hear movement on her end of the phone until a message comes through.

God, I love to torture myself.

She looks like a fucking vision in my black non-descript T-shirt. I can see the swell of her breasts as she lies on her back, her hair ruffled around her head, those fuck-me lips puffy as if she's been sucking on them.

"You are a goddess, Ivanna. I wish I was there with you."

"Really?" She's acting coy. "Whatever would you do?"

"Oh honey, I would do so much to you. I'd start by sucking those pretty little nipples through my shirt. Biting and sucking until you grind that sexy little body against mine. I'd make you beg for my cock before I'd relent, only I wouldn't give you my cock. I'd slide down your body, bury my head beneath your shirt, suck your clit into my mouth as I licked you dry, only that would never happen because with each lick, you'd give my greedy mouth more, wouldn't you?"

Her breathing is increasing as I talk so I'm not surprised when I hear a moan. "Yes. I'd be so wet for you. I'm wet for you now."

"Reach under my shirt and tweak those nipples for me, baby. Only the nipples. Don't you dare touch that cunt. It's mine."

She groans, but I hear the change in the sounds when she puts me on speakerphone to do as I ask.

"Good girl. I'd keep sucking on you until you were so turned on you weren't speaking any known language anymore. Only then would I slide my fingers inside your wet heat."

"God, Dimitri. I need you. I feel so empty. Please."

"Not yet, *printsessa*. Be patient. Keeping you on edge will only make the reward that much better."

I hear her let out a frustrated huff, but she relents.

"Okay. Tell me more."

"That's my *printsessa*. Behave and I'll make you feel good. I promise. Slowly drag your fingers down your body and drag them through your wet pussy. Don't play though. I only want you to gather enough to paint your lips. Then I want you to suck them into your mouth and tell me what you taste like."

As she does what I ask, I pull the blanket back, stroking my dick as I spread out the precum beading at the end of me.

"I taste like I need to be fucked," she moans out.

"Yeah? You need my cock, baby?"

"So bad."

"I want you to circle your clit three times before pressing two fingers inside of you."

"D, I've never." She sounds nervous suddenly.

"I know. Only go until you feel like you can't anymore. You're going to stretch yourself out for me. So one day I can fuck you."

I smile at the noise she makes. She likes the idea of me taking her.

"Okay," she hiccups on a breath. "I'm doing it."

"Good. Now set a pace with me. Circle your clit while fingering that little pussy. I'm stroking my cock, imagining I'm burying myself deep inside you. I can just imagine how warm and wet you'd be. Can you feel that?"

"Yes. It's so tight. Every time I clench, I can feel myself tighten even more. It's, god, it's hot as fuck."

"Good girl. Pick up the pace. I want you writhing as you moan out my name."

I pick up my own pace as I hear her making several keening noises as she pleasures herself. My own breathing is labored as I try to keep from coming too soon. My woman needs to come first.

"That's it. Imagine me fucking you with my cock. How I would fill you, making you feel as if we are one. We are one, Ivanna. Taking you will only be the final step to making it permanent. Once I fuck that cunt, you'll never leave me. You'll be mine. Forever. You'll let me spill my cum into you and grow my babies. You'll take everything I give you."

"Fuck, Dimitri," she screams out, her breathing hitching as I hear her blankets rustling on the other side of the phone.

"Such a good girl, coming for me. Ride out that high, baby," I tell her, stroking faster. "Ivanna," I call out, finally letting myself chase that same high.

I spill my cum all over my stomach, but I don't care. All I can focus on is the euphoria that fills my veins, along with the sound of her own pleasure through the phone.

"That was," she starts, groaning. "My pussy keeps clenching."

"Aftershocks, *printsessa*."

"Is that how it always feels?"

"It will for you. I'll make sure of it."

She giggles. "That was unexpected."

I smile, looking down at my cum-covered stomach. "That it was. Was it okay?"

"Better than okay. Thank you."

"Anything for you, *printsessa*."

I hear her yawn, making me look at the time. It's two sixteen in the morning.

"Go to sleep. I'll come see you tomorrow."

"Promise?" she whispers.

"Promise."

"Good night, Dimitri."

"Night, Ivanna. Sweet dreams."

The last thing I hear before she hangs up the phone is that angel voice whispering, "Only of you."

CHAPTER
NINETEEN

Ivanna

> Kiera: Are you coming to the social club tonight?

> Me: Nah, I'm going to sit this week out. You?

> Kiera: I'm going to go for a bit. Want to hang out in our room after? Watch a movie or something?

> Me: I would love that.

> Kiera: Cool. Get the snacks ready! I'll be back around eight.

I've read our text thread for the fourth time as worry eats at me. My eyes drift to the clock and I see that it's almost eleven. Kiera has never been late. One of the things I like about her is she's punctual and always shows up when she says she will.

I should have gone to club with her tonight. After talking with Dimitri the other night and knowing that he's worried, I decided to take it upon myself to limit my activities. I've even been inviting the guards along with me more. I wanted to show him that if he left my safety up to me, I would take it seriously.

Now I'm regretting that decision. What if something happened to her when she was walking home?

Swiping across the screen, I pull up the number and press call without thinking twice. As it rings, I chew on the side of my finger.

"Hey, *printsessa*. Is everything okay?" Dimitri's drawl gives me some level of comfort.

"I think something happened to Kiera," I blurt out.

His tone is stone in an instant. "Are you in your room?"

"Yeah."

"I'll be up in a minute," he says before hanging up.

I don't even let my mind wonder why he's downstairs right now. He texted me earlier letting me know he was on an errand for Nik and then again when he was done, but I didn't think to ask him what he was doing after that.

As I wait for Dimitri to knock, I pace the room back and forth. Am I overreacting? Maybe she decided to hang out with Josh.

Dimitri's heavy knock makes me jump.

"For fuck's sake, Ivanna," I scold myself quietly as I walk to the door.

"Thanks for coming up," I say as I open it.

"Always," Dimitri says as he steps inside.

After I shut the door and lock it, he grabs my hand and pulls me to the bed. He sits down and pulls me into his lap.

"Dimitri..."

DIMITRI

"Just let me hold you for a minute," he says as he squeezes my thigh. "Now tell me what's going on."

I sigh as I relax into his body. "It could be nothing."

"Or it could be something. Now tell me."

"Long story short, this afternoon we decided to hang out tonight. She was going to go to the social club." I feel Dimitri tense beneath me but keep going. "Then come home right after. We made plans to watch a movie. Eat snacks. She said she would be back around eight."

"And she's late."

"She's never late." I shake my head. "I thought maybe she got held up but I don't think so."

"Do you think she went to her boyfriend's?" he asks as he rubs my leg.

"I thought about that, but Kiera is one of the most considerate women I've ever met. She would have texted me, even if it wasn't right away."

"Have you called her?"

"I've called and texted," I confirm. "I'm just really fucking worried."

Dimitri reaches into his jacket pocket and pulls out his phone. "Do you know where her boyfriend lives?"

"Brighton Hall. I think she said room one sixteen."

He texts for a minute before setting his phone down on the couch next to us. "I asked Oleg to go check the building the social club is held in and he's sending Linc over to Josh's just to make sure she's not there."

"Thank you."

"Of course."

Closing my eyes, I bury my face into his neck, taking the comfort he's offering.

"What if they don't find her?" I ask quietly, saying my worst fear out loud.

"Then we will call Alexei and he will search the cameras. Don't worry, we will find something."

"I hope you're right."

"I am. Now how about you find something to watch while I go make you a snack?"

"I'm not hungry."

"In case you change your mind then."

I nod as I crawl off his lap. Dimitri stands and walks away. I watch him as he moves around the little area we have set up as a makeshift kitchen. He looks as at home here as I do. He knows where everything is without having to ask. Something about it screams this isn't right and I can't stand it.

Sighing, I tear my eyes away from him and grab the remote. I start flipping through the channels. After a few minutes, Dimitri comes back with a bowl of popcorn in one hand and an unopened bag of peanut M&M's in the other.

"Thank you," I say as tears fill my eyes.

He made my favorite snack.

Dimitri leans down and brushes a kiss against my forehead. "I'm going to step out and talk to Ilya."

"Please don't leave me," I beg, reaching out to hold on to him.

"Hey, I'm not going anywhere. I promise. Just give me a minute, okay?"

I nod and smile weakly. "Yeah, okay. Sorry, I'm being ridiculous."

"Nothing about you is ridiculous," he says as he presses a kiss to my forehead before leaving.

I watch him walk out the door before turning back to the TV. I find a romantic comedy movie. Before I know it, I fall into the story about a guy who's always had feelings for the girl. Meanwhile, she's always thought he was an ass. Her sister is marrying his best friend and on the joint bachelor and bachelorette trip, they room together and, I'm sure, fall in love. The things that happen to them make me laugh out loud.

I mean, who accidentally sprays glitter body spray between their legs?

At some point, Dimitri comes back in and sits down next to me and starts watching with me.

A knock at the door makes me gasp and move to get up.

DIMITRI

"Stop," he says as he puts his hand on my chest, holding me in place.

"But…"

"It's not her. It's just Maxim."

"Oh," I say as I lean back into the couch.

Dimitri gets up and lets the other man in.

"Hey, Ivanna."

"Hi, Maxim. How have you been?"

"Better than you." He turns toward Dimitri and hands him a bag I didn't realize he was holding. "Everything you need is in there. I'll be out in the hall. Let me know if you need any help."

"Thanks."

Maxim leaves as Dimitri walks toward me.

"What's going on?"

Dimitri sits down on the coffee table and sets the bag next to him before reaching out and grabbing my hands.

"D, you're scaring me."

"I don't mean to."

"They didn't find her. Did they?" I ask, even though I know the answer already.

"I'm sorry, *printsessa*."

"So what happens now?"

"Alexei has already started going through the footage. Maxim and I are going to go check some places ourselves."

"Let me help," I say as I start to slide off the bed.

"Ivanna," Dimitri says, holding me in place. "I'm not saying you can't help at all, but not tonight. It's late and you have class in the morning."

"I don't give a fuck about class. My roommate is missing, D!"

He continues on like I didn't cut him off. "If you go out there right now and start looking, all we're going to be paying attention to is your safety. We might miss something because of you."

"So you want me to sit around here while you go play with things that go bump in the night?" I scoff.

"Yes."

My jaw clenches. "I hate this."

"I know," he says as he stops me from digging my nails into my palms.

"What's in the bag?"

Dimitri looks at me hesitantly.

"Just tell me."

"It's a tracker."

"I thought you tracked my phone."

He nods. "I do, but this is different."

"Is it like a necklace?" By the look on his face, I know it's something else. "What is it?"

"It's a tracker that goes in you."

I lean back, eyes wide. "You want to put a tracker in me? Like. I'm. An. Animal?"

"Just until this is over. After that, we can take it out. I promise."

"Ab-so-fucking-lute-ly not," I say as I slide out of his reach and start pacing the room.

"I'm not asking."

"You can't do it. I'll tell Nik." I shake my head, grasping at straws.

"Nik is for it. The only people who will have access to the information are me and Alexei as backup. You know he won't betray your trust by looking for shits and giggles."

"I don't understand. Why this? Why now?"

"Let me paint the picture for you, *printsessa*," Dimitri says harshly. "You were taken from me once before and I won't let it happen again. It fucking killed me thinking I wouldn't make it to you in time, but I did. Now, years fucking later, you eat some pizza and end up drugged. I didn't tell you this before, but we believe that's how they've been getting people off campus. They drug them and make them sick so they can snatch them," he says, making me flinch, but he keeps going. "When you got sick that night, you have to know they were watching. The only thing that kept you safe was me being there. Had I not been, they would have taken you. They may have taken your friend too," he says, pointing right at me. "I would like to think that no one will grab you, but it's happened before. This time I'm not taking chances. You mean too much to me. So you'll let me cut you and place the tracker under your skin, so if god forbid something happens, you don't have to wait as long for me to get there this time."

I feel the tears track down my face as everything he said hits me all at once.

She was taken by sex traffickers. I could be taken again.

My body shivers at the memory of all those years ago. Being stuck in a room with Lia. Stripped down naked and repackaged to be sold to the highest bidder. Revulsion fills me with memory.

"Okay." The word is a whisper on my lips.

Dimitri jerks back like he wasn't expecting me to give in so easily. "Okay."

"Where do you want to put it?" I ask as I rub my arms.

Dimitri runs a hand over his jaw, thinking. "What about in your upper thigh? I can make a small cut inside one of your stretch marks."

"Then, if they find it, they won't think anything of it," I say, making him flinch.

"Nothing's going to happen to you. This is just a precaution."

"Right."

I don't know who he's trying to convince more, himself or me.

"Javier Medina called asking for a meeting," Nik says as soon as I walk into his office.

I curse under my breath.

The Medina Cartel are heavy hitters from Mexico. Nikolai made a deal with them when he took over, allowing them to traffic their drugs through our territory to ensure a safe route. Of course, it costs them, but it's a win-win. Nikolai isn't against the drug trade. If some junkie wants to get high and overdose, it's not our problem. It's easy money allowing them to run through here, especially since it's basically a licensing agreement. We don't have to do anything except let their people go through our territory. Sometimes it's their own people, while other times, it's the motorcycle club they are working with out in Nevada. The Lotus MC doesn't cause trouble for us, so we leave them be.

So if he's asking for a meeting with us, something went down. Something bad.

"When?" I ask, thinking about my plans for this afternoon.

Ivanna doesn't like the idea of the tracker, but it'll give me peace of mind. I'm surprised she agreed to it. I expected more of a fight. Maybe losing her roommate has scared her more than she's letting on.

"This evening."

"Fuck. That club Ivanna's roommate goes to is tonight. Ivanna is going to go and play decoy. She's going to see if anything happens."

Nik frowns. "You're using my sister as bait?"

I hold up my hands. "Not my idea. It's hers. She's not going to sit idle while her friend is missing."

"I don't like this. I need the tyrant back. You're conceding too much to her. She's going to get hurt."

I rub my hand over my face. "If I let her think she's helping, she stays out of trouble. Do you think I will actually let her get snatched? Of course not. I've got ten guys on her at all times. Besides that, Alexei checks the cameras on every route she takes hourly to ensure they are still working. I'm going insane with this intense need to lock her in a room and never let her out, but I made her a promise."

"Break it," Nik demands.

"You want me to push her away even further? Aren't you the reason she was going on those dates? Isn't it because you said you couldn't stand seeing her miserable?"

"That was before all of this. Someone is taking girls from our streets. I won't let her get kidnapped again. I don't know how Jan is doing it, but he's targeting her college. When I find the proof, I'm going to war and we are calling in all of our favors. I'm going to wipe the Polish from this fucking country."

"Mass genocide? That's your plan?"

"I don't care what you call it. None of those flesh-selling Polish bastards will be breathing when we are done with them."

I shake my head. "I need you to trust me. I love Ivanna. I will not let harm come to her."

He grimaces. "You better not. I'll put a bullet in your head myself."

I nod. "I'd stand still for you. Now if we are done here, I need to take Ivanna to see the doctor."

He frowns. "What for?"

"She agreed to put a tracker inside her. I was going to take her this evening, but with Medina calling a meeting, I want to get it done now."

His eyes widen. "She agreed to this?"

"She wants to help. It's a condition of her involvement. I refuse to lose her again, Nik."

"That's smart. I'll talk to Lia. She should get one too. Matter of fact, I think I'll make it a requirement. All men, women, and children will be required to have one implanted. We will never lose one of our own again."

I bow my head slightly. "I'll let Alexei know to order in bulk then."

Standing, I turn to head toward the door.

"D?" Nik calls out.

Turning back to him, he smiles. "I'm glad you fixed whatever it was you broke. I couldn't pick a better man for her."

"I was never going to let you. Fate chose her for me. It was always going to lead us here."

I nod once. "I don't know what we did to get fate to treat us so kindly. Don't fuck it up."

I leave him behind as I pull out my phone to text my woman.

> Me: Printsessa. Be ready in twenty.

"Is he really the only person who can do this? Why can't you do it?" Ivanna asks, turning to me from the passenger seat.

"He's a doctor. I'm medically trained, but only for combat. I don't want to fuck anything up. You mean too much," I tell her, taking her hand into mine.

She looks back at the clinic, her nose scrunched. "Dr. Daniil creeps me out."

I stiffen. "What do you mean?"

She shrugs, looking back at me. "I just don't like him. Let's get this over with."

She goes to get out, but I pull her back. "I'll find a new doctor. If you don't like him, you don't have to see him."

She chuckles. "Tone it down, big guy. It's a small incision. It'll be okay."

"I never want you to be uncomfortable. I'll find a new doctor."

"He's been our doctor my entire life. More than my life actually."

"Fine. We will let him do this, but then we get a new doctor."

She rolls her eyes. "Yes, sir."

Moving in closer, I press a kiss to her lips before whispering, "I like you calling me sir. Stay in your seat until I come get you."

She does as I ask, letting me come to help her out of the car. Then I thread my fingers with hers as we head into the clinic.

The receptionist isn't the same one as the last time I came in. This one is just as young though.

"Can I help you?" she asks with a friendly smile.

I ignore her, moving past her into the back.

"Hey. You can't just go back there," she calls out.

"Dimitri, that girl is just doing her job."

I sneer back at the hussy now on the phone.

"She's not even a real receptionist. He only hired her to fuck her. If he hasn't already, he will. It's his MO."

Ivanna shivers. "See, I don't like the guy."

I think about it for a moment. Shit, I bet he's hit on her or something. I'm going to kill him.

"Relax. You're with me. He won't do anything," Ivanna whispers as I escort her into an empty exam room.

"I'm going to kill him. After we find a replacement, he's gone," I vow to her.

She shakes her head. "Let's just get this over with. We should be out there looking for Kiera."

I haven't told her about my meeting yet. She's going to be pissed, but it's unavoidable. Besides, it could be related.

"Dimitri, to what do I owe the pleasure?" Dr. Daniil says from behind me.

"I need you to put a tracker in my woman."

His eyes widen. "I'm not sure I can do that. Ivanna, is that what you want?"

I step between them so he can't look at her.

"Don't you dare look at her."

"Dimitri, he's going to have to look at me to put it in."

I growl, "He can look at your arm then."

We agreed on placing it on her inner thigh, but since the doctor makes her uncomfortable, that's not happening.

"Yes, Doctor," Ivanna says from around me. "I want the tracker."

He clears his throat but moves to the wall to grab gloves. "Very well. You have the device, I presume?"

Reaching into my pocket, I pull out the box holding the small device Alexei provided me.

He takes the item, setting it on a tray before going to grab his instruments.

"Dimitri," Ivanna whispers.

I turn to her, taking in her face. She's nervous.

"What can I do?" I ask, knowing she knows I see her.

"Instead of boxing me, will you hold me?"

Swallowing hard, I nod, moving her so I can sit on the exam table. Then I pick her up, set her in my lap, wrapping my arms around her center.

She lets out a relieved breath as the tension releases from her body.

It's a heady feeling knowing that I caused that. I can take her stress away.

"Which arm?" the doctor asks, only meeting my eyes.

Fucker got the point.

"Right," I murmur, pressing a kiss behind Ivanna's ear.

The doctor sets up and then pauses.

"This will sting a bit."

"Wait." I stop him as he puts the scalpel near her skin. "You have local anesthesia that you can give her."

He nods quickly, going to get it. I frown at him. He's definitely dying. I don't think he forgot that he could cause her less pain. He just didn't care.

He comes back, giving her the shot before going to work. It's a quick procedure, but it seems like it takes forever. Especially watching Ivanna's reaction. Her eyes are closed as she leans into me, trying not to react to what he's doing.

When he's finally finished, I throw cash at him, pulling her out behind me. I wait until we get to the car to kiss her until she's breathless.

"What's that for?" she asks.

I shake my head. "You did so good. I'm proud of you."

"Whatever. Are we going to search for her now?" she asks.

I press my forehead to hers. "I have a meeting. Before you get mad at me, it's related. I would take you with me, but it is not the sort of meeting you take your woman to. Can you hang out at your dorm for a couple hours? I'll come to you right after. I promise."

She looks disappointed but gives me a small smile. "I'm going to hold you to that promise."

I know she will, which is why I hope I'm wrong.

I hope this has nothing to do with her friend at all because if it does, then this is bigger than we ever thought.

CHAPTER
TWENTY

Ivanna

I hate waiting.
I've been pacing my dorm room for hours, waiting on an update from Dimitri. He texted me to tell me he was going to his meeting and wouldn't be available for me.

I won't lie. A pang hit my heart at that. Realistically, I know he can't be at my beck and call, but something about knowing if I called him and he wouldn't answer makes me anxious. It makes me feel alone.

Not that I'm alone. Oleg is outside my door. I know Alexei has a direct link to my tracker too. Dimitri called him to make sure he was pinging me before he left.

I want to be mad at him, but it makes me feel adored. Fucked up as it is, knowing he can find me with the touch of a button is comforting. I think I may even start to enjoy the freedoms he has allowed me.

Dimitri is making concessions for me and I love him for it. I know he wants to take over my life completely. He craves that control. He's not though. He's compromising. He's making deals with me so that we can both be happy.

For once, I feel like he sees me as an equal. I'm not his ward he has to keep locked away.

I'm his woman.

A knock at my door pulls me out of my thoughts. I open it, knowing Oleg is on the other side.

"This young man would like to speak with you."

I look over and find a dejected-looking Josh.

"Come on in, Josh." I open the door wider.

Once inside, I go to close the door, but Oleg stops me, cracking the door.

I give him a brief nod, getting what he's saying. He doesn't like a strange man he doesn't know in my room alone with me.

"Have you heard from her?" Josh asks.

He looks so sad. I wish I could tell him the truth. When I found out Kiera was missing, I asked Dimitri if we should file a report.

He brought up a good point though. The more noise we make, the less likely they will keep her alive. Problems are often dealt with quickly and permanently in the meat markets. It's better off letting the school think she left on her own.

"She's with her mom. I told you that, Josh."

He shakes his head. "I know, but it doesn't make sense. She doesn't have a good relationship with her mom. Besides, she's not answering me. What did I do wrong?"

The boy is heartbroken. My heart wants to break along with his. He's hurting because he thinks the girl he loves abandoned him when the truth is she was taken.

"Her mother is sick. She went home to reconnect with her. You

DIMITRI

know how life-threatening situations can change a person's mind. I'm sure she wants to text you back, but she's going through something traumatic right now. You have to give her time. She loves you. She will come back to you."

His eyes snap to mine. "She loves me?"

I want to curse. She hadn't told him? I mean, she never said the words to me, but I recognized the signs. She always wanted to be with him. When she wasn't, she found a way to bring him up in every conversation. She'd get that dopey look on her face too. She's head over heels in love with the boy.

I only hope when we get her back, he can help her through the mental issues she's going to be facing. I know it wasn't easy for me and they didn't have me that long. They've had her four days now. Who knows what she's going through. The only thing keeping me sane is the fact that Dimitri knows the auction schedule. They won't be having one for another week. That's not to say she's not being hurt now, but as a last resort, we should be able to find her then.

"Of course she does. You are all she ever talks about. Give her some time. I'm sure she wants to talk to you but doesn't know how. Not with her mind being a mess. Promise me you'll give her some time and when she does come home, you'll be there for her. Support her no matter what."

His eyes harden with resolve. "I'll never leave her side. She's my whole world. I've not been able to eat or sleep without her. I promise I'll be there for her no matter what."

I nod once. "Good. Go home. I'll let you know if I hear from her."

"Thanks, Ivanna. You're a good friend to her. I'm glad she has you."

I force a smile, my eyes tearing up.

I only hope I continue to get the chance to be her friend.

As he leaves, I stop at the door to watch him.

"He's a good kid. I personally looked into his background. He comes from money, but he's not a little prick like most trust fund kids. Seems his mom grew up poor and taught him the value of a dollar.

That's why he's here instead of an Ivy League school," Oleg whispers to me.

"He loves her. You think he will be able to handle whatever we bring her back from?"

Oleg is quiet for a moment. "I think that if you love someone, then your love can handle any hurdle. If they are meant to be, he will toughen up. He will use all that money he has saved to get her the best therapist money can buy. Then he will stay by her side through the thickest part of it. If he does, then they will make it out the other side. It won't be pretty, but they will have each other."

"That's awfully insightful, Oleg. I didn't know you had it in you."

"My sister was raped when she was sixteen. It was a hard few years, but with love and devotion, we helped her through it. She still has some hang-ups, but it's been fifteen years now. She's made it through. Your Kiera is strong like Minka is. She will make it too."

"Do you think we will find her?" I whisper.

"I think Dimitri would go to the ends of the world to save you from pain. If anyone can find her, it will be him. Trust in him."

"He's still at that meeting, isn't he?"

Oleg hesitates. "He would be here if it wasn't important. You know that, right?"

I sigh. "I do. Thank you, Oleg."

"Of course, Miss Ivanna."

Logically I know Oleg is right. Dimitri is always here when I need him unless he's trying to fix the problem.

Shutting myself in my room, I start the routine over again.

Pacing until my man comes home to me.

My skin is crawling. Something is off. I don't know what it is, but this is all wrong. We haven't had to meet with Javier Medina in years. In fact, he usually has one of his men meet us instead to make any exchanges.

So the fact that he is here himself spells trouble for us.

My fingers itch to reach for my phone. The need to know Ivanna is safe is overwhelming. I push it down though.

Nikolai set up for the Medina men to meet us at our bath house. It's a popular meeting place for businessmen, so no one would think twice about the Mexican men being here.

"Thank you for meeting with me last minute," Javier starts the conversation.

"It's my pleasure. What can we do for you, Mr. Medina?" Nik asks him point-blank.

Javier chuckles. "This is why I like you. You've always been blunt."

"No point in beating around the bush. We have had a deal for several years. This is the first time in that span of time that you have personally requested a meeting with me. So tell me what it is you think I can do for you."

He rubs his chin. "I have to admit, my old man wanted to handle this a completely different way. He thought you had turned into your father and wanted to wipe you off the map. I told him he acts too hastily though."

My stomach churns at the mention of his father. Before Nikolai took over, Rafael Medina, Javier's father and the head of the entire Medina Cartel, had an ongoing war with the Petrov Bratva.

Nikolai's father would pick off any of the Medina men who would enter our territory. In retaliation, the Medinas would seek out our men. It was bloody, but neither side was willing to concede.

When Nikolai took over, one of the first things he did was request a meeting with the Medinas. The meeting wasn't pleasant, but it opened the communications for a truce.

Several meetings later, Nikolai negotiated the deal that's been in place ever since.

"I assure you, I will never be like my father. What seems to be the problem?" Nik asks coolly.

"One of our mules has gone missing. They stopped over in the business district here for a drop before they were to head on. Seems they've vanished into thin air."

My blood chills as my mind goes back to one particular woman who had gone missing recently. She's one of the poor ones who we believe were a test subject for the bioweapon we believe the men are using to take women.

"I can assure you we have nothing to do with your missing product or your mule."

Javier nods. "I believe you. That's why I did some digging on my own. Now I am going to handle what I need to on my end, but I believe in professional courtesy. The kind which will give us a discount for the next year on our deal."

Nik thinks about his words. "Fifteen percent off for the year."

"Twenty," Javier counters.

"Twenty for seven months."

This time Javier pauses for several minutes.

The entire room is quiet.

"Deal. Seems there is a new player in town, but they aren't our usual suspects. They are into shit even we don't get involved in. The Ukrainian men have settled into your territory. Rumor has it they harvest organs and sell them on the black market. There's a high demand for the wealthy and hospitals that are desperate. Then there's the small number of cannibals who like to purchase for personal consumption. Either way, they are here and trying to set down roots.

This is bad for business. Not only mine but yours. So I'm going to make you a deal. We will be looking into this. If we find anything, we will reach out to you. You will offer us the same. Then we will take care of this problem together. Let me be clear, I'm going to be involved. They killed one of my favorite mules. I will have blood for it."

Nikolai considers his words. "What do you know of this organ harvesting?"

Javier laughs. "It's been going on for years down in Mexico. They made a deal with Rafael to take anyone not involved with the cartel. It's how he keeps his men in line. He offers protection in exchange for their loyalty. I've kept it away from my business. The government here isn't like back home. They watch too closely. This operation is new. I'm just not sure why they've chosen here. You would think they would be worried to be so close to the infamous Petrov Bratva."

That's the crux of it all. Why would they choose here? Nikolai has made himself a name by being ruthless. He takes care of the people in his territory as if they are his own flesh and blood.

"Thank you for bringing this to my attention. I will admit that we did know that there was a pest problem in the city and have been working to eliminate it, but you've offered invaluable information. For that, I'll agree to the twenty percent for the full year in hopes that you see that we put a lot of value into this partnership."

Javier smiles wider. "Of course. As we do as well. This has been beneficial to us all. We will be in touch shortly."

Nikolai stands, so I move forward. He shakes Javier's hand before watching him leave. Once the guard indicates he's left the building, Nikolai curses.

"This isn't good, D. If they are harvesting organs, that means Kiera could already be dead," he whispers.

I clench my fists. "Or it could mean she's still alive. I'd assume they would need a buyer. They would probably keep the women alive until they have one. Many organs need to be transplanted within a certain amount of time in order to be viable."

"Unless some cannibal wanted it."

"I refuse to give up hope. If I do, then it means I've already disappointed Ivanna. I won't do that again."

Nikolai kicks the chair he had been sitting in, sending it flying.

"I want Alexei on it. They may be Ukrainian, but they chose this territory for a reason. I think our Polish problem has something to do with it."

"I'll call him on my way to Ivanna."

"Don't let her out of your sight. If some asshole tries to take my sister's organs, I will go to fucking war."

"I'll be right there beside you."

CHAPTER
TWENTY-ONE

Ivanna

"Ivanna, baby. Wake up."

His voice is the first thing that registers.

I wasn't trying to sleep. I wanted to wait up for him, but after a while, my eyes closed on their own.

"Dimitri?" I whisper, turning over to face him.

"It's me. I need to hold you. Come here."

He pulls me into his body. I relish the heat wafting from him.

"What happened?" I whisper.

He tensed. "We still don't know who has her, but we have a lead. I'm working on it."

"We still have time, right? She's alive and will be sold next week, you said."

He hesitates several moments. It makes me think he knows more than he's telling. Or maybe he's just hesitant to promise me that she's alive.

"We are going to find her. I won't stop until I do."

"I know. I know you will. I love you, Dimitri."

He breathes out an exhale. "Say it again."

"I love you."

"I love you so much it hurts, Ivanna. You are embedded in my soul."

"That sounds like it hurts," I joke, trying to lighten the moment.

Pulling back from me, he leans down, pressing a kiss to my lips.

"I mean it, *printsessa*."

Instead of answering him, I lean up, pressing my lips to his. He lets me take the lead, kissing him softly. I nip his lip until he opens his mouth, allowing me to slide my tongue inside.

He holds me tighter as he follows the movements of my lips on his. When I push him back, sliding on top of him, the entire vibe of the room changes.

The sweet, sensual feel is replaced by electricity as he takes control of the kiss, devouring my lips. His hands slide up the back of my thighs until he's gripping my ass, rocking me against him. The feel of his hard cock against my pussy is almost too much.

I want more.

No. I need more.

"Dimitri," I manage to gasp between kisses.

"Shh. Let me love you," he whispers.

I pull back from him. "I want you to love me. Please. I want you inside me."

He freezes. "Are you sure? I don't want to rush this. We have all the time in the world."

"I don't want to wait anymore. I feel like we've been building up to this for years. There's nothing I want more than to know if you live up to my fantasies."

He growls, flipping me so I'm on my back. "You fantasized about me?"

Biting my bottom lip, I nod.

"Fuck. I've jacked off more times than I could count to the thought of you in the room right next door. I've wanted you for far longer than I'd care to admit. If you truly want this, then there's nothing I want more."

"You did?"

His hands move to my sleep shorts, pulling them down my legs.

"Every single night. Do you know how hard it was not to do it in the room with you when I had to stay with you when Lia was in trouble?"

I gasp as he fingers my slit softly, collecting my wetness to paint my lips with it.

"I imagined you taking me those nights. Of how it would feel to have you inside me," I admit softly before licking my lips clean.

He groans, leaning down to take my mouth with his.

"You are so sexy," he murmurs against my lips, his hand pulling my shirt up between us.

He pulls back, stripping me of my shirt until I'm naked beneath him.

As he takes me in, my hands go to his shirt, pulling it up. He lets me take it off him, leaving his bare chest in its wake. Fuck, I've imagined licking his chest for far too long. Between his chiseled abs from all the training he does and the tattoos decorating his body, I'm not able to look away.

My hands feel his skin, my eyes taking in tattoos that I've only ever seen from a distance. When I get to the one at his heart, my breath catches.

His hand catches mine as he holds it in place.

A crown fit for a princess is right in the center of his heart. Weaved in and out of the crown is ivy.

It's as if the tattoo is for me.

I look up into his eyes, mine filled with tears.

"You've always been my *printsessa,* Ivy."

His use of my childhood nickname, along with the nickname only he has ever called me, causes my heart to swell with warmth and love.

This is how my mother always said I should feel. So overfull with love that I could burst at any second.

"Pants off, Dimitri. If you aren't inside of me in the next two minutes, I cannot be held liable for what I'll do."

Dimitri grins, pushing up to his knees to unbutton his pants. Then he stands, stripping them down his legs slowly, taking his boxer briefs with them. Once he's naked, he stands there, letting me take in his body.

My eyes zero in on the baseball bat he carries between his legs. Fuck, he looks bigger than the guys in porn look. I thought they were supposed to be unrealistically big. I guess Dimitri didn't get the memo.

"Don't look so scared. It'll fit. It will just take some work."

He climbs back onto the bed, making his way between my legs.

"I'm not scared. I'll admit I didn't really get a peek last time and it's bigger than I imagined, but I've never seen another in real life. I trust you, D. If you say I can handle it, then I will because I'd do anything to make you proud."

Leaning in, he kisses me as his fingers start playing with my clit.

"I'm always proud of you. Even when you fight me. I love that you don't roll over and let me bulldoze you. I'm not in love with who you can be, Ivanna. I'm in love with who you already are."

My heart soars at his words as my body starts to chase that familiar high.

"That's it. Show me how much you want this dick," Dimitri whispers as he nips the skin on my neck.

I give in to the pleasure, letting the orgasm take me over.

"So beautiful," he whispers as he lines himself up at my opening.

Looking down, I see he's bare.

"Condom?" I ask, swallowing hard.

His eyes meet mine. "There will never be anything between us. I know you're on birth control, just like I also know you aren't ovulating.

I know every single thing about you. I won't force a child on you until you're ready, but I won't ever use protection with you. The idea of my cum living deep inside of you strokes a primal part of me. I need to know part of me will live in you forever."

My pussy clenches at his words. They are so dirty. I should be repulsed, but I want that too. I want to keep part of him in me.

"Shit, Ivanna. Look at you. That turns you on, doesn't it?" He presses forward slightly, the tip sliding inside me.

It burns, but I don't make a noise. I don't want him to stop. I know the first time isn't pleasant, but I'll endure it if only to get to the other side when I know it will be magical.

He pulls back, pushing in more, making me wince.

"I know, *printsessa*. It's going to hurt, but I'll make it up to you after. I promise."

He keeps up a slow pace, allowing me to adjust as he moves in and out of me. As he does, he continues to talk.

"I'm going to mark you from the inside out. I know I can't breed with you while you're on birth control, but that doesn't mean we can't practice. I'm going to show you how good it feels."

His words distract me from the burn, keeping me in the moment with him. I hear myself breathing heavier as he picks up his pace until he's fully inside me, his body brushing against my clit with every thrust.

"One day, when you're ready, I'll bury my cum so deep inside it sprouts a seed. You'll carry my child. God, I can't wait to see your stomach swell with my baby. You're already a fucking goddess."

He's losing control. I can tell by the way his rhythm hiccups every now and then as he thrusts inside me.

It still burns, but the spark of pleasure is there too. I know I won't come from it, but it's enough to keep the pain from overtaking the entire experience.

When he finally comes, he roars out my name, a sense of pride filling me.

"Fuck yes, *printsessa*. You're fucking perfect."

Pulling back, he looks down at his blood-soaked dick. The purely animalistic look on his face is enough to have me panting for more. I don't care that it burned. I want the feel of him inside me always.

Before I can say a word, Dimitri sinks between my legs, licking from slit to clit.

"Dimitri," I gasp out, mortified about my blood being down there.

"Hush, Ivanna. Lie back and don't you move again."

My body jolts at the commanding tone.

I don't disobey him. Instead, I grow wetter at the dominating demeanor.

Once he's sure I'm listening, he goes back to his feast. His fingers probe me, pushing his cum back inside as he licks and nibbles my clit until I'm screaming.

When I finally combust, I scream out his name, my body shaking with the overwhelming sensation of pleasure.

It takes me several minutes to come down from that high. When I do, I find myself in Dimitri's arms. He's curled around me with his fingers buried inside my pussy.

"Dimitri, your fingers are inside of me," I whisper.

"Go to sleep, *printsessa*."

I wiggle, never having felt something inside of me for an extended amount of time.

He pulls his fingers out, but only enough to smack my clit, making me jump.

"Stay still. I'd prefer my dick be inside of you, but you're going to be sore, so for tonight, it's my fingers. I want part of me inside of you every night when we sleep. Now sleep."

I feel him press his fingers back inside as he kisses the back of my neck.

It takes me a moment, but I relax, clenching around his fingers to ensure he's there. He doesn't move. He just lies there, content to be inside me.

So I let myself cuddle back into him until I fall into a blissful sleep.

DIMITRI

Leaving Ivanna sleeping in bed without me was the hardest thing I've ever had to do. She looked so freshly fucked, making me feel proud as hell.

I made her feel good even though I knew when I had fucked her, it wasn't pleasant. There was no way it would be. I'd done my research when I decided she was going to be the one. I knew that I'd need to eventually take her virginity and while the thought of her being in pain kills me, it was a necessary evil.

She needed to feel it in order to get to the good stuff.

Just remembering how tight she squeezed my cock has me rock hard and ready to go already.

Ivanna doesn't know this, but I gave up fucking other women when she was sixteen. Back then, I attributed it to the fact that I was too busy handling her rebellion, but I think I always knew she was going to be it for me. I just needed her to grow up first.

Now here we are. I have everything I could ever want right in the palm of my hand.

I better not fuck it up.

Walking into Nik's office, I take in his sour face.

"What happened?"

He shakes his head. "Nothing. No new people have been reported missing. We have no leads. Alexei is trying his best to breach their server on the dark web, but he's coming up empty-handed. They speak in code, but he has no idea what any of it means. He could pose as a buyer, but without knowing the code, he might fuck himself over and tip them off. Then who knows what they will do."

It's not looking good. I had hoped overnight we would have found them and put an end to this. The longer Kiera is missing, the more Ivanna is going to blame herself for her disappearance. I know she feels guilty for staying home that night.

As fucked up as it is, I'm glad she did. It could have been her instead.

"What do you want me to do?" I ask, ready to be the soldier he needs.

"Javier asked if I could send someone to help him. He's got his men working on this, but he could use a hand. I need you and Maxim to go. It shows we respect his position by offering my top two men. Stay vigilant though. I don't like that his father's first reaction was to take me out."

"Of course. Maxim know already?"

He nods. "He's downstairs waiting on you."

"I'll get down there then and keep you updated."

As I leave the office, I think back to my promise to Ivanna.

Pulling out my phone, I send her a quick text letting her know I'm handling business and I'll be back as soon as I can.

Maxim is waiting for me inside the SUV when I get outside, so I slip inside quickly, needing this over.

We need to find Kiera.

The drive down to the warehouse Javier asked us to meet him is silent. I'm lost in my thoughts of Ivanna and how I can protect her.

Maxim isn't his usual jovial self either. He seems to be as intense as I am.

I know he has issues with human trafficking because of his history, so I don't prod. If he wanted to talk about it, he would. That's the kind of man he is.

"Keep your eyes open," I remind him.

He nods once.

He's not exactly under me anymore. More like adjacent. I'm still Nik's second, but Maxim is like my second in a way.

Javier meets us at the door, a wide smile on his face.

"I've got good news, friends. We stopped a kidnapping in progress. We were going to question them ourselves, but you know, I thought we could have a party instead."

The pure delight on his face is unnerving. I mean, we kill without remorse when needed, but this man revels in it. I wouldn't be surprised if he got off on it.

"Show the way," I tell him, following him into the rank warehouse.

It's obvious this is a place they keep when their people need to stop in our territory. Not only that, but the dried blood tells me that they use it for interrogations as well.

It smells nasty as fuck, but all of that fades away when I see the woman lying on a dirty mattress on the floor. She's knocked out, shivering.

She looks young. Younger than college age.

"Do you know who she is?" Maxim asks.

Javier shakes his head. "Caught him grabbing her as she walked home from the high school. Figured when we were done, you could take care of her. I know how you feel about getting rid of the innocent. She hasn't seen anything and even if she had, she wouldn't remember."

"Maxim, why don't you go ahead and take her? Drop her at the emergency room. You can swing back and get me later."

He gives me a sharp look. He doesn't trust Javier. I don't blame him. They could use this as an opportunity to take me out, but my gut says they won't.

"Very well."

I watch as Maxim makes his way to the girl, picking her up in his arms. Javier's man follows behind him, opening doors. I wait until we are alone to turn to the man strung up in the middle of the room from a meat hook.

"You haven't asked him anything yet?"

"Nah, amigo. I left that up to you. I wanted to see how you Russians work."

I nod once, moving in front of the man.

He sneers at me, spitting.

I laugh right before punching him in the kidneys.

He groans.

"Now that we've been properly introduced, how about you answer some questions?"

"Fuck you."

"Very well. I don't think you'll like it much though." I turn to Javier. "You got any pipes in here? Maybe something to lube it with? I don't care if it hurts, but I don't want him bleeding out."

Javier's eyes light up. "We will get you some."

He and his men go to work as I walk around the stoic man hanging in front of me. Grabbing my knife off my belt, I cut away his clothes.

I snort when I see his tiny, shriveled-ass dick.

"No wonder you kidnap people. With a dick like that, it's probably the only way you get to fuck. Tell me, do you fuck their bodies before or after they are harvested?"

The man doesn't respond, not that I expected him to.

"Here you go. It's the best we got."

I chuckle at the tire iron and pint of oil.

"It'll work."

Pouring some oil on the end of the tire iron, I turn it in my hand a bit. Then I pour some down the man's back.

"What are you doing?" He seems a bit panicked.

"Sodomy is an interesting thing. It goes one of two ways. Either you find out a new kink you never knew you had, or you are in agonizing pain. I wonder which you will be."

"Oh, he's going to love it," Javier pipes up.

"You could tell me what I want and we won't find out," I offer him.

He doesn't speak, but his face is much paler.

I shrug before moving behind him. He tries to struggle, but it's no use. After a few tries, I shove the tire iron all the way up his ass.

He screams out in pain. I hold it there before thrusting it. It's disgusting, but hearing his cries is music to my ears.

"Okay. Please."

The man breaks easily. I knew he would. He seemed like a low-level thug.

"Where is Kiera? She's the redheaded girl you took from Western U several days ago."

"We took her to the drop-off point. They had a buyer lined up, but he didn't want her right away. Something about wanting her body soft and pliable. That's all I know. I swear."

"I want that drop-off point."

"It changes. We take them there and get them set up in the room. The doctor puts them under. Once that's done, we collect our money and leave."

"Then how do you know about Kiera?"

"I'm fucking the doctor. She tells me things. The girl you described is the perfect match to some sheik's heir. They need her lungs. Until his son can make the trip, they will most likely keep her in a coma. I could be wrong though. Nonetheless, he's not healthy enough yet, but will be soon."

I nod. "Do you know anything else?"

"I can give you names. My contact at the college is Richard Lamington. He's a professor. He gets DNA from them or takes their blood somehow and matches them. Then he administers the drug and we wait outside for them. Sometimes it happens quickly, but other times they will make it home before it sets in."

I swallow hard. "What happens if you can't grab them? There was a girl a few weeks ago you didn't grab."

He shrugs. "Wasn't my job, so I don't know. It's not good if you don't get the mark. You only have one shot. If you try a second time, it looks suspicious."

"Do you guys not care that you are going against the Bratva?"

"What? I don't know anything about the Bratva. We were told this was prime hunting grounds. The higher-ups made it seem like this is our territory now."

I grimace. This isn't good at all.

"I'm done, Javier. Would you like me to end it?"

His smirk grows. "No. Let me have the pleasure. Please stay for the show."

That night I regretted sending Maxim off.

That night I met the devil.

CHAPTER
TWENTY-TWO

Ivanna

"It was perfect," I tell Lia, smiling down into my popcorn bowl.

"Oh my gosh. I am so excited," she squeals.

I've just finished telling her all about my first time, with Dimitri.

Okay, I didn't tell her all of it. I'm still a little embarrassed that he had eaten me out with my blood and his cum down there. Hell, I don't think I realized it last night, but this image of him with blood on his face has been locked in my head. It's oddly erotic.

"Me too. He was gone this morning, but he sent me a text like he promised, telling me he had business to attend to."

"I'm glad you finally talked to him."

I nod. "He promised that anything pertinent to my safety and well-being he would tell me. Not only that, but he seems to be keeping me in the loop with Kiera too. He knows this is important to me. I finally feel like he's treating me like his equal instead of the girl he has to look after."

"Good. He needed to get his head out of his ass."

The fifth guard walks by, looking into the room before moving on.

"Things around here are eerie," I tell Lia.

All morning, the guards have been walking around with a sense of doom.

"Yeah, well, with everything going on, everyone is on edge."

I sigh. "I know. I thought we had solved all of this Polish shit when we were kidnapped."

Lia tilts her head, looking confused.

"Polish?"

I nod slowly, feeling completely blindsided. "Yeah. Dimitri said Kiera was kidnapped for human trafficking."

Lia's eyes widened. "Oh. Um."

"What is it that you know?" I ask as my heart pounds, waiting for the blow.

"It's nothing." She shakes her head, refusing to make eye contact.

"No. You are my best friend first. What do you know?"

She blows a breath through her lips. "Nik told me that it's the Ukrainians. That they are harvesting organs. He wanted me to be aware so I know to be on the lookout while I'm at school. He's even asked me to stop making any extra stops."

I'm frozen at her words.

Nik told her all of that, but Dimitri didn't tell me anything. Nik's the hardest man I've ever met. He is pakhan to the damn Petrov Bratva, and he still found time to tell his girl what was going on.

Dimitri, who promised me he would tell me these things, hasn't said a word.

He had an opportunity too. I asked him about it last night.

"What does this mean?" I whispered to her, my body feeling numb.

"It means we have a new enemy. One who isn't waiting for an auction to sell off women. They are taking men and women to sell their body parts. Nik said he hoped Kiera was still alive, but you should prepare yourself. If they've already lined up a buyer, we might not find her alive. Or if she is, she might not be whole."

I swallow hard, my eyes prickling, but I force it down.

I'm done.

I asked for some very specific promises. It didn't even take him long to break them.

"Thank you for telling me. Is Nik in his office?" I ask as I push down the anger.

Lia reaches over to grab my hand. "Don't do this. Talk to him. Give him the benefit of the doubt."

I shake my head and laugh darkly. "He had the opportunity to talk to me last night. When did you find out about this?"

She frowns. "Last night after their meeting."

"So he knew when he came to me. He lied to me. I asked him about it. He said we still had time until the auction. The auction that doesn't matter because they don't have her."

"Ivanna..."

I shake my head. "No. I'm going to talk to Nik."

Standing, I leave her on the couch. I know she means well, but she doesn't understand how this feels.

I feel like I've been betrayed. I think I'd rather he had cheated. At least there would be someone I could blame.

I can only blame myself for believing him and his lies.

Once I'm in front of Nik's office, I pause.

Do I really want to do this?

I don't see another choice.

Taking a deep breath, I lift my hand and knock on the door.

"Come in."

Opening it, I slip inside and see Nik standing behind his desk.

"Hi," I say as I shut the door behind me.

As I approach, he walks forward and gives me a hug, kissing my cheek.

"Sorry for interrupting you."

He nods. "Must be important since you know I'm doing everything I can to find your friend."

I wince at that. This is not the time, but if I don't do it now, I might lose my nerve.

"Have a seat, Ivy. You look pale."

Wordlessly, I do as he says and watch him move back around his desk and sit. He rests his elbows on the arms of his chair and steeples his hands in front of his face.

"What's wrong?"

I shake my head. "My life is a mess, Nik. Do you think I'm messed up?"

"Of course not. What happened?"

"Dimitri made me a promise. One that he knew if he broke that, I would be done with him. He broke it anyway."

"Why is everything so black and white with you? Have you talked to him about it?"

I shake my head again. "He knew my stipulations. I need you to start the dates back up."

He glares at me.

"Does Dimitri know?"

"He will." I nod, my tongue feeling heavy. "I'll tell him."

Nik hums but doesn't say anything for a few minutes.

He leans forward and rests his elbows on his desk as he stares me down, shaking his head. "You know, Ivanna, you've pulled a lot of shit over the years. You've been reckless and gave no fucks when it came to your safety or those around you. I chalked it up to teenage rebellion, but after you were taken with Lia, you calmed down for the most part. I thought you were growing up."

"I am. I have," I snap as I cross my arms over my chest.

He ignores my response and keeps going. "But I was wrong. You're childish, self-centered, and have no regard for those around you. Most of all, you're a fucking coward."

I tense, refusing to show him how much his words cut me. "Excuse me?" I ask quietly.

"You heard me."

My eyes narrow as I glare at my brother. "I'm not a coward."

"Yes, you are. You're running away from Dimitri before you even give it a chance. You are scared and instead of facing the fear of things changing, you're turning tail and running. That man is out there right now busting his ass to find your roommate because she means something to you. To be honest, had it been left up to me, I wouldn't be expending all of my resources to find her because, in my head, she's a lost cause, but not to him. He's fighting for her because you want him to. This is how you do him? You wait until he's gone to come and ask me to give you to another?"

I look down at my hands and shake my head. "How can I ever trust him if he can't even keep his word to me? I asked for something simple. I asked him to treat me as an equal. To keep me informed when it is directly related to me and he can't even do that."

Out of the corner of my eye, I see Nik shake his head. "We can't always tell you everything. You grew up in this. You know this."

"Really? Then why does Lia get to know? That's the only reason I know he blatantly lied to me last night. Lia told me what you told her. If she can know, why can't I?"

He looks a little shocked. Seems he might be having a chat with Lia, but it will do no good. We always said that we had each other's backs.

"Talk to Dimitri. See why he made the decision he did."

"Does this mean you won't schedule the dates for me?"

"I'll think about it. You can see yourself out. I have to get back to work," he says, looking down at his desk.

I choke back the tears as I watch my brother pick up a pen and start reading a piece of paper.

This is the right thing to do.

Standing, I head toward the door. Just as I step outside, Nik calls my name.

"Ivanna."

I look over my shoulder. "Yeah?"

"I love you, but I'm disappointed. When you're standing on the edge of the cliff about to jump into the unknown, it's scary. All your senses tell you to run, but if you run, you will never know what it means to be loved unconditionally. I didn't want to fall for Lia, but she made it impossible not to. Don't be afraid of how D makes you feel. Embrace it, otherwise you will be cold for the rest of your life and will never know true happiness." He pauses. "Make sure this is what you really want because once it's put into motion, there will be no going back."

I nod my head and shut the door. As I walk down the hall with heavy legs, I try and convince myself that this is right.

Dimitri and I will never work.

But are you sure? a little voice whispers in the back of my mind.

Dimitri

"You need to talk to Ivanna," Nik says before I can even take a seat in the chair.

My heart is pounding in my chest. "What happened?"

He quirks an eyebrow. "You tell me. She came in here asking me to arrange a date for her."

"If you do that, I will kill every man she meets." My hands fist.

"It's not my choice. You lied to her about something and she found out from Lia and it's a fucking mess. She's making a rash decision like she always does. It's my fault, really. I coddled her too much as a kid trying to make up for our shitty father. She cuts and runs before shit gets hard."

"What the fuck did I lie to her about? I've not lied once," I grunt.

"I don't know, but she's downstairs, so how about you find out? I'm about sick of these games. You need to lock that shit down."

I stride from the room in front of him, stopping in the middle of the foyer at the bottom of the stairs.

"Ivanna, get your ass in here," I scream.

It only takes a few minutes for both she and Lia to filter into the room.

"Why are you yelling?" Ivanna spits out, folding her arms over her chest.

She's angry. Good, so am I.

"What is this about wanting to date other men? I thought you understood. You are mine." I move toward her, but she takes a step back, looking uncertain.

I'm sure it's the crazy look in my eyes. I'm going to lose it.

She's finally done it. She pushed me to my breaking point.

"Don't talk to me like that. You made me a promise, Dimitri. You said we were in this together. Then you lied to me without me even prompting you. I told you that I needed you to treat me as an equal. I can't trust you."

"Trust? Are you serious right now? I live my life for you, Ivanna. There is not a single step I make that you aren't right there with me, helping me make it. You can't trust me? Why? Because I didn't tell you something the way you expect me to? We agreed to this, yes, but you also agreed to have patience with me. You agreed to allow me some grace because I cannot change decades' worth of conditioning overnight. So tell me, what did I lie to you about? How did I hurt you? Tell me so I can fix it."

The tears shining in her eyes are killing me. I want to take out my gun and turn it on myself. I hate that I've hurt her again. It seems to be the only thing I'm good at.

"You said Kiera was taken by the Polish. That we still had time to get her before the auction. Lia said that her organs are being harvested by Ukrainians. You didn't tell me that. I have a right to know. She's my friend."

I rub my hand down my face. I knew I should have told her last night, but I stupidly thought we would have time to talk about it today. I didn't want to stress her out in the middle of the night.

"Ivanna, you can't jump to the worst-case scenario every time something doesn't go your way. I won't live with the threat that you will leave me every time I do something that upsets you. Had you waited just twenty-four fucking hours, you would have known that I didn't tell you last night because it was late and we both needed rest. I was going to tell you today."

"Oh, we needed rest so much that you fucked me instead of telling me about my friend?"

"Jesus fuck, woman! Are you being for real right now? This is some bullshit. I wanted you to rest. You started that. Not me. And before you fucking crucify me, I wanted to, but I wouldn't have pushed the issue. God, is this how it's always going to be with us? You running at the first little sign of trouble? Me chasing you over and over again? What can I do to prove to you that I'm one hundred and ten percent in this with you? Tell me and it's done."

"There's nothing you can do. I want to marry another."

I shake my head, my body starting to shake. "Never. You will never marry another. You will marry me. You will only ever marry me."

"You can't make me."

The laugh I let out is scary even to my own ears. Was I just saying that Javier was the devil? I feel like I'm channeling him in this moment.

The red seeps in as I look at the woman who owns me. She wants to hurt me. I can see it.

She's succeeding.

"I will give you a choice. Marry me, Ivanna. You're mine. Let me make you mine for the world to see. If you don't, then I will kill any man you attempt to marry. Any man who touches your body. That is the deal I will make with you."

DIMITRI

The fire in her eyes does nothing to deter me.
I will own her once and for all.

CHAPTER
TWENTY-THREE

Ivanna

"I will give you a choice. Marry me, Ivanna. You're mine. Let me make you mine for the world to see. If you don't, then I will kill any man you attempt to marry. Any man who touches your body. That is the deal I will make with you."

I let the tears fall freely as my body rages. How dare he make demands of me? Can't he see we are no good for one another?

"No. I won't," I tell him.

I want to. I wish I could, but I can't. Not while knowing he can never truly give me what I need. I love Dimitri with my whole heart, but I can't be the one who loves the most. It might be selfish, but I need more.

"Yes." He moves to step toward me, but Nik stops him.

"Back off, D. She said no. She's made her choice. You need to respect it."

Dimitri pushes back against Nik.

"Fuck you, Nik. You gave her to me. She's mine. I won't let you take her from me."

Nik moves in closer to him. "Don't do this, brother. I don't want to have to kill you."

Dimitri doesn't even hesitate. He pulls his gun, pointing it at Nik's head. Nik responds the same way.

I stand there watching as the two men I love stare each other down, ready to murder one another all over me.

When did it come to this?

"Please," I cry out, the anger seeping from my body being replaced by despair.

Lia catches my arm, pulling me back. I can tell she's as worried as I am, but she's watching out for me. Not Nik, but me.

"D, I need you to lower the gun. Let's be rational here."

Dimitri shakes his head, the anger falling off him in waves. "There is no rationale. She's mine, and I will kill anyone who tries to take her away from me. Even you."

I gasp, my hand finding my mouth.

Dimitri looks at me then, his hand never wavering. "You said you needed me to beg and plead. That I needed to prove to you that I'm in this one hundred percent. You said you needed me to grovel until you felt like I meant the words I spoke. I've done everything I can to prove it, but none of it has been enough. I love you, Ivanna. I always have, but those feelings changed somewhere along the way and I no longer loved you like the girl you were. I fell in love with the woman you are now. I refuse to live this life without you by my side. I will *never* let another man touch you. So make your decision now. Either you marry me and be mine, or I will take you by force. If you choose option *B*, know that one of us won't walk out of here alive. Either Nik or I will die because I'm not leaving here without you and he will never agree to allow me to take you without your permission."

I sob, shaking my head. "Don't, Dimitri. Don't hurt him. Please."

"What will it be, love?" His own eyes have a sheen to them, almost as if this is hurting him as much as it is me.

"He's your pakhan. If you kill him, they will kill you. Is that what you want?" I cry out.

He laughs, but there is no humor in it. "This life isn't worth living without you in it. Fuck the Bratva. Fuck the hierarchy. In the end, only one thing truly matters. That's you."

My heart feels like it's about to beat out of my chest.

Moving forward slowly, I shake Lia off. Then I keep taking steps, my eyes locked on Dimitri until I'm right next to him.

Then I step in front of him. Nik drops his gun immediately, not wanting to point it at me, but Dimitri keeps his training on Nik.

"Why are you doing this?" I whisper quietly.

"You don't believe my words. The only way to get it through your thick head that I love you is to take action. I'm proving it to you. It's you or nothing for me."

"You would kill my brother if you can't have me?" I ask.

"I would burn the fucking world down if I can't have you. I know you want your freedom and to make your own choices, but this is one choice I can't let you make. The only way you will ever truly be free of me is if you kill me."

Dropping his arm, he turns the gun in his hand, pressing it into mine. I try to stop him, but he holds it in my hand, pointing it at the middle of his chest.

"My life is in your hands, Ivanna. Make your choice."

It feels like the whole world stops in that moment. All I can do is stare into the darkness in his eyes, praying for an answer to come to me.

I always said looking into his eyes feels like he's taking my soul from me, but in that moment, I'm the one in control. I'm the one staring at his soul, stealing from him.

Then a memory resurfaces.

"You never settle, my little one. You wait for a man who would stop

breathing before he would let any harm come to you. He should be hopelessly devoted to you. Never settle for less. You deserve so much more."

I haven't heard my mother's voice in so long, but hearing it now, I know that she's the reason I've held out this long. She's the one driving force behind my feeling so unsettled with men.

In that moment, I know she'd approve of this man.

He has killed for me. He will continue to if he needs to. Not only that, but he would die for me. Over and over again.

"You," I whisper.

"What?" he asks.

"I choose you."

Slowly, he allows me to lower my hand until I drop the gun on the ground.

Then I'm in his arms, my tears coming fast and hard.

"I choose you. I'm sorry. It's always been you. I've always wanted you."

"Shhh," he whispers, peppering kisses on my face. "Don't be sorry. You never have to be sorry."

He bends, his hands grabbing my ass as he lifts me. I wrap my legs around him, squeezing him so tight I know it has to hurt. I don't stop though. I need to be close to him.

You could have lost him.

"Dimitri." Nik's commanding tone comes from behind me.

I try to lift my head to look at him, but Dimitri presses it back against his throat as he whispers sweet words to me.

"Dimitri, we need to talk about this."

Dimitri freezes. I can feel the tension radiating off him.

"No, Nikolai. You made me make a promise. You don't get to be upset because I upheld that promise. Do you remember what you said to me that day?"

I want to question what he's talking about, but I don't. I keep my mouth shut.

"You held a gun to my head," Nik scoffs. "I'm your pakhan."

"I would do it again too. You said that she is to come first, even

DIMITRI

before you. From that moment on, I've made my life based on that. There's no changing it now. She will always come before you. That includes if you try to interfere with our relationship. I will not tolerate it."

Nik growls, but it's Lia's voice that calms him.

"Nikolai," she says. "What would be the harm in letting this go? He's your best friend. He's going to be your brother for real now. How about we let bygones be bygones?"

"*Kroshka*, I can't let him get away with it. It will be seen as weakness."

I hold Dimitri tighter.

"It's okay, *printsessa*. I've got you. Nothing will ever come between us again," he whispers.

"Who is going to see it as a weakness? There's no one here but us," Lia spits out.

"Fuck, Lia. He held a fucking gun to my head."

"And he would do it again for the love of his life. Let me ask you this. If it were between him or me, would you choose him?"

"That's not fair."

"Isn't it?"

The room is silent. All I can focus on is the feel of Dimitri stroking my back.

"Never let it happen again," Nik grumbles.

"Never try to take my woman from me again," Dimitri responds.

"You little shit. You better treat her right. I'll fucking end you if you don't."

"You won't have to. I would end myself first."

"Good."

"Good."

"Are we done with this macho bullshit?" Lia interjects.

Nik sighs. "Figure your shit out. I expect you both at dinner tonight."

I hear their footsteps leave the room, leaving Dimitri and me alone.

After a few moments of basking in him, I finally speak, "What does this mean now?"

"What do you mean?" He pulls back, tilting my chin so he can look at me.

"Do we go back to how we were before?" I whisper, hating that I don't know if I want the answer.

"No, baby. Never. This is going to be a new us. A better us. A partnership like you asked for. You will always have guards on you. Believe it or not, you're going to be in more danger. Not only will you be the pakhan's sister, but you'll be his second's wife. That will put a bigger target on your back. We can't avoid that though, because I plan to let the whole fucking world know that you are mine."

"You're mine too," I argue.

His face softens. "That I am. You're more than welcome to tell anyone you want."

Leaning forward suddenly, I sink my teeth into his neck. He groans but doesn't stop me. I bite until I taste the metallic tang of his blood. When I finally pull back, I smile.

"Does it look good?" he teases.

"Everyone who sees that will know that I own you now."

He chuckles. "Alright, my little temptress. I think we need somewhere a little more private for my branding. I need to leave marks all over your body."

My thighs clench at the thought. I've missed him more than I care to admit.

"Take me to bed then, Mr. Lukin."

He gives me a wicked smile. "Your wish is my command, Mrs. Lukin."

"You know, when I said to take me to bed, I didn't mean at your house. The one upstairs would have sufficed," Ivanna snarks.

My hand clenches on her thigh. "I'm going to fuck you hard and make you scream a lot. I figured one round with Nik was enough for today."

"Don't ever do that again," she says, suddenly solemn.

"Do what?" I ask, needing her to say it.

"Try to hurt yourself. Even if I'm mad at you, I can't imagine a life without you in it. I'd never want that."

"I'd never want to live a life without you either, so maybe don't leave me? Stay and fight with me even when I make mistakes."

"I will. I'm sorry. I shouldn't have done that. I don't know why I am the way I am."

I give her a sad smile. "Your person died when you were young. All you've known is abandonment. It's easier to run and hide from the pain than process it. It's a conditioned response, one we will work on breaking. I don't want you beating yourself up about it. We have all the time in the world."

"I know we do. Still, I don't like the thought, so don't do it again."

I grasp her hand, pulling it to my lips as I pull into the driveway.

"Let's get you into your new home."

She waits until I help her from the car to speak again. "We are going to live here?"

"After you graduate, yes. I already cleared it with Nik. I want you to make this place our home," I tell her as I unlock the door with my hand.

"What if I want to move in here sooner?" she whispers.

I look down at her as I close the door behind us.

"You wanted to room with Kiera again next semester."

She frowns. "If we find her alive, she's not going to want to room with me. She's going to need therapy."

Cupping her face, I pull her head to mine. "When we find her. Tomorrow we are going to go over the plans to do so too. The guys are getting some last-minute intel, but as soon as they have it, we are moving out. So be ready. If she doesn't want to room with you, then you can move in here. Maybe we can get her and that boyfriend of hers an apartment and set her up with a therapist. The best one money can buy."

Her eyes are wide. "You'd do that."

I nod. "He seems to care for her and if her getting better makes you happy, then I'll do it. Although I have a feeling her boyfriend will want to handle it on his own."

"I love you. I'm so sorry for tonight. I went insane. I lost it for a bit."

Leaning down, I shut her up with a kiss.

"It's in the past. We won't be living there."

She smiles up at me. "You'll let me help plan tomorrow?"

"Yes."

Her smile grows wider. "Good."

I chuckle. "I have something for you. Come on."

She lets me pull her into the living room, where I have her wrapped gift sitting on the table.

"What's this? It's not my birthday." She looks up at me.

"Something I want you to have. I don't need a reason to give you nice things."

She melts. "You're spoiling me."

"I'm going to spoil you for the rest of your life. Now open your gift so I can take care of that needy cunt."

Her cheeks redden as she leans over to the table to grab her present. I slap her ass, making her squeak before glaring back at me.

"Punishment for trying to leave me."

She shakes her head but opens the package. Her eyes tear up as she notes the item.

"Is this a hairpin dagger?"

"Yep. It's only made from the best steel too."

She holds it to her chest. "It's perfect. I'm going to wear it all the time."

Leaning down, I press a kiss to her forehead. "That's what I bought it for."

Setting the hairpin back in the box, she sets the box on the table before dropping to her knees.

"What are you doing, *printsessa?*"

"Begging for forgiveness. On my knees," she whispers, her hands going to my pants.

My dick twitches in anticipation.

I should tell her she doesn't have to, but fuck it. She does. She made me feel like my world was ending. The least she can do is let me know what it feels like to have her mouth around my cock.

I won't come in her mouth though. No, that's saved for her pussy. Something about the idea of breeding her is erotic to me. Like it's my own personal kink. Whatever the reason, I will never waste my cum anywhere but her pretty little cunt.

My pants drop to the floor as she gasps at my dick.

"No underwear?" she asks.

"Felt like freeballing today."

She laughs but leans in closer to me. Then she kisses the tip of my dick, making it jump. She presses several more kisses to my shaft before finally sucking me into her mouth.

It's heaven. Everything about her is perfect. If I died in this moment, I would be complete.

"Fuck, Ivanna. You feel so good. Strip," I demand.

She hums around me, making my body jerk forward. She gags a little but takes it like a champ. It makes me wonder what she practiced on because there's no way she's this good this quickly.

Pulling back, she quickly strips off her clothes before going back to her task.

Threading my fingers into her hair, I guide her head gently at first, showing her the pace I want. When I feel her hands gripping my thighs as she rubs her legs together, I take control altogether, picking up the pace. I start to face fuck her hard, loving the way her cheeks turn red as her eyes look up at me, all watered with tears in them. She doesn't try to stop me though. Instead, it's like she's egging me on. When she's not gagging, she's swallowing, making me harder.

"Good girl. Take my cock. Swallow it all. Show me how good you can be for me."

My praise only ignites the fire in her eyes. She seems to be trying even harder to get me to come.

She almost succeeds. I pull out just in the nick of time, stopping her.

The spit dripping from her lips onto her heaving breasts is a sight I will never forget. She sits back on her heels, her breath slowly becoming more steady.

"I want you bent over the couch, ass in the air. I'm going to fuck you hard and quick. You're going to come and then I'm going to take you upstairs and spend the rest of the night taking it slow, making you beg me for more."

She whimpers a little as if the thought is as torturous as it is pleasurable, but she does as I ask.

Once she's in position, I line myself up. She's so wet that I slide right in. I pause once buried inside, leaning over to kiss her neck and shoulders.

"Does it still hurt?" I whisper.

"It burns a little, but it feels good. I like it," she admits.

I smile, kissing her shoulder one more time.

Then I straighten up and thrust into her hard. She gasps but doesn't make another noise.

I continue to thrust into her, picking up my pace. She's panting and moaning underneath me. Wrapping her hair in my hands, I pull her head back as my other hand slides between us to play with her clit.

"I want you squirting all over my cock. Are you going to be a good girl and squirt for me?"

"Dimitri," she moans out.

I slap her clit once, making her eyes snap open.

"I asked you a question."

"Yes. I'll squirt for you, daddy."

My dick surges at the new nickname. I kind of like it.

"Fuck," I murmur against the side of her head. "Do it then. Now, *printsessa*."

She squeezes against me twice. Then I feel it. The liquid runs down my dick as she comes. Her body goes slack in my arms as I continue to fuck her until I spill my own release inside of her. I hold her until she can talk again.

"You good, Ivanna?" I ask her.

A smile comes across her face as I hold her back to my front, my lips on her cheek.

"More than good."

"Daddy, huh?" I ask.

She tries to shrug, but her body is still shaking with her release. "Sounded appropriate."

"I liked it. You'll call me that every time we fuck now."

Her core clenches against my dick, still buried inside of her. I chuckle.

"Seems like you like that idea."

Turning her face, she takes my lips with hers. "I like everything as long as it's with you."

I slip out of her before picking her up in a bridal hold.

"You shouldn't have said that. I think it's time for round two."

Then I carry my girl to our room and show her exactly why she will always call me daddy.

CHAPTER
TWENTY-FOUR

Ivanna

"Okay, last topic of the day," Professor Lamington says, making everyone quiet down. "Which is better for the environment, gas vehicles or electric?"

As Dean debates Stacy, I stay quiet, keeping my opinions to myself. On the outside, I appear calm, my face blank, only engaging when I have to. On the inside though, I'm a bundle of nerves for what's to come.

This morning was a shit show. Dimitri and I argued for an hour over my involvement in this little operation. Seems he found out that Professor Lamington is directly involved with the Ukrainians and is likely the reason Kiera is missing. He wanted me to take a back seat and let him handle it.

I wanted to be the bait so we could finally find this place.

We aren't the perfect couple. We yelled back and forth, each wanting to be heard, but at the end of it, he agreed to let me do it. Not because he wanted to. He allowed me to do it because he saw reason.

I'm the best chance we have of finding Kiera alive. Her clock is running out and without anything more to go on, Professor Lamington is our last shot at this.

Dimitri and I debated how to approach Professor Lamington and if I should wear a wire or not. I told him about how smart the man appeared to be and how I didn't think I could pull off a wire. Dimitri cursed up a storm when he realized they didn't have any more microscopic microphones and the next shipment wouldn't be here in time.

In the end, we settled on my computer recording everything. Dimitri wasn't thrilled, but it was better than nothing.

"All right, that's all for tonight. I'll see you guys again next week."

As the classroom empties, I stay seated. Blood rushes through my ears as anticipation hits me full force.

It's go time.

"For the love of God, Ivy, don't do anything fucking stupid." Dimitri sighs.

"Don't worry."

"Ivanna, I noticed you were quiet tonight. Everything okay?"

"Honestly? No," I say, making my lips tremble with fake worry.

"Do you want to talk about it?" he asks as he takes a seat on the desk in front of me.

"You know Kiera is my roommate, right?" I ask, looking up at him through my eyelashes.

Outside of the corner of his eye twitching, he doesn't flinch.

"Of course." He forces a smile.

"Well, I'm worried about her."

"Oh?"

I lean forward in my chair, pushing my breasts together. On the inside, I gag as his eyes drop, checking out my cleavage.

DIMITRI

"She hasn't come home and that's not like her. Last week she was acting off too."

"How so?"

"Just distant. I figured maybe she was busy with school or maybe preoccupied with something else. We share a room, you know." I watch him nod. "Well, a couple times, she unknowingly woke me up in the middle of the night. I don't know if she was coming or going. I'm just worried."

The entire time Professor Lamington's face barely changes, but he's grown tenser by the minute.

He takes a deep breath and leans forward, reaching for my hands. Instinctively I want to jerk away, but I can't. I have to keep up the charade.

"You know, I'm glad Kiera has someone like you in her life. She's very lucky."

"You think so?" I ask softly.

"I know so. She told me how close you two had gotten."

"I didn't know you two were close."

Professor Lamington's eyes shift from side to side. He's trying to figure out what to say next.

"She actually came to me. The stress of school and the future were eating at her. She was having trouble sleeping, as you know. Ivanna, I hate to say it, but Kiera was troubled."

"D-do y-you think she did something to herself?" I gasp, pulling my palm out of his hand and bringing it to my chest.

I know he's fucking lying. Kiera has a job lined up here in the city. She just told me how excited she was for a trip to London she had planned. A graduation present for herself, she called it. Not to mention her budding relationship with Josh. She would have never up and left. Not to mention we know for a fact she was kidnapped. He's an idiot if he thinks I'm buying this, but I have a role to play.

"I was worried about it. That's why I took Kiera to get some help."

My shoulders drop and a fake smile spreads across my face. "You know where she is?"

"I do." He pauses. "Would you like me to take you to her?"

"Yes, please."

"This place is top of the line. They have celebrities and have very strict rules. You know, to protect their guest's privacy."

"You were able to get her into a place like that?"

"I have a friend who works there. He pulled some strings." He smiles.

"Okay, what are these rules?"

"I'm going to have to ask you to leave your electronics here. I can either lock them up in my office, or we can drop them by your room."

"What else?" I ask, mind spinning.

He tries to look apologetic. "I'm going to have to check you for a wire. Not that I think you have one."

I raise my eyebrows. "I wouldn't even know where to get something like that honestly. Do you want to check me now?"

Professor Lamington stands and I follow. I hold my hands out to the side and move into a wide stance.

"I'm sorry."

"It's okay," I lie.

As he checks me, I try to stay calm even though my heart races. I'm so fucking thankful that we decided to play it safe. My stomach rolls as he touches between my breasts. Thank God Dimitri isn't seeing this. He's going to be so mad that I'm going off-script.

One of Dimitri's stipulations was that I didn't leave with the professor, but it's an opportunity that I have to take. Who knows if we will get another chance.

Besides, it's not like he won't be tracking me.

He will be right behind me. I have nothing to worry about.

"There, all good. I'm sorry about that."

"Like I said, it's fine." I force a smile.

"Did you decide what to do with your things?"

"If we could drop them in your office, then we can just get on the road."

"Sounds good."

He turns and starts walking toward the door. I follow behind him like a good little student. After walking down the hall, Professor Lamington pulls out his keys and unlocks his private office. He flips on a light, and I follow him inside. I look around the room and can't help but wonder if there's anything of use here.

Does he keep a list of girls he wants?

Has Dimitri gone through everything here?

I set my bag down and smile at the professor. "Ready."

I follow him out, knowing that when I return to campus later, my bag will safely be in my room. The guys won't take a chance on him going through my things.

In what feels like a blink of an eye, we leave campus and drive a little ways off campus. Professor Lamington pulls his clunker of a car into an empty parking lot with only one light at the very back. His headlights hit a dark brick building.

Everything about this place has me on edge. It's the type of place I would avoid at all costs.

"This is…" I trail off.

Professor Lamington shuts the car off and then reaches over and squeezes my hand. "Trust me, it's fantastic inside. A place like this has to go under the radar to protect the guests."

"Makes sense."

Taking a deep breath, I reach for the door handle and get out. Reluctantly I follow the professor toward the building. I watch as he knocks in a five-knock pattern on the door. A man in black opens the door and lets us in.

"Who's this?" the man asks as he shuts it behind us.

"A friend. We're here to see the girl I brought."

The man grunts as he looks me up and down. "Have you checked her?"

"Of course, Preston," Professor Lamington says, sounding offended.

It takes everything in me not to laugh at the slipup. Clearly, the professor isn't a professional if he's dropping first names by accident.

"Go on then. You know what to do," the man says ominously.

The professor starts walking down the hall and I follow. The entire time, I fight the urge to look behind me at the doorman. I can feel his eyes on me.

As we reach the door at the end of the well-lit hall, Professor Lamington grabs something off the hook next to the door and holds it out to me. "I'm sorry, but I need you to put these on."

Dread fills my stomach as I take the black hood from him.

Part of me wants to put up a fight, but I know I can't.

Slowly I place it over my head. I hold out my wrists and feel him wrap the rope around them. I hear the door open and the professor pulls me out of the room like I'm an animal on a leash. My legs feel like lead as he ushers me through the room. With the loss of my vision, my sense of hearing seems to grow the farther we go.

I've always hated elevators, but riding in one with a fucking hood on makes it so much worse. When the doors open and we slip out, I feel the chill in the air. A shiver racks my body at the sound of metal and keys clanking together.

"In you go," Professor Lamington says as he pushes me.

Instantly I rip the hood off and turn toward the man. I watch as he locks the door and gives me an unapologetic shrug. "I would say I'm sorry, but I'm not."

"Professor. What's going on?" I ask, infusing my voice with worry.

He doesn't answer and walks away.

Turning, I take in the room and realize I'm in a makeshift cell. There are no windows or anything. I spot several women lying out on the cold concrete. They don't even flinch. Looking down, I work the ropes off my wrists.

Clearly, Professor Lamington isn't the brains of the operation because he barely tied my hands together and the rope is easy to get off. Gingerly, I start checking the girls. Everyone seems to be alive but drugged. Finally, in the very back, next to the wall, I find her.

Kiera.

Leaning down, I press my fingers on her pulse in her neck. It's there but thready. I let out a breath I didn't realize I was holding and drop my head to my chest.

I found her.

She's alive.

And now all I have to do is wait for Dimitri to come in and get us.

Dimitri

Bile burns my throat as I watch her get into the car with the professor.

"We should end this now," I rasp.

Nik shakes his head and places his hand on my shoulder. "No, we have to let this play out."

I turn, glaring at my best friend. "She's with a psychopath. We don't know where he's taking her or what's being said. We didn't wire her."

"Ivanna can take care of herself. You made sure of that," he says, squeezing my shoulder. "Now sit down. The best chance we have is following them."

"Okay. You're right."

"Of course I am." He turns away from me and looks at Maxim, who's sitting in the driver's seat of the van. "Follow them."

Maxim nods as he turns on the van.

While he drives, I lean against the wall and close my eyes. I hate everything about this. I know Ivanna can protect herself. From listening in to the conversation she had streaming to us from her laptop, I know we made the right choice in not wiring her up. That doesn't mean I like it, though.

Different scenarios go through my head as we follow behind them from a safe distance.

What if we're too late? What if he hurts her?

You have a tracker in her arm, I remind myself.

I feel the car start to slow down and open my eyes. "Where are we?"

Nik shakes his head. "Industrial district."

"They just pulled into a parking lot," Maxim tells us.

"Drive past and I'll jump out the back on your signal. Use the building as cover."

Nik moves toward the back of the van and grabs the handle as Maxim slows down further.

"Go," Maxim tells him.

Nik opens the door and jumps out. Leaning out, I grab the handle and shut it behind him. Then I move forward and get into the passenger seat.

"You hanging in there?"

"Barely."

Maxim shakes his head. "I don't know how you do it."

"She's worth it. Loving her is worth all the fucking bullshit she throws at me."

"I hope I never fall in love." Maxim circles the block and pulls into a parking lot close by.

Getting out, we grab our weapons and make our way to Nik. We find him hanging out in the shadows, watching the building.

"Anything?" I ask as we approach.

"They were let into that building." Nik tips his chin toward the brick building.

"Anyone with them?" Maxim asks.

"I know there's at least one other person in the building. I called Alexei. He's already sent me the building plans and is currently trying to get into the cameras. Backup will be here in ten."

"We shouldn't wait." I shake my head.

Nik shoots me a glare. "We wait. Gather as much intel as possible. According to the blueprints, this is the only way in and out."

"But Ivy is in there," I grind out.

"Ivy will be fine. She's a fighter," Maxim chimes in.

Time feels like it crawls by as we watch the building. Everything around us is still and almost unnaturally silent.

"This place is fucking spooky," Maxim says quietly.

"I was just thinking the same thing," I confess.

Nik looks around. "It doesn't feel right, and that's saying something coming from me."

Nik looks down at his watch. "Backup's approaching."

Soon we see men approach from in front of us. Using the cover of our target.

"Behind," Oleg says.

Turning, I see my friend approach from behind us. "Thanks for coming."

Oleg tips his chin. "Always. I brought Javier and his two men as well." He looks over at Nik. "Alexei sent these."

He holds out his hand and has three ear mics, one for each of us.

"Thanks," Nik says as he grabs one, placing it in his ear.

Maxim and I do the same.

"Can everyone hear me?" Nik says over the comms.

One by one, guys chime in. Even Javier and his men.

"Alright. We know Ivy is in that building next to you guys." He points to the guys in front of us. "We don't know how many people are in there, but the blueprints only show one exit and entrance. Did you guys bring the grappling hook?"

"I got it," Stepan says from across the street.

"Think you can scale the building? Go in through the rooftop door?"

"Easy," Stepan says.

"Good. You take two guys with you up top. Check the windows on your way up. If any of them open, send a couple more guys up to go through them. I want as many of us in there as possible."

"Cameras?" Linc asks.

"None on the outside and Alexei hasn't found any inside either."

"Amateurs," Maxim mumbles under his breath, and I can't help but agree.

Nik continues on. "Everyone with me, we'll breach the door. Everyone knows what they need to do?"

"Da," murmurs through the comms.

"Everyone get into place, then go on my count."

Silently, in a black mass, we work our way across the parking lot and get into place. As I lean against the building, I hear the sound of something whizzing through the air. The grappling hook. We give the guys a few minutes to work their way up the building.

"Ready?" Nik asks quietly.

"Da," Stepan says.

"Go," Nik says as he moves to stand in front of the door.

I stand off to the side next to him. He nods at me as he knocks on the door five times. Slowly the door opens and a man peeks his head out. He doesn't see me at first but does when I grab him, pulling him out by the front of his shirt. Before he can get a word out, I'm behind him and have him in a choke hold. When he stops fighting and his body goes limp, I drop his body.

Nodding at Nik, we head into the building and start sweeping it, knowing two of the men will stay back and take the man to the van.

It's time to find my woman.

CHAPTER
TWENTY-FIVE

Ivanna

Running my hand through Kiera's hair, I shiver. Even though I'm wearing a long-sleeve T-shirt, it does nothing to fight off the chill. I push it from my mind as I look down at Kiera. I don't know how long I've been in here, but she hasn't stirred once, but her pulse is still there.

"You care for her."

Turning my head, I find one of the girls has finally stirred.

"I do."

"Must be nice."

"I'm Ivy."

"Sloane," she rasps.

Her voice is rough and not in the normal way. Almost as if she's had damage done to her vocal cords.

"They will be coming for you soon."

"Why do you say that?"

"Because they haven't drugged you yet." She smiles. "It's the best time of day."

"How long have you been here, Sloane?"

I silently tack on, How long have you been an addict?

"Who knows." She shrugs.

The sound of footsteps has us falling silent. I listen to them talk to each other as they approach. Two of them speak what sounds like Ukrainian. I can't fully understand them, but I know a lot of the language is similar to my own.

About fifty percent of the Ukrainian and Russian overlap I read once.

As they come into view, I study them. Three men in total. What surprises me the most is one of the men speaking Ukrainian is Professor Lamington.

I didn't see that coming.

"Up!" one man with a heavy accent says as he unlocks the cage.

Ignoring him, I stay in my spot. Going easy isn't in my DNA. If they want me to comply, they will have to make me.

Two of the men, Professor Lamington being one of them, step into the cell. The one drops next to the girl and sticks a syringe into her arm with zero hesitation.

I can't help but cringe as she moans in pleasure.

She's fucking crazy.

Professor Lamington manhandles me until I stand. "Come on, be a good girl."

I struggle with him but ultimately give up.

As he pulls me out of the cell, I look back at Kiera. I hate leaving her, but sitting in here does neither of us any good.

"Why are you doing this?" I demand.

The man I don't know snaps, shaking my other arm. "Shut up."

They come to a stop and open a door, pushing me inside. I flinch as I hit the floor, the pain ricocheting through my body.

That's going to leave a fucking bruise.

I hear the door lock and look over my shoulder and see Professor Lamington leaning against it.

He smiles wickedly. "Now it's just you and me... you can't get out until I let you."

I look toward the doorknob and see it's one of those with a fingerprint sensor.

"Why?"

He saunters over to me and grabs me by the arm and drags me across the tile floor. He comes to a stop next to the bed and sits down. For a moment, fear consumes me. I'm locked in a room with a psychopath and a bed.

Fan-fucking-tastic.

"Let me tell you a story." He reaches out and runs his hand from my jaw down my neck.

It takes everything in me not to pull away from him.

"The first time I saw you, I wanted you. You brushed right by me as you were walking out of one of the buildings on campus. I had no idea who you were. Then Kiera brought you to the social club and I knew it was meant to be."

"What?" I ask, completely confused.

He continues on like I never said a thing. "See, I made plans to take you the night they came for Kiera. Only nothing went according to plan. I dropped the bioweapon into Kiera's drink. It was supposed to knock her out, and the men were supposed to take her. Instead, she gave it to you. I planned on slipping her another dose I had while she fawned over you, but instead"—his jaw clenches—"that man came in and took you away from me." He slaps his chest. "He thought he had the right to touch what was mine."

"I'm not yours," I hiss.

He lunges forward and tries to pin me to the ground. When my head hits the ground, I feel the sharp pain from my hairpiece.

Yes! I just need to get it and use it.

I catch him off guard by wrapping my legs around his waist and flipping us over until I'm on top of him. He wraps his hands around my neck and starts choking me. Reaching behind me, I find his zipper and undo it. I slip my hand into his pants and find his balls and start twisting as black dots fill my eyes.

Professor Lamington loosens his hold on my neck as he howls in pain. With my free hand, as hard as I can, I punch him in the jugular. His eyes bulge as he grabs his throat. Removing my hand from his pants, I reach for my hairpin and remove it. With zero hesitation, I stab him in the eye with it.

As Lamington goes limp beneath me, my head drops to my chest as I try to catch my breath.

Holy shit. That just happened.

With shaky hands, I remove the hairpin from his eye and then begin checking his body for anything I can use.

"No, no, no..." I mumble as his pockets come up empty, with the exception of a key ring.

I have to get out of here.

Standing, I drag his limp body toward the door. Grunting, I move his body so he's leaning against the door. My hand moves to his neck, feeling for a pulse. When it bumps beneath my fingers, a small part of me is relieved to find it. I honestly don't know if I want a body count of my own.

Grabbing his hand, I bring it to the doorknob. Right away, the middle of the knob goes from red to green. As soon as the lock unlatches, I open the door and peek my head out.

Gripping the hairpin, ready to use it if needed, I make my way back toward Kiera. I need to get her out of here before it's too late.

Room by room, floor by floor, we clear the building. Men are stationed on the main floor, covering the front door, the stairwell, and the elevator. No one is coming or going without us knowing. The men we find who don't put up a fight are cuffed with zip ties and taken out to be interrogated. The others fall like hot potatoes as our guns take them out with barely a sound.

My anxiety grows the further we go without finding her. The only thing that gives me the slightest relief is knowing that her tracker says she's still in the building. Every time I check, Nik looks at me as if I've lost my mind, but I know he would be doing the same if he could. Especially if it was Lia we were searching for.

Using the stairwell, we approach the basement but come to a halt as we hear the door open. Weapons raised, we're ready to fire when he comes into view.

"Drop to your knees now!" Nik says harshly.

The man is missing an eye and has blood trailing down his face, soaking his shirt.

"Please, d-don't shoot," he pleads as he falls to his knees.

As soon as I hear his voice, I race forward and grab him by the neck. I move his body so he hangs over the stairwell. The drop wouldn't kill him where we're so close to the basement, but it's enough to throw his body off balance.

Professor Lamington claws at my wrist. "What are you doing!"

"Where is she?" I demand.

"Who?"

I shake him, making him cry out as the railing digs into his back. "Don't play stupid. Where. Is. Ivanna?"

"I-I d-don't know!" He shakes his head. "S-she attacked me and when I woke up, she was gone."

"She did this to you?"

The man nods so fast he almost tips himself over. "Yes."

With my free hand, I reach up and dig my thumb into his empty eye socket. Professor Lamington cries out as he pisses his pants from the pain. "Stop!"

"My wife," I grit out. "Wouldn't have done this unless pushed. What did you do to her?"

Before he can respond, Nik places a hand on my shoulder. "Hand him off. We haven't found her yet, so she has to be close by."

Reluctantly, I pull him back from the edge and hand him off. Once he's in Nik's hold, Nik spits in his face before passing him off. The other men do the same until he gets to the very back.

"Go," Nik orders.

Taking a deep breath, I raise my gun and continue on. Stepping out of the stairwell, we walk into a cold basement with minimal lighting. It looks like something out of a horror movie. The sound of movement at the end of the hall has us speeding up, knowing the men behind us will clear the rooms we pass by. Not letting anyone get us from behind. Coming to a door, I stand off to one side as Nik takes up the other.

He nods and I open the door. As it swings open, he steps inside first. He comes to a stop so fast that I slam into his back.

"Holy shit."

Stepping around him, I forget how to breathe as I eye the cages filled with women.

"Ivanna," I call out.

"D?"

The sound of her voice sends relief through me.

She's here.

As soon as she steps forward, we rush toward each other. She jumps into my arms. I bury my face in her neck as I hold her tight.

"You came," she murmurs quietly as everyone else moves through the room, checking the women.

"You knew I would."

She pulls back slightly and smirks. "Took you long enough."

"Yeah? I saw some of your handiwork."

Her eyes flash in anger. "Professor Lamington didn't escape, did he?"

"No, some of the guys took him so we can interrogate him."

Her shoulders drop in relief. "Good."

"Nice work on his eye though," I say, raising a brow.

"Thanks. The hairpin proved to be handy."

My eyes move off her face and eye the hairpiece that's firmly holding her hair back, blood crusted on the tip. It looks so fucking wrong, but something about it turns me on.

"If you two are done having a moment."

Ivanna jumps down from my arms and rushes her brother. "Hi."

As soon as she pulls back, he cups her face. "Do you need the doctor?"

She shakes her head. "I'm fine. Honestly, it's them I'm worried about. Especially Kiera. I don't know what they drugged her with."

"Alright. How about you let Dimitri take you home while we get them taken care of? We can talk after," he tells her.

"But Kiera. I don't want to leave her."

Nik looks down at her softly. "Go home, get a shower. You won't do Kiera any good like this."

"I don't want her to be alone," she confesses.

"Come on, *printsessa*. One of the guys will stay with her in your absence."

She looks back at me and bites her lip. "If you're sure."

"Hey Ivanna, glad to see you're safe."

"Good to see you in one piece too, Maxim."

He turns around and starts walking backward as he walks into one of the cages. "Oh, hey, congratulations on getting married. If I would have known about it, I would have gotten you a gift."

Nik starts laughing as soon as the words leave Maxim's mouth.

Ivanna turns to me, eyebrows raised. "Married, huh? And who am I married to?"

I shrug as I pull her out of the room. "Me, obviously. I might have slipped and called you my wife."

Her breath hitches and I keep going. "It's not that big of a deal. I mean, it's only a matter of time."

"You're something else."

"But I'm yours." I look down at her and smirk as I weave my fingers through hers.

A pretty blush covers her cheeks. "That you are."

CHAPTER
TWENTY-SIX

Ivanna

"So you girls are sisters?" the doctor asks as he shines a penlight in Kiera's eyes.

I figured we would talk to Dr. Daniil, but it seems my psychotic husband killed him because he creeped me out. I have no idea when he did it, but all I know is Nik is now looking for a new doctor. So I guess we are testing this guy out. Dr. Rami.

"We are," Lia tells him.

He chuckles. "Genetics is an interesting thing. You two look nothing alike."

Lia shakes her head. "Oh no, I'm married to her brother."

"I'm sorry." The doctor shakes his head. "You just look so young, and I assumed."

"It's okay," Lia reassures him.

"How's Kiera doing?" I ask.

The doctor pockets his penlight and picks up a clipboard, checking it over.

"I think she will be just fine. She was slightly dehydrated and had a fever, so we're giving her some fluids. As far as I can tell, she will make a full recovery."

"And when will she wake up?" I ask as I bite my nail.

The doctor shakes his head. "That depends on her and when she's ready. It could be any minute or tomorrow. Her body is doing what it needs to do right now and resting. It's all on her schedule for now."

"I hate waiting," I groan.

The doctor looks at me with a soft smile. "Do either of you have any more questions?"

"No," we say in unison.

"All right. Just hit the call button if either of you needs anything or when our patient wakes up."

"Thank you," Lia says as he slips outside the door.

The room is silent with the exception of the monitors they have her hooked up to as a precaution. I eye the screens, wishing like hell I could understand what they all mean.

"How are you?" Lia asks from the other side of Kiera's hospital bed.

"I'm okay. I'll be better once we get an update on her."

Lia looks over at me with that look that screams don't bullshit me. "Ivy, don't downplay it. Talk to me."

I look around the room before looking back at her. "This really isn't the place."

Lia rolls her eyes. "You and I both know no one is coming through that door randomly and the room has been cleared. It's safe."

I sigh as a weight of exhaustion hits me. "What do you want to know?"

"How are you feeling about being kidnapped again?"

"I went willingly," I point out.

DIMITRI

Lia continues on like I didn't interrupt her. "Did the professor hurt you? How do you feel about what happened to him?"

"I'm fine, I promise. I knew what I was doing when I walked into that classroom. I'm glad we were able to save Kiera and those other girls."

"What else? Keep going."

"I hope we found something in the building. I want the entire operation shut down."

"You and me both." Lia sighs.

A knock at the door has us pausing.

"Hey babe." Lia smiles as Nik walks in with Dimitri and Maxim on his heels.

Nik walks over and gives Lia a kiss. "How's the patient doing?" he asks after he pulls away.

"Doctor says she should be fine. He gave her something for the fever. Hopefully she will wake up soon," I tell him.

Dimitri walks over to me and stands behind me. He places his hands on my shoulders and kisses the top of my head. "How are you feeling?"

"Fine."

Maxim grunts as he sits down on the open couch under the window. "Fine. One word a man should fear coming from a woman."

"Why is that?" Lia asks with humor in her voice.

"Because when a woman tells you she's fine, she's clearly not."

"Oh really?" I tease. "Tell me, what do you know about a woman not being fine?"

Maxim opens his mouth, but Nik cuts him off. "You three can banter later. Right now, we need to talk."

Lia stands and Nik slides into her seat before pulling her onto his lap. "Now, Ivy, I need you to tell me everything that happened after you left the school."

Taking a deep breath, I jump into a full recap. I tell them how he covered my head with a hood and brought me down to the basement before tossing me into a cell. I mention how one of the girls woke up and managed to tell me a few things, but nothing really useful. How Professor Lamington came in and grabbed me before taking me to a private room and the events that happened after. Everything.

Nik's jaw clenches. "Are you sure he didn't touch you inappropriately?"

Dimitri's hands tighten on my shoulders and I can't help but reach up and squeeze them. Offering him a little bit of comfort. "I promise you, nothing happened. At no time did I really feel unsafe."

"Is there anything else? Did you hear them talking or anything?" Nik asks.

Biting my lip, I think about it, replaying everything in my head.

I snap my fingers. "I almost forgot. I heard another language."

"What did you hear?" Dimitri murmurs.

"I'm ninety-nine percent sure they were speaking in Ukrainian." I look over at Maxim. "It's just like Russian, right?"

Maxim nods. "It's not exactly the same, but if you can speak one, you can vaguely understand the other."

"Interesting..." Nik muses.

"So what now? Did you guys find anything?" Lia asks.

"What about the other girls? Did you find anything out about them?"

"They are all being treated. We are just waiting for them all to wake up," Dimitri tells us.

Nik chimes in. "Alexei is running their photos through the missing persons database and checking to see if they are in any systems."

"What about the first two missing girls from school?" Lia asks softly.

"We found them," Maxim says. "Everyone should make a recovery as of right now."

"Did you guys find anything else?" I ask.

The three men share a look but keep their mouths closed.

"Let me guess, you can't talk about it." Lia shakes her head.

Nik smiles at her and teases, "Now you're learning."

"But it was worth it?" I press.

Nik looks at me and nods. "You did good. I thought I was going to have to knock D out at one point to keep him from charging in too early, but other than that, it went well."

"No one was hurt," Maxim says, answering my unasked question.

"Good." I sigh.

It was worth it.

"Ugh," Ivanna groans as she falls back onto the couch.

"You alright?" I chuckle.

"I could sleep for a week."

Picking up her legs, I sit down and lay them across my lap. "Hate to break it to you, but that can't happen if you still want to graduate."

"Way to rain on my parade." She pouts as I take off her shoes.

Slowly, I start to rub the arch of her foot, making her sigh.

"You're too good at that."

"Do you want me to stop?"

Ivanna glares and points at me. "Don't even think about it."

"Whatever you say, *printsessa*."

After a few moments of silence, Ivanna speaks. "So what now?"

"What do you mean?"

"What do we do now that all that bullshit is over?"

"Well, technically, it isn't over," I point out.

Ivanna rolls her eyes. "You know what I mean. What now?"

I take a deep breath and choose my words carefully. "I know what I would like to happen next."

"What's that?"

"I want you to move in. I want to see your clothes mixed in with mine in the closet. In the mornings, I want to curse you as I fight for a sliver of counter space in the bathroom. I want you to decorate this place the way you want. Really make it a home. Most of all though, I want you to become my wife."

I look over to Ivanna to see she has tears rolling down her cheeks.

"I can't wait to marry you."

"Me either. Haven't you figured it out yet, Ivanna? I want everything with you."

"So if I tell you I want no kids..."

I shrug. "It's your body. Would that make me sad? Yeah, maybe a little, but it's not a deal breaker."

"What if I tell you I want five?"

I raise a brow and tease her. "That might be pushing it, *printsessa*. We don't want to be outnumbered."

I'm lying through my teeth. If I can keep her knocked up, I will.

Ivanna giggles, making me smile.

After a few moments of silence, she speaks. "I want all of that too."

"Then I'll make it happen."

"When can I move in?"

"As soon as you want."

"You know..." she says lightly. "Nik will probably want me to wait until after we're married."

"Do you want to move in before then?"

Ivanna nods her head. "Then I'll handle your brother."

I push her legs off my lap and stand. Reaching down, I pick Ivanna up bridal style.

"Ah! What are you doing?" she squeals as I walk down the hallway.

"I'm taking my woman to bed. Do you have a problem with that?"

Ivanna leans forward and nips my earlobe. "Never, daddy."

I growl, moving faster. "For that, I'm going to fuck that ass of yours. You're going to love it."

As I toss her down onto the bed, I stare down at the girl who has been my past and who is my present and future.

"I love everything you do to me, Dimitri. I love calling you daddy and letting you dominate me. I love fighting with you and being a hellcat. I love every single second with you."

Leaning over her, I press a hard kiss to her lips. "I love all that too. I love our life together. You're mine, *printsessa*. You will be mine for eternity."

"Well then, you better show me what my eternity is going to look like."

"Lie back on the bed. I command her."

She does as I ask without complaint.

"If you promise to be a good girl, I promise I'll make you feel good, but if you disobey me, you'll be punished."

Her eyes look mischievous as she nods her head. "Of course I'll behave, daddy."

If it wasn't for the look in her eye, I might believe her. Her tone is innocent, however I know her. She's going to test me and I'm going to love it.

Starting at her ankles, I press kisses slowly up her calves until I reach her thighs. I smirk to myself when I hear her breathing increase. Right when I'm about to get to her center, I stop, letting a breath out so she can feel it. She hisses but doesn't make another noise. I skip over her center, making a path back down the opposite leg. She lets out a little noise of disapproval but otherwise doesn't make another sound.

I know I should probably just let her have it, but I'm not giving in so easily this time. She thinks that she can top from the bottom, but I'm not going to let her. I'm going to show her why she calls me daddy.

"Dimitri, please, I need more. Touch me."

I ignore her pleas, continuing to trace the skin on her legs.

She huffs out of breath, leaning up to reach down to grab my head so she can put me where she wants me.

I let out a dark chuckle. "I told you to behave, *printsessa*. This isn't behaving."

"It's not fair. You're teasing me for no good reason. I told you I'd behave and I am."

"No, you're not. You're trying to control this. It's going to take some time for you to learn, but when it comes to the bedroom, you're not in control. I am. I'm feeling charitable. I'll let you lie back down on your own and you'll accept every excruciating moment of what I plan to do to you."

"I'm not lying back down if all you're planning to do is tease me until I can't breathe. I need you, daddy, so give it to me."

I shake my head. "Such a commanding little girl. You'll learn though."

Standing from my position at her feet, I moved toward my dresser. She lets out a noise of complaint. When I glance back, I find her with her hands between her legs, pleasuring herself as if it's a punishment for me.

"You'll stop that right now if you know what's good for you. If you make yourself come, I won't let you come for a week, so make your decision quickly and be smart."

Her eyes flash mine, heat behind them. She's judging whether or not I'll follow through with it. She should know by now that I always mean what I say.

Reaching into my drawer, I grab the ties that I put there earlier. I always knew it was going to come to this. That I was going to have to tie her up one day. My dick twitches at the thought.

I've had years to perfect all the fantasies that I plan to enact on Ivanna's perfect little body. She has no idea what she did when she decided to dance with me.

When I turn back toward her, I find her lying there, hands away from her perfect little cunt.

I smile. She's learning.

"That's a good girl. Now I'm going to tie you up so you can't think about doing that again. Then I'm going to suck on that pretty little clit of yours until I've had my fill. If you lie still and hold off until I tell you you can come, I'll fuck you. If you don't obey, then I'll edge you until you feel like your body can't handle any more."

She lets out a whimper, but then her sweet voice whispers, "Yes, daddy. Whatever you want, daddy."

My body heats at her words. The pure submission washes out the defiance in her eyes.

Leaning over her, I tie her hands to the headboard. Once I'm happy with how tight they are, I move to her feet as well. She jumps a little, not having expected me to make her completely immobile.

This is just step one in her training. I took it easy on her the first couple times, but that won't happen again.

From this day forward, she is my wife and I will treat her as such. That means I'll bring her the most pleasure she will ever have imagined in her life. It also means I'll teach her to love the punishment she'll receive when that feisty little mouth spouts off, writing checks that her ass can't cash.

Once she is secured, I place kisses all over her body, avoiding her most erogenous areas.

I revel in every whimper and whine that comes from her as she attempts to obey me while also giving in to her body's needs.

I wait until I think she's about to break before I move back to her pussy. Then I feast on it the way I've been wanting to since the moment I realized that I needed Ivanna to be mine.

With each sound escaping her lips, I ramp up the pressure. I need to know if she can hold off her orgasm simply on my command. I'm going to push her past every comfort zone she has until she doesn't even realize what a comfort zone is anymore.

As I suck on her, I let my fingers play in her wetness, slicking them up for what I'm planning to do next.

Once I'm ready, I slip them down to that little forbidden spot in the back, knowing that she's never imagined anything ever going there.

Then I put pressure on it, circling it as I let the tip of my finger slip in.

"Oh fuck, daddy! I can't handle it anymore. I'm going to come if you don't stop."

Her warning is music to my ears. It means that even though she's being pleasured, she still has enough sense of mind to know that she needs to obey me if she wants to be rewarded.

And reward her, I do.

"Come for me, *printsessa*. Shower my face with the proof that only I can make you come." My tongue goes back to her cunt as I start to push my finger in and out of her ass. She clenches around me, her body giving in to my command.

And when she comes, it's beautiful. Divine even. Like nothing I've ever been able to imagine before.

With her submission comes the beauty of what our love will be.

She screams out my name, making me only want her more.

Pride fills me, knowing that only I have made her scream that way. The one to make her come the way she just did. I'll be the one to teach her what pleasure means and how to find it in every little kink.

We'll explore every avenue until we find exactly what her limits are and what will make her scream the most.

When she finally comes down from her orgasm, I slip my fingers out of her ass and kiss my way up her body. My face soaked with the proof of how good she feels.

"Daddy, I want you to feel good. Please use me. Fuck me until you come inside me."

I growl at the erotic word spilling from her mouth. I know what she's doing. This is her way of trying to top once again by wanting me to spill before I am ready.

That's okay though. We have a lifetime to learn who's boss.

So I take my time. I bring her to the edge over and over with my mouth and my fingers. I even make her ride my thigh at one point.

I bring her higher and higher until the pain of not taking her is too much for me.

Only then do I let myself slip inside her sweet cunt.

Only then do I use her body to pleasure my own.

And only when she screams so loud she loses her voice, unable to call me daddy anymore, do I finally give in to the pleasure I find inside her.

It takes several minutes for me to be able to hear again, my orgasm so intense that it clouds my ears.

Ivanna's not much better. She's passed out beneath me. I can hear her breathing, feel her pulse against my hand, so I know she is alive and fine. She just passed out from the pleasure I've caused her body.

Pulling out of her body, I untie her, then I rub each one of her extremities. Making sure that the blood flow is back to them.

Once I'm sure she's okay, I climb back onto the bed, pulling her on top of my chest. My already hardening dick slides into her easily as I hold her to me.

I'll let her sleep as long as she needs to and then when she wakes, I'll claim her all over again.

I'll fuck her and keep fucking her until she doesn't remember anything outside of me.

I'll be her entire world, as she's already and always has been mine.

EPILOGUE

Ivanna

Grunting, I drop the screwdriver and pick up the instruction manual.

Who knew putting together a bookshelf would be so hard?

"What are you doing?"

I look over my shoulder and see Lia and Kiera standing right inside the door.

"I didn't hear you knock." I frown.

"That's because we didn't..." Kiera asks as she looks around the room. "Do we want to know what all this is?"

"I'm building a bookshelf." I shrug.

"Why..." Lia asks as she shuts the door.

"The other night, I was scrolling through Pinterest and saw this beautiful living room set up. A TV in the middle with bookshelves on both sides with the fireplace underneath." I wave toward the wall in question. "The only thing I was missing was the bookshelves, so I had these bad boys next-day delivered," I say as I slap the box next to me, still holding wooden pieces.

Kiera chuckles. "How's that going for you?"

"Honestly, I thought it would be easier than it is." I shrug. "But with Dimitri out of town, it gives me something to work on while he's gone."

Kiera laughs while Lia groans, pinching the bridge of her nose.

"We don't have time for this," Lia moans. "Did you forget what today is?"

She looks at me and rolls her eyes, seeing that I have clearly forgotten. "You have your bridal appointment today, Ivy. We're supposed to go find you a dress."

"Oh shit!" I yell as I jump up.

The board that was resting on my lap lands on the top of my feet.

"Motherfucker!" I cry out.

The door slams open, and Oleg and Ilya rush in, guns drawn.

"What happened?" Oleg demands.

Ilya frowns. "Is anyone hurt?"

"Only my pride," I mumble under my breath.

"Ivy, go get dressed and do something with that hair." Lia turns and looks at the guys. "Do you think you could call some of the guys over to put these together for her? The last thing we need is her getting a splinter while D is gone."

"I'm on it," Ilya says as I leave the room.

I walk right into my closet and grab a strapless bra, a pair of pants, and a loose shirt. After putting them on, I head into the bathroom and run a brush through my hair. Grabbing my mascara, I put some on and pinch my cheeks, adding some color to my face.

Looking into the mirror, I hardly recognize myself. Over the last few months, so much has changed. My eyes are brighter, my skin is clearer, and most of all, I look happy. I never realized how unhappy I was until I let Dimitri in.

And today I'm going to find my wedding dress.

THE BRIDAL DRESS consultant huffs as she walks away.

"Someone needs an attitude adjustment," Kiera says quietly.

"Honestly, I'm starting to feel so petty that even if I love something that she has me try on, I'll deny it," I say, making the girls giggle.

"I think the next dress you try on should be the one I picked out for you," Lia says.

"If she ever comes back," I quip.

Lia stands and walks toward me. "Come on. I'll help you get into it."

"Shouldn't you wait before you piss her off anymore?" Kiera questions.

"If Miss Bad Attitude has anything negative to say, we will just have Oleg or Ilya step in," I say as Lia grabs my arm and drags me into the fitting room.

Quickly we strip me out of the ugly cheap feeling ballgown.

"Did you see the price tag on this thing?" Lia asks quietly.

"Do I want to know?"

"It's nowhere near where your budget is and while that's fine, I almost feel like she did it because she didn't think you're willing to drop what you said."

"I wouldn't be surprised," I say as I hang the dress, even though I want to toss it into the trash can.

"What do you think?"

My breath catches as soon as I see the dress in Lia's hands.

It's off-white with a deep V-neck in the front and back. The bodice is lace and delicate looking while the skirt is simple and full.

"It's beautiful."

Lia helps me into the dress and while she does up the back, I keep my eyes closed and head down.

"What do you think?"

I shake my head. "Before you even put it on me, I was thinking it was the one. I want to step out so Kiera can see it at the same time and so I can see your guys' reactions."

Wordlessly, Lia grabs my hand and leads me out of the room.

Kiera sucks in a breath. "Yeah, we are going to need all the details on that dress to buy it somewhere else."

I step onto the stage and open my eyes. Instantly my breath catches. It's everything I didn't know I wanted. It makes me feel soft, feminine. Words I never thought of when describing me.

"Wha—" the bridal consultant huffs as she comes back into the room. "You aren't supposed to get into a dress by yourself. Especially one that is clearly over your budget."

Looking through the mirror, I glare at her. "And we're done. Congratulations, you just lost a sale. Kiera, babe, will you please take a picture of the tag so we can call around and see where else you can get this dress?"

Kiera jumps up, tapping on her phone. "On it."

Lia steps toward the bridal consultant. "While they are busy, why don't you introduce me to your boss?"

As they walk away, Kiera chuckles. "It's never a dull moment when I'm with you two."

"I'm glad you feel that way since you're stuck with us now."

I study my friend as she stands next to me. Every day she amazes me. She hasn't let being taken hold her back. As soon as Kiera woke up, she agreed to start going to therapy and has continued to go without fail. Honestly, I think it's safe to say Josh is still having a harder time than she is. Poor guy doesn't like it when she leaves his sight, but he's working on it.

Kiera stands to full height and tucks her phone into her pocket. "So is this the dress?"

I run my hands over my hips and smile. I can picture Dimitri

DIMITRI

standing at the end of the aisle as I walk toward him in this dress. The way the dress would move as he spins me around the dance floor.

"This is it." I nod with tears in my eyes.

Kiera pulls me into a hug. "I can't wait to see Dimitri lose his mind when he sees you in this. What do you think he will love the most about it?"

"How easy it will be to take it off me at the end of the night."

Kiera tosses her head back and laughs.

"What's so funny?" Lia asks as she walks back into the room.

I ignore her question. "Did you get everything taken care of?"

"Yep. Fired on the spot. Apparently she has a history of being a bitch to clients."

"Talk about great for business," Kiera quips.

"Come on, let's get you out of that. The owner told me who else might have it in stock here in town."

"That was nice of her," I say as I walk toward the room.

Lia shrugs. "Eh, I think she was hoping we would be willing to buy it since she fired Miss Grumpy."

I roll my eyes. "Figures."

Dimitri

THE SOUNDS of slot machines and gambling makes me wince as we pass through the casino. I don't know how people can put money into a machine without the promise of getting it back. A security guard sees us approaching and lets us pass through the velvet rope, blocking off the hallway. Getting into the elevator, we descend into the basement of the casino. As soon as we step off the elevator we hit a security checkpoint.

"Please remove your weapons," the guard tells us.

Reluctantly Maxim, Nik, and I do. Even though it goes against our instincts when we are on neutral territory. We watch as the guard places them in a locker before handing us the key. The guard steps forward and opens the door. Maxim walks in first, and I follow with Nik at my back.

As soon as we step into the room, everyone moves to greet one another. I can't help but eye Bastiano Catalini as he steps forward to shake Nik's hand. Even in California, it's known that he rules New York City with an iron fist and that his right-hand man, Lorenzo is a bloodthirsty motherfucker.

Bastiano's brother-in-law and head of the Westies in New York, Killian O'Reilly, steps forward next.

Haruaki Takahashi, head of the Yakuza in Chicago, nods from his place, keeping a healthy distance from everyone but his brother-in-law Callum Brennan, head of the Westies in Chicago.

Maxim breaks away and moves to talk to Kenji, Haruaki's right-hand man. He spent some time with the man when he visited Chicago earlier in the year.

"Congratulations on your engagement," Giovanni Catalini, Bastiano's adviser and third in command, says to me.

"Thank you."

"If I may, I recommend eloping." Killian smirks as Bastiano shoots him a dirty look.

I fight back a smile. "I'll take that into consideration."

While the wedding won't be big, I know it's something Ivanna wants and after Nik playing referee between us for so many years, it's the least I could do. Hell, I overheard him and Maxim talking about their plans to kidnap Ivanna for ransom, a Russian wedding tradition that makes the groom do several challenges to win her.

"Let's get started," Bastiano says.

Everyone moves toward the table, and we all sit down with our families. I fight back a smile when I see that the table is round, preventing a fight about who would sit at the head.

"Before we get started, I would just like to say thank you for coming," Killian says diplomatically.

"Thank you for traveling so far from home." Nik dips his chin.

"Tell me, what is this about?" Haruaki asks from his spot.

Bastiano nods toward another man. "Tristano, if you will."

Tristano Ferrari, twenty-five, works as one of Bastiano's tech guys.

The man hits a couple of buttons on an iPad and the lights dim on one side of the room. We all look over and see he has a projector set up.

"For a while now the team I'm part of has been tracking a trafficking ring," Tristano says.

No one moves but you can feel the tension in the room ramp up.

Tristano shakes his head as he jumps into the finer details. Once in a while, Declan O'Brien speaks up, adding more. Unsurprisingly, the Irish and the Italians have been working together tracking this thing. For so many days a number of girls and women go missing from one city and then they suddenly stop, only to be picked up in another.

The map lights up on the wall showing that each of our cities are being hit back-to-back and never at the same time.

"Do you have any idea who's behind it?" Haruaki asks.

Tristano looks over at his boss. Bastiano nods, giving his approval. "At first we thought it was the Polish." He looks over at us. "We know that they had an operation in your area under the previous leader."

"They still do," Nik confirms.

"We don't think they are working alone though," Declan adds.

I look over at Nik before chiming in. "I think you're right."

"What do you know?" Bastiano asks.

Nik tips his chin toward me, so I fill the other men in. I tell them about the girls on campus going missing, the bioweapon, how Ivanna went on a rescue mission and that we discovered the Ukrainians are making a move into the organ game.

Nik's eyes narrow. "What are you smiling about?"

Killian shakes his head. "I think we need to keep your sister away from my wife. They would get along a little too well, if you know what I mean."

"We need to keep all of our women away from each other or we will never sleep again." Lorenzo smirks. "Then again, it was Greer," he says, referring to Killian's wife and Bastiano's sister. "That discovered this was happening."

"Who runs the world...girls," Tristano sings under his breath.

Bastiano shoots him a dirty look before looking back at the heads of the table.

"All of our families have one thing in common. You don't mess with our women or children. The skin trade does just that. I think we all need to work together to take the Polish and the Ukrainians."

"What do you have in mind?" Haruaki asks as he adjusts his glasses.

"We put our tech people in contact with each other. Have them work together to track this," Killian says before looking at Declan.

"Right now we only have four of us working on it and it's not getting all of our attention because of our other family obligations."

Tristano elbows Declan and shoves his tablet in the man's face.

"What is it?" Bastiano asks.

"Do any of you happen to speak Ukrainian?" Tristano asks.

Out of the corner of my eye, I see Maxim's hands flex under the table.

"Why?" Nik asks coolly.

"Because if it's legit, I just found a countdown to an auction," Tristano says.

"What kind of auction..." Conor, Killian's right-hand, asks.

"Skin. Organs. The whole shebang," Tristano confirms our worst fears.

"When is it for?" Kenji asks.

"The countdown itself is for the announcement of what the stock will be. Date and invitation will follow," Declan murmurs as he scans the screen.

"We need to keep an eye on it and try to get an invitation," Killian says.

"I'll do it," Maxim says, making us look his way. "I can speak Ukrainian."

"Are you sure?" Nik asks.

Maxim turns toward Nik and nods. "This needs to end."

"With the help of Alexei, we can hook you up with a new identity and cover," Declan offers.

"I don't know how long you'll have to go under, but you should have plenty of time to get your shit in order at home," Tristano adds.

"I have no one waiting for me, so it won't be a problem. I can start whenever, as long as my Pakhan agrees," Maxim says.

Nik nods his head, giving him permission.

"So are we all in agreement? We work together to end this once and for all?" Bastiano asks.

Killian dips his chin. "All in favor, say aye."

"Aye," everyone says.

"Then let's get to work," Tristano says, rubbing his hands together.

The End.

AFTERWORD

Thank you for reading Dimitri. We hope you loved this story as much as we do. Want more of the Syndicates Series? Check out, Tristano available now on Amazon and Kindle Unlimited.

Read Tristano Here!

Want to stay up to date on our newest releases and access to exclusive content? Sign up for our newsletter now!

Newsletter

About the Author

Author Bio

Cala Riley, better known as Cala and Riley, are a pair of friends with a deep-seated love of books and writing. Both Cala and Riley are happily married, and each have children, Cala with the four-legged kind while Riley has a mixture of both two-legged and four. While they live apart, that does not affect their connection. They are the true definition of family. What started as an idea that quickly turned into a full-length book and a bond that will never end.

Acknowledgments

Husbands/Family- Thank you for loving us through the crazy and listening to us ramble.
Louise O'Reilly- Thank you for being you.
Jenny Dicks- Thank you for all the swoons & ideas.
Aimee Henry- Thank you for going through everything.
Stefanie Jenkins- Thank you for the motivation & play by plays. Your reactions keep us going.
Nikki Pennington- For always being a cheerleader and listening to us rant.
My Brothers Editor/ Elle- Thank you for being the most laid-back editor and making the entire process painless.
Dark Ink Designs/ Jo- Thank you for the beautiful formatting.
Grey's Promo- Thank you for the killer promotion.
Books and Moods- For always killing it on the design front.
Our ARC/Street Team: Thank you for always cheering us on. We love you.
Bloggers/Readers- Thank you for loving our stories as much as we do and spreading the word.

Also by Author

Mafia Royalty Series

Mafia King

Mafia Underboss

Mafia Prince

The Syndicates

Matteo

Killian

Haruaki

Nikolai

Enzo

Callum

Kenji

Dimitri

Tristano

Shadow Crew Series

Redlined

Friction

Shift

Finish Line

Brighton Academy Series

Unbidden

Unpredictable

Undeniably

Unapologetically

Standalones

One of Them Girls

You Kissed Me First

Love Off the Field Collection

Scandalous: A Why Choose Romance

Forbidden Noelle

Lotus MC

Reaper

Serenity Valley Series

Wild Hearts

Trailer Park Girls

Mayhem

Harmony

Where to Find Us

Facebook

Instagram

Bookbub

Amazon

Goodreads

Cala Riley's Boudoir of Sin

Website

Printed in Great Britain
by Amazon